Praise for
CHRISTINA DODD'S
Paranormal Series
Darkness Chosen

"[A] fast-paced, well-written paranormal with a full,
engaging mythology and...memorable characters."
—*Publishers Weekly*

"[A] phenomenal paranormal series."
—Fresh Fiction

"[An] emotionally intense paranormal tale that
readers will find both entertaining and passionate."
—*Affaire de Coeur*

"[An] adrenaline ride....A multilayered
heroine and a sizzling-hot hero give readers
plenty of emotional—and physical—action."
—*Booklist*

continued . . .

"A sweeping saga of good and evil, the series chronicles the adventures of four siblings who try to redeem their family from a pact an ancestor made with the devil a thousand years earlier. This latest promises to be one of her best to date." —*Library Journal*

"Filled with action and adventure . . . a must read."
—*Midwest Book Review*

"Christina Dodd demonstrates why she is such a popular writer, in any genre. The characters are boldly drawn, with action on all sides. Readers will be riveted until the final page." —*A Romance Review*

Scent of Darkness

"The first in a devilishly clever, scintillatingly sexy new paranormal series by Christina Dodd." —*Chicago Tribune*

"[A] satisfying series kickoff . . . [a] fast-paced, well-written paranormal with a full, engaging mythology and a handful of memorable characters." —*Publishers Weekly*

"Dodd kicks off her new Darkness Chosen series with a bang. A multilayered heroine and a sizzling-hot hero give readers plenty of emotional—and physical—action, and the relentless game of hunter and prey adds an adrenaline ride for good measure." —*Booklist*

"Multigenre genius Dodd dives headfirst into the paranormal realm with . . . a scintillating and superb novel!"
—*Romantic Times* (top pick, 4½ stars)

. . . and Her Other Novels

"Dodd delivers a high-octane, blowout finale. . . . This romantic suspense novel is a delicious concoction that readers will be hard-pressed not to consume in one gulp." —*Publishers Weekly*

"Warm characterizations and caperlike plot make Dodd's hot contemporary romance a delight, and the cliff-hanger ending will leave readers eager for the sequel." —*Booklist*

"Dodd adds humor, sizzling sensuality, and a cast of truly delightful secondary characters to produce a story that will not disappoint."
—*Library Journal*

"Sexy and witty, daring and delightful."
—Teresa Medeiros, *New York Times* bestselling author of *After Midnight*

Other Books by Christina Dodd

Christina Dodd's The Chosen Ones Series
Storm of Visions
Storm of Shadows

Christina Dodd's Darkness Chosen Series
Scent of Darkness
Touch of Darkness
Into the Shadow
Into the Flame

Christina Dodd's Romantic Suspense
Trouble in High Heels
Tongue in Chic
Thigh High
Danger in a Red Dress

CHRISTINA DODD

STORM of VISIONS

THE
CHOSEN
ONES

A SIGNET BOOK

SIGNET
Published by New American Library, a division of
Penguin Group (USA) Inc., 375 Hudson Street,
New York, New York 10014, USA
Penguin Group (Canada), 90 Eglinton Avenue East, Suite 700, Toronto,
Ontario M4P 2Y3, Canada (a division of Pearson Penguin Canada Inc.)
Penguin Books Ltd., 80 Strand, London WC2R 0RL, England
Penguin Ireland, 25 St. Stephen's Green, Dublin 2,
Ireland (a division of Penguin Books Ltd.)
Penguin Group (Australia), 250 Camberwell Road, Camberwell, Victoria 3124,
Australia (a division of Pearson Australia Group Pty. Ltd.)
Penguin Books India Pvt. Ltd., 11 Community Centre, Panchsheel Park,
New Delhi – 110 017, India
Penguin Group (NZ), 67 Apollo Drive, Rosedale, North Shore 0632,
New Zealand (a division of Pearson New Zealand Ltd.)
Penguin Books (South Africa) (Pty.) Ltd., 24 Sturdee Avenue,
Rosebank, Johannesburg 2196, South Africa

Penguin Books Ltd., Registered Offices:
80 Strand, London WC2R 0RL, England

First published by Signet, an imprint of New American Library,
a division of Penguin Group (USA) Inc.

First Printing, August 2009
10 9 8 7 6 5 4 3 2 1

For Susan Mallery
We've survived so many years in publishing
and celebrated all the ups and downs with friendship
and laughter.

It's time we split another bottle of champagne.

ACKNOWLEDGMENTS

Launching a new series involves hours of plotting and planning, glorious moments of exultation, and humbling hours spent desperately looking for inspiration. Luckily for me, I'm not alone—I have the wonderful team at NAL backing me up. Thank you to Kara Welsh for giving me the opportunity to introduce The Chosen Ones and encouraging me to link it to my beloved Darkness Chosen series. Thank you to my editor, Kara Cesare, who generously gives me her inspirations when mine are lacking. Thanks to Frank Walgren and the production department. Thank you to the art department led by Anthony Ramondo, the publicity department with Craig Burke and Michele Langley, and of course, the spectacular Penguin sales department. Thank you all.

A special thanks to Shelley Kay of Web Crafters for designing a fabulous new Web site worthy of The Chosen Ones.

Long ago, when the world was young, a young woman lived in a poor village on the edge of a vast, dark forest. The face she saw in the reflecting pool was glorious in its splendor, and all the men of the village competed for her favors, each desiring her as his wife.

Their good opinion of her was matched only by her good opinion of herself, and she declared she would take only a man whose magnificence matched her own. She scorned the metalsmith with his blackened face, the woodsman with his hand that lacked fingers, the warrior with his scarred chest, the farmer who was stooped from planting the soil.

She took instead the eldest son of the local lord, a lazy lad as famed for his dark, wavy hair and deep-set blue eyes as for his vanity. Together they rolled on the bed, made passionate love, and talked of the comely family they would have. Before the year was out, she grew large with child. She strutted, if a woman great with child could be said to strut, and imagined how she would present the lord's son with a strapping boy who would bind him to her forever.

But in the spring, when it came time to deliver her child, she gave birth not to one healthy male, but to two scrawny, wailing, red-faced babes. Worse, on closer examination, the two babes were not like her and her lover.

They were not perfect.

The elder looked as if red wine stained him from the tips of his tiny fingers to his bony shoulder.

The younger, a girl, had a dirty smudge in the palm of her hand that to the mother looked exactly like . . . an eye.

Disgusting. And terrifying.

These children would not do.

The mother rose from her birthing bed. She ignored the lord's messengers, ignored the dismay of the women who attended the birth, ignored her own bleeding body. She took her children, the children she had brought forth from her womb, and disappeared from the village on a mission that made the midwife huddle by the fire and mutter a prayer.

She took the trail that wound into the deepest part of the forest where, it was said, the old and hungry gods waited to devour any human who dared venture close. There she abandoned the boy.

The girl she tossed into a swiftly running stream.

At the moment when she turned away, abandoning her children without a backward glance, they were left devoid of the gift every child is automatically given at birth—a parent's love. In that moment, their small hearts stopped beating. They died. . . .

And came back to life changed, gifted, the vacuum in their hearts filled by a new gift, one given in pity and in love.

These two children were the first Abandoned Ones.

They didn't perish, as their mother intended.

The boy was picked up by a group of wanderers, and carried by them into the subcontinent of India, where he grew into manhood. There he became a legend, for he created fire in the palm of his hand.

That was his gift.

As he grew in age and wisdom, he gathered around him others like himself, babes who had been tossed aside like offal and, as amends, had been given a special gift. They were the Chosen Ones, seven men and women who formed a powerful force of light in a dark world.

The girl floated down the cold torrent, bobbing to the surface and screaming when her tiny body caught on a branch. A woman—a witch—heard the shrieks and pulled the baby from the water. Disappointed by the scrawny, worthless thing, she intended to toss her back . . . until she saw the eye on the baby's palm. She knew then that the child was special, so she took her to her home and raised her, starved her, tormented her, used her as a slave.

She taught her how to hate.

On the day the girl became a woman, and her first menstrual blood stained her thighs, she looked at the witch and, in a vision, foresaw the old woman's future. In a voice warm with delight, she told the witch a horrible death awaited her.

The girl was a seer, and that was her gift.

Determined to evade her fate, the witch set up an altar to her master, the devil, and prepared to sacrifice the girl. But as the girl had grown up, the woman had grown old, and the girl took the knife and plunged it into the witch's heart.

The devil himself took form.

He scrutinized the girl, as beautiful as her mother, yet not heartless. No, this girl was steeped in anger, and with her gift, she would be a worthy instrument in his hand. So he showed her his wonders, promised her a place at his right hand, and commissioned her to find others like herself and bring them to him to do evil in the world. Around her, she gathered six other abandoned children—warped, abused, and special—and they were the Others.

The girl designated their first task. They found the

poor village and the lonely, miserable woman who fourteen years before had given birth to twins, and they killed her most horribly.

Then the Others used their powers to cut like a scythe through the countryside, bringing famine and fear, anguish and death.

So through ages and eons, through low places and high, in the countryside and in the cities, through prophecies and revelations, the battle was joined between the Chosen Ones and the Others . . . and that battle was fought for the hearts and souls of the Abandoned Ones.

That battle goes on today. . . .

Chapter 1

---◆◈◆---

Napa Valley, California

Jacqueline Vargha dug her corkscrew out of her jeans and, with an expert twist and pull, opened another bottle of Blue Oak wines. The tasting room hummed with the conversation of two dozen happy tourists—happy because everyone was engaged in sampling some of the best cabernet sauvignon in the valley.

She poured generous glasses for the young couple before her. They had money, they thought they knew a lot about wines, and if she handled them right, she could sell a case, maybe more, of the high-end wines. "Blue Oak Winery grows our grapes exclusively in our own estate vineyards, one in Napa Valley and one in Alexander Valley." She'd given this speech a thousand times, and it wasn't always easy to make it sound fresh. Maybe if she'd gone to Juilliard and taken acting . . . "As you sip the pure cab, you'll notice the rich cassis and berry flavors that form the base of the wine; then you'll pick up the spicy, peppery flavor and a hint of cherry."

They sipped and nodded, their brows furrowed.

At the other end of the long bar, Michelle explained to the newest arrivals, two recently returned marines, "It's twenty dollars to taste the wine, but we refund that amount if you buy a bottle." Leaning forward, she placed two glasses on the counter, and the Blue Oak logo on the crest of her right breast strained at her thin blue T-shirt.

The guys' eyes glazed over, and they dug out their wallets without a hint of protest.

Jacqueline grinned. She swore the vintner hired his female help by the size of their chests and how well they used them. How Jacqueline, with her B-cups, had gotten the job, she did not know. Maybe because the vintner's wife had wandered through during the interview and it had been politic to employ the woman with the little boobies. Probably because Jacqueline was twenty-two and levelheaded, the kind of worker who could keep the tasting room under control, and did. Certainly because she was tall and long-legged, and smiled like Miss America accepting the crown.

It was a character flaw created by a mother who nagged at her to *smile* until it was easier to give in than fight.

But she could never fill a Blue Oaks T-shirt the way Michelle did.

A party of six finished their tasting and left, muttering about the heat.

They were right. Spring had come with a vengeance, and the temperature had been unrelenting, like an upwelling of hell.

Jacqueline lifted her shoulder-length hair off her neck and wished for a breeze.

An upwelling of hell.

Hell . . .

The world took on a sepia tint, and the word echoed in her mind, a soft, foreboding whisper. . . .

Hot. Explosively hot. Flames spurting . . .

Hell.

Hell.

Jacqueline's breath slowed. Her eyes narrowed. Her hands, clad in fingerless leather gloves, curled into her hair. She stood, frozen in place, caught by a vision that clawed its way up from deep inside her, overwhelming her, taking her somewhere she did not wish to go.

Then she faintly heard the sound of water dripping, and a cold gust of air brushed the back of her neck.

She snapped back to the moment, to the tasting room, to her job behind the counter serving wine to a dozen thirsty tourists, to Michelle's voice whispering, "Dibs, Jacquie. He's divine. Dibs. Dibs!"

What could have pulled Michelle's attention away from the buff young marines?

Jacqueline glanced at the guy who stood in the doorway—and froze in wary appreciation.

He was a dark silhouette against the bright sunlight: long and lean, narrow hips wrapped in fitted, faded denim, and a black silk T-shirt stretched across broad shoulders. He stood aggressively, with his arms held away from his body, like a bullfighter prepared to face the final challenge.

No wonder Michelle was impressed. He was her kind of guy. He was trouble.

Jacqueline had had enough trouble in her life. She dropped her hair, flexed her hands to rid them of the betraying stiffness, and in an undertone, said, "He's all yours."

"That's right, sweetheart. Because I called dibs, and don't you forget it." Raising her voice, Michelle called, "Come in, sir, and take your place at the counter. There's always room for another connoisseur of fine wines."

Two of the older ladies glanced back, did a double take, and moved aside to let him in. Because they might be schoolteachers, and married, but when a guy walked like Mr. Aggressive, like a stalker on a mission, he commanded adulation.

They were glad to give it to him.

Michelle gave her speech about the tasting fee and the refund, and almost vibrated with excitement as Mr. Aggressive put his twenty on the counter. She poured a generous glass of the first cabernet sauvignon, and avidly watched as he swirled it, his gaze on the brilliant garnet in the glass. Without even trying, Mr. Aggressive demanded the notice of everyone in the tasting room. He was one of *those* guys, filling the space, taking the oxygen, putting his stamp on the place, the hour, the atmosphere.

Unbidden, Jacqueline's attention wandered his direction.

He breathed in the bouquet, then lifted the glass to his lips—and with a swift, sideways glance, speared her with his gaze.

The image of him seared into her brain. Dark hair, close cut. Olive skin. Sinful cheekbones. And blue eyes. Pale, brilliant, cold eyes like blue diamonds that held her prisoner in his gaze.

She couldn't look away. Not while he sipped, tasted, and approved with a slow, steady nod. Not when his gaze dropped to her leather-clad hands. Not when he lifted his glass in a salute to her. Not until he looked away, back to Michelle.

Michelle spoke clearly, loud enough for Jacqueline to hear her, loud enough for everyone to hear her. "That's Jacquie. She's our resident nun. She doesn't date; she doesn't care for guys at all; she only works and hikes and reads."

Jacqueline flushed. *Thank you, Michelle. That was something everybody here needed to know.*

"Really?" The guy had a great voice, warm and deep, vibrant in a way that made a girl strain to listen to him. Not that Jacqueline wanted to hear him, or even tried, but like Michelle, he pitched his tone loud enough for her to hear. "Is she gay?"

"I guess." Michelle glanced at Jacqueline, and something in Jacqueline's face must have made her change her mind. "No, she's just not interested in sex."

"Maybe she hasn't met the right man," he said.

It sure isn't you, you conceited bastard. But Jacqueline gave no indication that she heard.

Yet a glance at his half smile proved he had plucked the thought from her mind.

Oblivious to the undercurrents, Michelle stepped back to open a new bottle and murmured to Jacqueline, "Look at the quirk in his cheek. Look at that crooked smile. Give him a martini and a license to kill, and he'd be the new James Bond—you know, the rough one."

"Give him a sailor hat and a can of spinach, and he'd be Popeye." Jacqueline returned Michelle's shocked look with a cool one. "I'm just sayin'."

Middle-aged, well-dressed, two married couples stood a little apart, drinking their wine, chatting and laughing. The Fun Four might buy a bottle, no more, but they were good for the tasting room, giving it the warmth and ambiance of a sophisticated party, and Jacqueline was grateful when the gray-haired man caught her eye and changed the subject. "It's warm in here. Can I turn on the ceiling fans?" he asked.

She sighed gustily. "I wish you could. You may have noticed that we're remodeling"—she indicated the old counter pushed off to the side and the half-painted wall—"and the electrician isn't done with the wiring."

She was determinedly not looking at Mr. Aggressive, yet she *felt* him frown. He exuded disapproval, and the others picked up on his displeasure.

If she didn't do something now, everyone would leave—everyone but him—and she'd lose the sale she'd cultivated so diligently. Lifting her voice, she called, "But if you'd like, I can top off your glasses and take you on a quick tour of the winery. It's cool down in the cellars." As she expected, the promise of more wine brought an enthusiastic response, and seven of the nineteen tasters followed her through the gift shop and into the working winery.

Mr. Aggressive stayed behind.

Yeah, Michelle's easy. Put the moves on her. Never mind that the idea raised Jacqueline's anger a notch.

A quick survey of the group proved that only the lady visiting from Wisconsin was a wine-tour virgin, so Jacqueline gave her the basics about wine making while lauding the awards Blue Oak Winery had won in the past year. The awards impressed her wine-buying couple and made the Fun Four seriously discuss whether to buy a bottle to take to dinner that night. As

they talked and laughed and lingered in the cellar—
Jacqueline was in no hurry to return to the tasting
room—that faint, cold and now-familiar breeze lifted
goose bumps on her skin.

Mr. Aggressive had found them.

He joined the group with an easy swagger. He stood
a little apart to listen as Jacqueline recommended Cole's
Chop House for steaks. The wine she dispensed so
freely was working on the guests now, and the food discussion turned serious. She found out that two of the
Fun Four, the gray-haired man and his blond, laughing
wife, owned a cattle ranch in Texas. They knew their
leather. "Those are fine gloves." The wife took Jacqueline's hand and examined the material and stitching.
"Are they in style, or do they protect your hands when
you open the bottles?"

When the woman ran her fingertips over the palm,
Jacqueline flinched and curled her hand into a fist. "A
little of both."

"So you're a slave to style?" Mr. Aggressive's voice
was as cool as his manner.

The wife didn't like his implied criticism, but nothing in her friendly, accented voice or vivacious manner
changed. "Bless your heart, sir, but we silly women do
love to follow trends and set the fashion."

Jacqueline glanced at him to see if he realized he'd
been mocked and put down, and by an expert.

He smiled crookedly, that half smile that made Michelle pant with desire. That smile clearly indicated he could withstand censure. That smile royally pissed Jacqueline off.

The blond wife turned back to Jacqueline. "Now, where should we have dinner tonight?"

Naturally, they knew their beef, too. Jacqueline was able to assure them that Cole's was consistently one of the highest-rated steak houses in the country with a wine list that won accolades from the top wine magazines. She casually mentioned that at Cole's, the Blue Oak eighty-dollar bottle of cabernet sold for one hundred and seventy-five. At that moment, she sold a bottle of cab to the Fun Four, a mixed case to her wine experts, and consoled the lady from Wisconsin about the high prices.

Then she briskly returned the group to the tasting room, where a disgruntled Michelle had lost her marines, lost her schoolteachers, and gained three new guests to tend.

Jacqueline noted with some satisfaction that none of them was likely to buy.

Normally, she would have stepped up to the counter to help. But the afternoon was waning. The Fun Four bought their bottle and moved on to the next winery. The wine experts fought about whether they should purchase another case. The lady from Wisconsin started talking to a new guy, the sunburned man from New Jersey; she'd obviously read the study financed by the wineries that declared tasting rooms were great places to meet men.

And Mr. Aggressive stood silently sipping his wine . . . and waiting.

To hell with him. He could wait forever.

Jacqueline slipped into the back room and picked up the house phone. When the vintner's wife answered, she said, "Mrs. Marino, the tasting room is slow, it's an hour until closing, and I'm feeling ill. Would it be possible for me to leave early?"

"Of course, dear." Mrs. Marino sounded surprised and kind—Jacqueline was never sick. "I'll come over in case we get a late rush. Will you be all right driving yourself home?"

"Yes. It's the heat that's bothering me."

"And you work too much. I suppose you'll be waitressing tonight?"

"I don't know. I may take the night off." Although she needed the money. It wasn't cheap to live in Napa Valley. Her tiny apartment near downtown San Michael, on the second floor of the early-twentieth-century Victorian, cost almost as much as her apartment in New York City, and that was saying something. She could have gone elsewhere—nothing held her in Napa Valley—but she loved the dry warmth, the long rows of grapes, the mountains that cupped the valley, the wineries, their rivalries and alliances, the food, the wine. . . .

She didn't love the weirdos who popped up occasionally. Guys like Mr. Aggressive, who acted as if he had rights she hadn't granted him. Rights she would never grant him.

Let Michelle have him. Jacqueline had had enough heartache in her life.

Chapter 2

Jacqueline pulled her backpack out of her locker and headed out the rear door to her car, parked under the broad branches of the two-hundred-year-old blue oak that had given the winery its name. The little Civic started right up, and she headed south on Highway 29, the windows wide and the wind ripping through her hair.

The color was like the shimmer of moonlight . . . or so she'd been told. She realized now she should have cut it, and dyed it black, or brown, or purple, or any color besides this freakish platinum. The blond was too distinctive, too easy to spot. More than once she glanced behind her, watching for a strange vehicle with the strange guy in it, but everything seemed normal. All she saw were SUVs full of tourists and faded farm trucks packed with workers. Then, as she pulled into San Michael, she spotted a black Mercedes SL550 with dark-tinted windows, and that chill rippled through her.

Was it him? Not necessarily. There was money here, and a lot of people who drove expensive cars.

But if it was . . . she couldn't outrun him. She had to outsmart him.

Rather than going to her apartment, she drove until she found a parking spot beside the old-fashioned town square. It was crowded here, part of the downtown renaissance. Quaint shops faced out on the park filled with grand live oaks and benches where tourists lolled in the shade. Directly across the way stood an old redbrick courthouse complete with white trim and a cupola. Jacqueline loved the courthouse; she liked to look at it, to feel the tug of the past in its ornate styling. She liked to imagine what this town, this wine-producing valley had been like a hundred years ago. When she talked about her decision to live in San Michael, she said the courthouse architecture and the styling of the town were the main reasons she'd chosen to stay in San Michael.

But of course, that wasn't true. The main reason she'd chosen to stay in San Michael was because it was as far away from New York City in culture and distance as she could be and still be in the continental United States.

Now she scanned the park, looking for Mr. Aggressive.

She saw nothing.

Plucking her cell out of her backpack, she called the winery.

Michelle picked up on the first ring. "Blue Oak Winery, where the hell are you, Jacquie?"

"I didn't like that guy, and you did, so I left."

"Like I need you to leave before I have a chance with him?" Michelle was always crabby, and never more so than when she was offended.

"You got a date with him?"

"*No.* About the time I realized you hadn't come back from the back room, he put the glass down and walked out."

No wonder Michelle was offended.

Michelle continued. "All he did was ask questions about you, and he didn't even finish his tasting. Twenty dollars and he didn't take his second glass. What a loser."

"Loser" was not the term Jacqueline would slap on that guy. "Okay. Thank you." She hung up while Michelle was sputtering.

She got out of the car. Locked the doors. Slung her backpack over her shoulder. And started walking.

In Hills's sales window, a pair of red satin heels with diamond buckles caught her attention. She stopped, stared, and wondered if she could ever afford shoes like that again—and at that moment, she caught her first glimpse of him, a dark reflection in the glass. The other people on the sidewalk hurried past, but he stood still, a little to the side, and when she glanced at him, the way you do in a crowd, without really looking at him—he was watching her.

Tall. Lanky. Dark-haired. Pale blue eyes with the chilling look of a hunter.

She had seen that look before.

Turning away from the window, she hurried down the street, that cold draft on the back of her neck.

Okay. So this wasn't some kind of bizarre coincidence. He wasn't here on vacation. He *had* followed her. He *was* there, part of the impersonal crowd that gathered by the crosswalk. No one else was looking at her. Just him.

The light changed. The crowd surged forward. She surged with them.

The heat rose from the sidewalk and through the soles of her running shoes, and in the odor of the hot asphalt, she could almost smell the flames of hell.

Hell . . .

For a moment, the colors around her faded, turned pale and sepia-tinted, and inside her head, she heard a faint, constant sound of water dripping . . . dripping. . . .

She staggered and went down on one knee, and the pain brought her back.

Thank God. She couldn't afford to do this now. She *would not* allow herself to do this now.

Bending her head, she pretended to tie her shoe,

and when she stood, Mr. Aggressive had moved on. Darting into the quilting shop, she walked swiftly toward the back.

With a smile, the lone, elderly clerk said, "Hi, I'm Bernice. May I help you with your quilting needs?"

"I'm just passing through." Jacqueline paused, her attention captured by the long row of scissors hanging from hooks on the Peg-Board wall. "How much are those?"

"The scissors? It depends on the size and the quality, and what you intend to do with them." Bernice bustled forward, ready to have a long, involved conversation.

Jacqueline scanned the selection, grabbed an eight-inch, fifteen-dollar pair, and flung it on the counter.

"That pair is good as all-around scissors, but if you're going to be cutting much material, you'd be happier with the slightly more expensive, chrome-plated Heritage Razor Sharpe shears."

Jacqueline dug out her wallet and flung a twenty on top of the scissors. "I'm going to stab somebody with them." The plan gave her a fierce satisfaction.

Bernice tittered; then as she stared into Jacqueline's face, her smile faded. "Well . . . then . . . I suppose they'll do."

She backed toward the cash register so slowly, Jacqueline knew she couldn't wait to be rung up. She had about a minute before Mr. Aggressive realized he'd lost her, retraced his steps, and picked up her trail again.

Grabbing the scissors, she said, "Keep the change," and swerved around the sales counter and into the back room.

"Hey!" Bernice called. "You can't do that. You can't do that!"

"Watch me," Jacqueline muttered. She slipped the scissors in her pocket, and was out the back door and into the alley before Bernice had a chance to say anything more.

Jacqueline took a left and ran hard for the next street. With a glance either direction, she caught another wave of the crowd and headed away from the courthouse. At an opportune moment, she dashed across traffic and ducked into another alley. She hid behind the first Dumpster, a hot, filthy metal bin that smelled like rotting Mexican food. She opened zippers and dug down to the bottom of her backpack, looking for her baseball cap. She found it, gave a sigh of relief as she tucked up her hair, and ran again, away from the crowds, and toward home.

Her apartment was two blocks away on the town's formerly fashionable drive. If she could reach the old house, she'd be safe. Her stalker would be behind her. She'd have time to figure out what to do.

Call the police?

Not even. Men like Mr. Aggressive had connections that law enforcement respected.

Pack her bags and get out of town?

No way. She'd run before. She wasn't doing it again.

Hide under the bed?

Yeah, maybe.

She turned onto her quiet street, with its massive oaks and shady yards, and slowed to a walk. She scanned the immediate area.

Mrs. Mallery's little dog Nicki came out and yapped at her. Nosy, retired Mr. Thomas stopped killing his weeds long enough to ask, "Hot enough for you?"

"Sure is," she said. "Have you seen anything interesting come down the street? Any strangers?"

Mr. Thomas leaned on his shovel. "No. Were you expecting someone?"

"Just asking!" She smiled at him.

His gaze dropped to her leather gloves. "Weird girl," he muttered.

She didn't care what he thought. She only cared that no *man* disturbed the even tenor of the neighborhood.

So she was hot and sweaty, but she was triumphant. Mr. Aggressive might be the world's all-time best tracker, but she'd lost him. That would teach him to terrorize a young, single woman, to think that he had the right to show up in her life again after so many years.

She climbed the wooden steps onto the wide porch and checked her mailbox. A catalogue and a bill. She used her key to let herself in the side door and climbed the stairs to the second floor.

The old house had been divided into four apartments per floor, with a tiny kitchen and a living room, and a bedroom the size of a closet. She was one of the lucky ones; she had her own bathroom with a black-and-white ceramic tile floor, a pedestal sink, and a claw-foot tub.

Still cautious, she tried the knob; her apartment was locked.

She pulled the scissors out of her pocket and held them like a knife. She inserted her key, swung the door wide, and looked inside. The living room and kitchen were empty. Everything was as she had left it.

Damn him. He really did have her on edge.

But better safe than sorry. Quickly, she shut the door behind her. She slid the scissors back in her pocket, set the dead bolt and fastened the chain, then dropped her backpack and hat by the door. Pulling off her T-shirt, she headed for the bedroom. She kicked her shoes toward the closet, peeled off her gloves—and paused.

She could hear water running. No big deal, because the lavatory upstairs was right over her head and the pipes ran through the wall. But this was in *her* apartment. She walked through the door into the old-fashioned bathroom, and the steam hit her in the face.

She'd left the shower running.

Sure, this morning she'd been in a hurry, distracted

by that sickening sepia world that hovered close to the edges of her consciousness, and the sound of water dripping . . . dripping. . . .

Now, for the briefest second, she closed her eyes and touched her marked palm to the place on her forehead between her eyes.

Her mind, her soul struggled to give birth to some . . . thing. . . .

She caught herself. Took her hand away.

She didn't want to acknowledge the ache that plagued her there. If she could just ignore it, it would go away. It always had before. . . .

The shower. She'd left the shower running.

How could she have been so careless? She had her hand on the green plastic curtain when the word echoed in her mind.

Careless . . .

And she realized . . . someone was in there.

Flinging the plastic curtain open, he pulled her inside.

Chapter 3

———◆———

Jacqueline landed on her rear in the tub. The thump was loud; her scream was louder. She caught a flash of naked guy—tall, lean, cold blue eyes—hovering over her.

Rage blasted through her. He would not win. Not this time.

Flipping onto her hands and knees, she groped in her pocket. When she came back around, she had the scissors in her fist. She stabbed at his ribs, ramming him with the point.

He flinched back. Hissed with pain. Recovered all too quickly. Caught her wrist as she wound up again. Twisted until her fingers went numb. She released the scissors; they clattered against the side and before they'd slid toward the drain, he'd kicked them through the plastic shower curtain in one smooth, forceful motion.

Her breath caught in her throat. She threw herself against the sloped back of the tub, hit hard, and slithered down, lashing out with her feet.

He went down, then recovered as quickly as a cat, landing on top of her.

Yet not too hard—he took the brunt of the fall on his hands and knees, protecting her from the full weight of his body.

But not for any good reason; before she'd finished sliding to the bottom, he'd grabbed the front snap of her bra and broke it open.

Enraged, outraged, she grabbed for his close-cropped hair. She gave a twist, but after forcing one satisfying yelp from him, she lost her grip.

He settled his hands on her breasts. And looked at her. Just looked at her.

Blood slid out of the wound at his side and, driven by the rush of water, washed along his sculpted ribs. Blood dripped onto her belly and down the drain.

She was proud she'd wounded him, glad he was in pain.

Then she looked deep into his fierce blue eyes, and her body was suspended in a bubble composed of an intoxicating cocktail of hatred and desire.

He used his thumbs to taunt her, caress her, offer a slow, sweet enticement.

The world inside the shower curtain was warm and intimate. Her nipples tightened, thrusting into his palms. The water rained down on them, wetting his shoulders, her face, their entwined bodies. The pounding of her heart slowed, and her eyelids grew heavy.

She took a long, measured breath. . . . Seduction was so easy for him.

She was so easy for him. The thought roused her, infuriated her. Shouting, "No!" she knocked his hands away and slammed her fist toward his nose.

She didn't make contact.

He was too fast. He was too experienced. He caught her around the waist and turned her onto her belly.

She got her elbows underneath her and easily levered herself up. Too easily; he was waiting for her.

He reached around her and unsnapped her jeans.

"You son of a . . ." She headed over the edge of the tub.

Again, she'd made it easy for him. He could never have wrestled the wet denim off, but he held her waistband and she crawled right out of them. He let her tumble out of the tub and onto the mosaic of cold ceramic tile, then followed her out. He grabbed her ankle as she rose to run. She let him jerk her off her feet, then kicked at the wound on his ribs.

The breath left his lungs in a wrenching groan. He lost his grip. Caught her ankle again. Wildly, she used her free foot to lash out at him.

But he dodged, dodged again, and the third time, he caught her other ankle. He had control of her legs. He yanked her knees out from under her. Her belly slid onto the cold tiles. He dragged her toward him, and when she tried to claw the floor and slow her progress, he laughed . . . softly.

It was like being drawn into a furnace fired by lust. Water dried on her skin as he pulled her into his grasp. He used his broad hands to open her legs, then walked them up her calves, her knees, her thighs. He reached her hip, and briefly his fingers lifted.

She took the opportunity to struggle another yard toward the bedroom.

He used both hands to rip one thin strap of her thong. Her panties sagged, hanging on one hip. Then he captured her again.

Her stomach twisted in fear and fury.

And, God help her, anticipation.

He kissed one buttock; then when she tried to reach around and slap him, he bit her, a small, sharp sting of retribution. He slid one arm under her hips and used that as leverage to push her underneath him. He rested on top of her, pressing her into the floor.

The tiles were cold. And hard.

He was heavy. And hot. And hard. His erection pressed between her legs. Nothing but the thin nylon of her panties barricaded her from his intrusion.

He smelled like soap and man and sex that lasted for languid hours.

He infuriated her. "You coward," she said.

"Coward? My darling, what do you mean?" His voice was a purr of satisfaction.

"Are you afraid to let me face you? Afraid I'll hurt you again?"

He stilled; then with his hands at her waist, he turned her.

She stared into his eyes, blue, but no longer cold. They blazed with passion, with need . . . with a knowledge she could not deny.

"My God, I have missed you." Reaching up, she grabbed his hair, damp from the shower, and pulled his face down to hers. She kissed him deeply, tasting for the first time in two years the flavor of Caleb D'Angelo, her one, her only lover.

Chapter 4

———◆◆———

Caleb responded to Jacqueline's aggression with an aggression of his own, thrusting his tongue deep into her mouth while his hands shoved her panties down one leg. He pushed one finger inside her, claiming her without a care to the years apart.

And her treacherous body, of course, did more than yield. It softened around him, grew moist in surrender, and she bucked beneath him, already on the edge of orgasm.

"Don't even think about finishing already." His voice grated in anger. "You ran away. You pretended not to know me. You are going to pay."

"You were an ass, so if there's payment to be made—"

"I've already paid. Every day when we were apart, I paid."

"Not enough. Whatever you suffered, it wasn't

enough." She tightened her inner muscles, massaging his finger.

His eyes narrowed.

"Imagine how good that would feel around your cock," she whispered, and did it again, a long ripple that made him hiss with need.

He wanted to dominate her? She had the weapons to fight the good fight.

And he had the toughness, mental and physical, to keep her subdued. In a gradual, torturous motion, he slipped his finger out of her.

She shuddered and grabbed his arms, wanting to be filled again.

He sat up between her thighs. She watched, mesmerized, as a drop of water gathered at his throat, then trickled down his breastbone, zigzagging along the path of least resistance, between muscles even more sharply defined than she remembered. Had he lost weight? Did he work out more than he had before? Or was reality simply so much better than memory?

The drop of water joined the slow ooze of blood from the wound she'd given him.

He must be in pain, but he didn't seem to notice. Of course not. Caleb had always been capable of proceeding on the course he'd determined, regardless of the pain he suffered . . . or the pain he would cause her.

And right now, his course had been determined by

his erection and his need. Curse him for making his need hers.

He widened his legs and folded them underneath him, resting on his heels so close against her, everything female opened to him like a flower in bloom. Her knees were crooked, her feet rested flat on the floor, and as he looked down, he slid his palms up and down the sensitive skin of her inner thighs. That distinctive half smile quirked his cheek. "You're swollen, Jacqueline."

He was looking. Looking and enjoying himself. She lifted her chin. "Yeah. So what? So are you." She glanced down at him. *Obviously.*

"So this makes even the smallest touch agony."

"That works both ways."

He pressed himself against her, a long, slow slide of his hips.

She wanted to writhe against him. She wanted to rub him until she found her own pleasure, then rub him until he found his.

But as always, he read her intentions on her face and caught her hips in his hands. "What is your desire, Jacqueline?"

She turned her face away, refusing to look at him, to give him the satisfaction of knowing her frustration.

"Jacqueline." He leaned over, slid his hands along the floor on either side of her back, under her arms, and up to cradle her head. He surrounded her now; his legs were under hers and against her hips. His arms embraced her body. His chest touched hers. He smelled like her soap, lemon and rosemary, and like himself, strength and power.

Yet one thing overcame her awareness of all that—his erection, heavy and hot, pressed at the entrance of her body.

His voice demanded and cajoled. "Jacqueline, look at me."

Damned if she would.

He smoothed his lips along her cheek, then kissed her neck under her ear, and nipped her lobe.

She jumped.

He laughed, his breath puffing against her skin.

In a flash, she turned her head and caught his lower lip between her teeth. She nipped, too, and released, and glared into his eyes.

"You don't know when to surrender, do you?" he asked.

He made angry blood roil in her veins. "I won't surrender to you again. All that got me was rejection and—"

He pushed himself the first inch inside of her.

She caught her breath in shock.

They'd done this before. They had. But it had been a long time, and he was bigger or she was smaller or . . . she'd forgotten what it was like to have a man, this man, fill her so gloriously full.

"All right?" he asked. But he didn't wait for the answer. He pushed again. He watched her, stretched her, wordlessly commanding she forget her anger, her resistance. He demanded all of her mind and all of her senses concentrate on him, on this grandeur, on this heedless, helpless desire.

He moved so unhurriedly, she moaned with anticipation. She sank her nails into his shoulders. She tried to lift herself, to hurry him along.

But he held her trapped. His chest rested on hers. He held her tightly in his arms. Below her, the tile was cool against her still-damp body. Above her, he burned with intensity.

She couldn't look away from his blue eyes, heavy with dark lashes and with passion, and when at last he had filled her with all of himself, she saw his flare of triumph.

But before she could gather herself to fury, he unleashed his control.

He thrust and retreated, thrust and retreated, progressing slowly at first, then with an ever-increasing rhythm. His thighs flexed against hers; his hips directed his power. She was open, wide-open, making each sensation new and fresh. With each advance, he rocked against her. With each motion, his dominion over her grew. She felt like a virgin again, taken from one marvel to another until her perceptions were overloaded. Dimly she was aware of crying out, over and over, as her soul stretched and reached, seeking release.

He slipped one hand under her head. The other

rested on her belly. Close against her ear, he murmured, "Not yet, Jacqueline. Wait a little longer . . . a little longer. . . ."

Wait for what? She tried to shake her head, to deny him. If he would just *stop talking* and let her focus on this one moment, she would . . .

The hand on her belly glided downward and, with the coordination of a born athlete, he slipped it between them and caught her clit between his fingers. He knew her body all too well; with one unique motion, he drove her from frantic deprivation to an orgasm so intense, she screamed with pleasure.

He let her scream, listening with a faint smile, as if the sound of her ecstasy was music.

Then the spasms in her body held him captive. The rhythm between them grew in speed and strength. Another orgasm caught her up, or maybe the first one never ended. She didn't know; she only knew he had reached the limit of his restraint, that he rested both elbows on the floor next to her, and his arms shook with the strain. She only knew that above her he panted and groaned, snared at last by the driving passion that existed between them; by the passion that went on forever.

As he thrust harder, as he came at last, he called her name, and she heard the anguish caused by their long separation . . . and in the midst of her climax, she knew that if he deemed it necessary, he would leave her again.

Chapter 5

———◆◆◆———

Caleb leaned, shirtless, against the kitchen counter and watched as Jacqueline cleaned the slice she'd put into his ribs. It was jagged, it was deep, it hurt like hell—and he felt a solid sense of pride in her accomplishment. He'd taught her to fight like that, and no man alive had ever done a better job of spitting him.

Of course, no man alive distracted him like a half-naked Jacqueline. After the sex on the bathroom floor, and the sex on the lumpy mattress, she had showered alone—she had locked the bathroom door and wedged the towel cabinet behind it—and donned ugly faded plaid pajama bottoms and a clean, baggy, short-sleeved T-shirt. He supposed that was her naïve way of saying *Hands off*.

Instead she looked sweet and clean, and smelled of soap and Jacqueline.

The California sun had loved her, caressed her, leaving her skin a beautiful pale tan color. As her hair dried, wisps of pale blond curled around her face and the ends kissed her neck. The shirt had a faded logo for Artie's Giant Ball of Twine, one of the first places she'd worked when she ran away, and her arms were buff. She'd been working out.

Of course.

He'd taught her to do that, too.

"You need stitches," she said for the tenth time.

And for the tenth time, he replied, "The scissors are new and clean, my tetanus shot is up-to-date, and I can get antibiotics in New York City. Just put a butterfly bandage on it. Then start packing."

She dabbed the paper towels into the basin of clean warm water, then carefully wiped the area around the wound. She didn't look up, didn't respond in any way.

His gaze shifted to the fingerless leather gloves she wore. They were well-made, almost the color of her skin, and supple enough to move as she moved. "You didn't used to wear gloves all the time."

"I still don't. Not all the time."

"Why wear them at all?"

"You heard me today in the wine cellar. It's a combination of style and protection."

"Protection?" He mocked her openly. "From the corkscrew, you mean."

This Jacqueline was wiser than the teenager he'd known, less likely to rise to the bait, more inclined to take her own time in answering him—or not answer him at all. "How did you find me?" she asked.

He laughed sharply, and winced at the pain that brought. "We never lost you." He had tracked her from the East Coast to the West Coast, through hardship and good times, for two long years of exile.

She picked up the scissors.

Although perhaps he could have been more tactful about saying so. He tensed, prepared to fend off another attack.

She glanced up and saw him watching warily. "Don't worry. I'm not going to stab you again." She cut strips of first aid tape and hung them on the edge of the Formica. "I mean, what else could you do to me? Screw me again?"

"*I* did *not* screw *you*," he said precisely. Did she think he had forgotten the second time, when she took control, led him to the bed, shoved him down, and mounted him? Did she dare imagine he would not cherish the familiar, sweet madness that gripped them both, the way she took him inside of her, the way he felt as he thrust, and thrust, and thrust, wanting nothing more than to have her today, yesterday, and every day of his life?

He never supposed that a man's thoughts resembled anything like a woman's, but for once, they must have been on the same track, for she said, "No. I suppose you didn't."

"And yes, if given the chance, I could do it again."

She didn't laugh. He hadn't been here long enough to tell for sure, but this Jacqueline didn't even seem to smile, and that was a change he didn't like.

"You could, huh? I suppose. Because it has been two years. That's a long abstinence." One by one, she cut the strips of tape into the butterfly shapes. "But I suppose I'm the only one who refrained."

He didn't answer. There was no point. No answer he made would make her happy.

For all her hostility, she used a gentle touch as she pulled the skin together and applied the first bandage. "She sent you, didn't she?"

"Your mother? Yes."

"It's the time of Choosing."

"Yes."

"I'm not going back."

He didn't answer that, either. She would go back whether she liked it or not.

Jacqueline layered another bandage across the jagged cut. "How is she?"

"Your mother? She's fine."

"I read about her in the tabloids. She's divorced again."

"Yes."

"Why this time?"

"I don't ask."

"That's right. Because it's none of your business."

"No."

"You merely do whatever she tells you to do."

"For which she pays me very well." An excuse. Normally he would never make an excuse, but Jacqueline always got to him.

And as involved as Jacqueline was in her own bitterness, she didn't even notice. "I'd venture to say she got a divorce for the same reason she always gets a divorce. Because she's bored. And she's got a new boyfriend."

"Why do you care? You barely met the last husband."

"I *don't* care. I just wish that for once she'd act her age." Picking up a large sterile gauze pad, Jacqueline savagely tore it open. "I suppose that's too much to ask."

In the last two years, Jacqueline had changed, had grown up in every way but one—she still despised her mother for being who she was. He could have told her that was a waste of time. He'd learned the hard way that parents were as human as anyone else, and sometimes their mistakes had dire consequences.

But Jacqueline wouldn't listen to him. She despised him, too. Despised him and loved him at the same time. It was a painful combination of emotions for him to watch, and for her to live with. He wished . . . Well, it was far too late for him to undo what he had done, and if he had the chance, he knew he'd do it all over again. Apparently, he could resist everything except temptation—and Jacqueline was the only temptation in his life.

She finished taping the gauze over the wound and stepped back to examine her handiwork. She nodded as if pleased. Then her gaze wandered across his shoulders, his chest, his belly. . . .

God. What she did to him.

And what he did to her. For she closed her amber brown eyes for one betraying moment, and turned away. "You can put on your T-shirt now."

He reached for it.

"And leave." She walked across the miniature kitchen and dining room and toward the door.

His hand hovered an inch above his shirt. Deliberately misunderstanding her, he asked, "You want to leave now?"

"I told you. I'm not going." She was smart enough to know she should keep an eye on him, so she turned back to face him. "I mean, what are you going to do? Shove me screaming and yelling through airport security?" Placing her hand on the knob, she said, "I don't *think* so."

Gently, he told her, "I don't have to take you through security. Your mother's new . . . boyfriend . . . loaned her his jet. It's sitting at the airport, fueled and ready to fly."

Jacqueline took a sharp breath, obviously torn between arguing the issue of her mother's boyfriend or her own return.

He didn't wait. "You have until tomorrow to make up your mind."

"My mind is already made up."

"Then—you have until tomorrow to change it. Until then—"

She saw the look in his eyes and, prey to his predator, froze for a fatal moment.

He took the two long steps that put him in front of her. Smoothly, he lifted her hand off the knob, carried it to his lips, and kissed her fingers. "Until then, I know what I would like to do."

"What?" Her hostility was apparent, in her stance, in her tone, in her expression.

But her desire glowed like an ember. He had only to breathe it to life, and she would be his. He leaned closer, pressing her against the door, and kissed her, a slow exploration that gained in heat and light with each moment, with each touch. Against her lips, he whispered, "I want to do this. All day, and all night. With you."

She drew in a breath to speak.

He didn't let her. He slid his fingers into her hair, that remarkable white blond that glowed like platinum and sparkled like diamonds. Tilting her face up, he kissed her until she forgot everything but him, kissed her until he existed only for her. He kissed her resistance away.

Yet when he lifted his lips away, he discovered he was wrong, for she said, "I won't go back."

She would. It was his job to make her.

But for now . . . Their only concern was each other. Only each other.

And the rest of the world could go to hell.

Chapter 6

If Aaron Eagle had had any doubt about the insanity of the people who ran the Gypsy Travel Agency, being brought into the lowest level of the New York subways and being told to stand inside a carefully drawn chalk circle pretty well settled the matter. The board of directors was certifiable, every last one of them, and if he didn't have his own reasons for giving in to their stupid attempt at blackmail, he would be out of here.

Unfortunately, his reasons were good. Better than good.

So he stood here and watched while some weird old woman directed the other five suckers to take care as they stepped in, and not smudge the chalk. Yeah, because if they smudged the chalk, something awful might happen, like all the New Yorkers who hurried past on their way home from work would stare at the odd mix of people high-stepping into a chalk circle underneath a subway stair. Hell, as long as no one got in the way, New Yorkers didn't give a damn if Aaron and his newfound compatriots gathered to perform Riverdance. Which Aaron truly hoped wasn't the next order of business, because he had to draw the line somewhere.

His gaze landed on the pristine, just-swept concrete floor enclosed by red and blue chalk, and he laughed, brief and bitter.

No, he wasn't going to draw any line. As long as this kept him safe, he was their man.

He was Aaron Eagle. He had given his word, and he always kept it. He only hoped to hell they would keep theirs.

One of the two females stepped up, offered her hand, and shook his enthusiastically. "Hi, I'm Charisma Fangorn from Oregon. Isn't this great? I can't wait for the party tonight."

"The party?" Remembering what he'd been told, he said, "At the Gypsy Travel Agency headquarters, you mean."

"Everyone associated with the organization comes in for it. All the old Chosen and all the old directors. There is a huge feast—think Hogwarts at Halloween—and lots of drinking and dancing, and then there's a ceremony where we're formally presented to the group." Her eyes shone with excitement.

"Sounds like a lot of silliness to me," he said, then felt a pang when her face fell. This was why he made it a policy not to hang with young women like this one. The Heidi outfit, studded dog collar and long black hair streaked with purple made him feel old—or at least older than his thirty-two years.

"But they have to present us, or the Chosen Ones from former years might mistake us for, you know"— she glanced around and whispered—"one of the *Others*."

"They could simply send our pictures around in an e-mail." Then he wouldn't have to be there for what sounded like a fraternity hazing.

"What if the e-mail is intercepted and the Others discover our identities?"

"Aren't they going to figure us out eventually?"

"Yes, but this gives us time to train under experienced Chosen." Which did make sense. Then her dimples peeked out. "Besides, the presenting is a tradition."

Yielding to her gusto, he said, "As long as it's tradition, then it must be done."

"Yes. In an organization like this, it's tradition that binds the company together. I read that in *When the World Was Young: A History of the Chosen Ones*."

"Right." The board of directors had presented him with a leather-bound copy, too. It had just never occurred to him to read it.

"Once my mother realized I had a gift, she held a

few séances, but of course, I don't have *that* kind of a gift." She took a place next to him and surveyed the others with enthusiasm. "I do stones."

She said it like he was supposed to know what she was talking about. "Stones."

"Crystals, mostly." She jangled the gold and silver bracelets that wrapped her wrists. "I can hear them sing."

"Sing." He noted the different-colored rocks attached to each bangle, and beneath them, the tattoos. Only he would be willing to bet that they hadn't been put there deliberately. Maybe they had spontaneously sprung up during adolescence. Or maybe she'd been born with them.

He only knew the manner in which the mark had appeared on him. Who knew how it worked with the others?

"I hear the earth song." She almost bounced with enthusiasm. "What's your gift?"

"Hm?"

"We are the Chosen Ones. We have gifts. What's your gift?"

"I don't talk about my gift." He had, they'd assured him, a lot in common with these people. Right now, he doubted that.

Unfazed, she asked, "You're American Indian, aren't you?"

Points for using the politically correct term for his people.

"That's why you're so silent and inscrutable."

Deduct points for heading right for the clichés. "Right you are." If Charisma could see him in his tux, holding a drink, talking finance to all the right men, charming all the right women, while none of them suspected . . . well. Almost none of them. If none of them had suspected, he wouldn't be here.

"What do you do for a living?" she asked.

"I'm a thief."

"Of course you are."

She accepted his statement so blithely, he couldn't tell if she believed him or not.

But it didn't matter because she lowered her voice and nodded her head toward the Blond Surfer Guy. "What do you think his gift is?"

Silent and inscrutable. She had decided Aaron was, and it suited his convenience, so he crossed his arms across his chest like Sitting Bull and shut the hell up.

Charisma sort of jangled her rock bracelets at the guy, and announced, "He's a weird jumble."

Surfer Guy turned. He fixed his mesmerizing blue eyes on her.

She looked back, searching his face, and in relief said, "Oh. Of course. He's Tyler Settles. He's a faith healer and a psychic. Just not a very good psychic."

The way she pronounced that, her certainty, took Aaron off guard, and he dropped the inscrutability. "How can you tell?"

"The stones told me."

That was just stupid, to think stones could gather information and hand it out at her whim.

But no one believed what he could do, either. Thank God, because he'd made a fortune off his specialty.

"Okay, what about him?" He indicated the other guy, swarthy, handsome, and with an indefinable air of authority.

She laughed. "He's Samuel Faa. He's a lawyer. He'll do anything to win a case."

"Being a lawyer is hardly a gift." Aaron had good reason to dislike lawyers. Half the Gypsy Travel Agency's board of directors was lawyers.

"It is when you can control minds."

"Ouch."

"Don't worry. He can't control yours. He doesn't even want to. He doesn't want to be here. They had to blackmail him to get him here at all."

There was a lot of *that* going around. "You got all that from shaking your stones at him?"

"No, from listening at the door."

Aaron viewed her with new respect.

She had emerald green, charcoal-rimmed eyes to go with that black and purple hair, a sweetly rounded face with dimples pressed into her delicately pale cheeks, and he realized she was laughing at him for his caution. This was a woman who embraced life and all its quirks. "How old are you?" he asked.

"Twenty."

"I would have said sixteen."

"Great! I've found people underestimate me when they think I'm young."

His respect notched up another degree. "You're smarter than you look."

"So are you."

The two grinned at each other, and a fast friendship was forged.

Not far away, a woman in her early twenties stood inside the circle. She had just the right hair, just the right makeup, and expensive designer clothes. Aaron's expert eye identified a conservative black Chanel suit offset by a trendy leopard-print Betsey Johnson bag and shoes, platinum-set one-carat diamond studs, and a three-carat platinum-set diamond ring on her right hand. Perfect Boston Brahmin, if her accent was anything to go by, but not so perfect after all. She had an exotic look; her bones were as delicate as porcelain and her eyes were faintly slanted. Somewhere in her unknown bloodlines, she boasted an Asian ancestor. She stood apart from the others, glancing at her watch, a vintage Cartier worth more than the rest of the outfit put together, with a smooth patience that would have done credit to a politician's wife.

"That's Isabelle Mason," Charisma told him.

"Of the Boston Masons." He knew the family, had attended parties at their home, but he had never met Isabelle. Probably she'd been at finishing school, or touring Europe, or doing something high-class and preppy.

Charisma continued to smile brightly, but her voice was subdued and a little depressed as she said, "I can't quite get a fix on her gift. She doesn't like it, doesn't acknowledge it, keeps it restrained."

Isabelle caught Aaron watching her and smiled politely. Caught the lawyer watching her and her expression became Botox smooth.

"Whoa. She doesn't like him," Charisma observed.

"No . . ." Aaron wasn't so sure. There was something between those two. He nodded at the young guy in frayed jeans, dirty running shoes, and a denim jacket. "Who's the kid?"

Charisma goggled at Aaron. "Don't you *know*? That's Aleksandr Wilder."

Aaron shrugged. He'd already figured out if he kept his mouth shut, she'd spill everything she knew.

She did. "Nineteen years ago, the Wilders broke their family's covenant with the devil. It was a big deal in the world of the Chosen Ones, and I imagine in the world of the Others, too."

"That would do it." The board of directors, a group of sharp-eyed, middle-aged men in suits, had given Aaron the barest outlines of the organization. They called themselves the Gypsy Travel Agency, located in a historic cast-iron building in SoHo. They were widely famous for leading treks into the wildest parts of the world, had been doing it since the late nineteenth century and apparently collecting a wad of money from satisfied customers. According to them, the agency had started because of their gypsy background and their dedication to combating evil.

None of the directors looked Romany to Aaron; more like a bunch of middle-aged white guys in suits with one politically correct clean-cut black guy. And none of them looked like they'd ever been in combat with more than a New York investment broker.

But then, he didn't really care who they were or what they did, because while they made it clear they would use him as a tour guide if needed, his real job for them related to his special talent—and they owned him and his talent for the next seven years.

"So, did the Wilders work for the Gypsy Travel Agency?"

"The Wilders raise grapes in Washington and sell wines in California."

Aaron blinked at Charisma. "Is that a cover like the Gypsy Travel Agency?"

"No. They really raise grapes and sell wines. They're completely out of the paranormal business now. None of them can shape-shift anymore."

Seeking a way out of his confusion, Aaron said, "Let me see if I've got this right—the Wilders broke a covenant with the devil that let them shape-shift."

"That's it."

"So what's the Wilder kid doing here? What's his special gift?"

The Wilder kid stepped close. "For starters, I've got really good hearing."

Aaron had to admire him for his poise, had to admire both the kids, because Charisma grinned and stuck out her hand. "Hi, I'm Charisma Fangorn. I'm *so* glad to meet you, Aleksandr."

Aleksandr shook her hand, then Aaron's.

"So what's your gift?" Charisma asked.

Aleksandr stuffed his hands in his pockets. "I don't have one."

Charisma looked affronted. "Of course you do. You walked through the fire with your mother."

"Yeah." Aleksandr paused to scuff his feet on the tile floor. "There's speculation, probably justified, that my mother's gift protected me."

Aaron's head swiveled between them. He had no idea what they were talking about, but he had to admit it was fascinating.

"Why justified?" Charisma asked.

"When I was thirteen, I decided maybe it was me, so I tried grabbing a burning stick. Man, did I get in trouble. My father and grandfather aren't exactly keen on teenagers who do dumb stuff." Aleksandr shook back his shaggy blond hair. "While we were in the emergency room, I thought my mother and grandmother were going to rip me a new one."

"So it was bad?" Charisma prompted.

Aaron figured the kid was exaggerating the extent of his injuries to impress Charisma.

Then Aleksandr held up his hand.

Burn scars rippled the skin, and two of the fingers were fused together.

Charisma winced.

"What the hell made you do that?" Snapping at Aleksandr made Aaron feel as old as the kid's grandfather, but . . . good God. That looked like hell, and he bet it had hurt forever. Maybe still did.

"We were out in the woods. My cousins were there. The Wilder cousins are younger, and I didn't care what they thought. But my grandmother's family is Rom, and they're all so wild and tough." Aleksandr hunched his shoulders and mumbled, "I wanted to impress them."

"Okay. I get that." Aaron did. He'd been a dumb kid himself once.

Charisma shook her bracelets at Aleksandr. Shook them again, and frowned. "You really don't have a gift?"

"Not that anybody can figure out," Aleksandr said.

"And you've got family? You weren't abandoned?" Aaron stared at the old woman standing on the outside of the circle, the one who had led them here, the one who was apparently some sort of dedicated servant of the Gypsy Travel Agency. "Hey! You! Martha!"

The woman turned to face him. Her brown face was creased with age. Her gray hair was long, braided, and wrapped around her head like some Austrian yodeler. Chalk dusted her gnarled fingers.

"The board of directors said there'd be seven Chosen," Aaron called.

"Sh!" Martha hurried—well, hobbled, really—around the outside of the circle toward him.

Aaron continued. "They said that we all had gifts that we'd received because we were abandoned."

"Mr. Eagle. We do not discuss this in public!" Martha stood inches away from Aaron, her toes almost on the circle, and stared at him with black, unblinking eyes.

Look at that. Aaron had just found the gypsy in the Gypsy Travel Agency. "Then we shouldn't be standing in the middle of a subway station, should we?"

"This is where Suzanne's powers are at their greatest." Martha spoke as if Aaron should know what she meant. "But I am not supposed to talk to you. Not while you're in the circle!"

"Then quietly, tell me about the kid." Aaron had Martha over a barrel.

And Martha knew it.

Charisma and Aleksandr edged closer.

In a low voice, Martha said, "In the last seven cycles, the gifts have been fading."

The Abandoned Ones were chosen every seven years. So, seven cycles times seven years . . . Aaron did the math. In the last forty-nine years, Martha was saying. "The gifts have been fading? What the *hell* does that mean?"

"Mr. Eagle, let us not mention *hell* when we're so close to its mouth I can smell the brimstone." Martha sounded so fierce, so convinced, Aaron looked around for the flames. "I mean the gifts given to you six are mere shadows of the gifts given in years past."

"Really?" Aaron had always been pretty impressed with his gift. But actually, lately, it *had* been fading. That was what had gotten him into this mess to start with. "Does anybody know why?"

"There is some talk that we've wandered away from our purpose, or that modern life has corrupted us, or—" Martha stopped herself.

"What do *you* think, Martha?" Charisma asked.

"It's not my place to say," Martha said primly.

"It's not your place to say, or you don't want to talk about it so close to hell?" Aaron hated this pussyfooting around.

"Are we done speaking in such an inappropriate manner?" Martha turned away.

Aaron started to reach out and grab her. And something zapped him, something like static electricity, but . . . dangerous. Much, much more dangerous.

Martha looked back at him, satisfaction cold in her dark eyes.

Aaron had stepped in the circle under his own will. He would leave when someone else allowed him.

So. He'd learned something today. Watch out for chalk circles.

"Was there anything else?" Martha asked.

Damned right, there was. "Let me see if I've got this right. You guys took the kid"—Aaron indicated Aleksandr—"because there was no one else, and you hope he develops a gift or some specialty you can use?"

"I'm not privy to the decisions of the directors," Martha said, but she nodded her head.

"Is that why there's only six? Because there have always been seven." Charisma did know her stuff.

For the first time, Aaron wondered if he should have glanced through the text he'd been given after he signed on the dotted line.

"We have one more coming. I hope." Martha sounded disgusted. Then she looked beyond them, and the old woman broke into a broad smile. In a voice hushed with pleasure and worship, she said, "Suzanne has arrived."

Chapter 7

Aaron gaped in amazement.

Martha hadn't been saying *Suzanne*. She'd been saying *Zusane*, and no wonder she looked like an awestruck teenage girl.

Zusane was . . . Zusane. One of those women who only had one name, who was famous for being famous, who was Hungarian or Romanian or some nationality that gave her a rich, smoky accent. Zusane had had more husbands—seven? eight?—than anyone could remember, all of them had been rich, and she'd left them all considerably less wealthy and a lot more whiny.

Now she was walking through the subway station, three bodyguards in front, acting like the prow of a ship to cut their way through the afternoon rush hour crowd, and another two bodyguards in back, making sure that no one crowded her from behind. Because dressed like that, she was one hell of a target. She wore a long, skintight dress covered with gold sequins from the low neckline, over every inch of her curvaceous body, and down to the weighted hem. With every step, she showed a flash of shapely leg, and she walked so smoothly on four-inch spiked heels, they might as well have been Reeboks. Her black silk gloves extended from her fingertips over her elbows to her well-toned upper arms, and she held a small evening bag decorated with Swarovski crystals. Like American royalty, she waved to the crowds, shook hands, signed autographs.

"Your jaw's hanging open," Charisma said.

She was talking to Aleksandr, but Aaron shut his mouth, too.

As Zusane stopped at Martha's side, the bodyguards took their places around the edge of the circle and turned to face the crowds.

Zusane put her hands on Martha's shoulders and kissed both her cheeks. She whispered something that made Martha nod, roll her eyes, and indicate the circle.

Lifting her skirt, Zusane carefully stepped inside.

As if by magic, people stopped staring and pointing at her.

As if by magic . . . Aaron looked around at the others. Was there something about the chalk circle that made them invisible to all the normal people and removed them from their minds?

Of course. *Magic* would explain a lot.

Zusane removed her long gloves, a slow striptease that titillated and entertained. And all the while she observed the six in the circle, her blue eyes thoughtful and perceptive. She tucked the gloves into her bag, then turned to Aaron. "Mr. Eagle. How good to see you again." Her voice was throaty and amused.

Aaron had run into Zusane one other time, about a year ago, right after he'd finished a job, and she'd looked at him and spoken to him as if she could *see* him.

Now he knew why. She *had* seen him. She had a gift, too. "I'll bet you're the reason I'm here," he said.

She laughed, throwing her head back to release a light chuckle. "You don't hold that against me, do you?"

"No. No, I wish I could, but I can't."

Up close, she wasn't as young as she first appeared. She had wrinkles around her eyes and a faint thin scar at her ear left by a chin lift.

It didn't matter. She was magnificent.

Taking her hand, he kissed the fingers. "It is good to see you again, Zusane."

"Charm is such a rare thing in an American." She placed one hand on his chest over his heart. For a long moment, she looked into his eyes, and he felt almost light-headed, a fly caught in a spider's seductive trap. "But in your business, it is a necessity, is it not?"

"One of many," he said.

"You will do very well," she said.

"Thank you." He supposed.

She lifted her hand away, and at once he was freed from her spell. He watched in curiosity and amazement as she turned to Charisma and offered her hand. In a brisk, businesslike tone, she said, "Hello, dear, how are you doing today?"

Charisma took the pale, slender hand. "I'm thrilled to meet you. You're a legend, the most famous of them all."

"Do not be misled by the glamour."

"I'm not." Charisma's enthusiasm was boundless. "I read about you in *When the World Was Young: A History of the Chosen Ones.*"

"You are having a wonderful time at the Gypsy Travel Agency, are you not?" Zusane took possession of Charisma's wrists, stones and all, and held them.

"Oh, yes!"

"Will you be ready for the challenges ahead?" Zusane's smile disappeared, and she looked almost grieved. "For you will be greatly challenged."

"I'm going to study. I'm going to prepare. And when it's my turn, I'll do what has to be done." Charisma was so young, so sure of herself.

"You will be afraid, and in the dark."

Charisma stared into Zusane's face, closed her eyes so slowly, she might have been falling asleep, then opened them again. When she did, Aaron was startled to see the irrepressible Charisma's eyes fill with tears. "Yes. I see. I am such a coward."

"No. A coward you are not." Zusane kissed Charisma's forehead, then turned to Aleksandr. In a voice like a whiplash, she said, "Look at me, Mr. Wilder. My eyes are up here!"

Aleksandr yanked his gaze from her cleavage to her face, and blushed scarlet.

"Let me see your hands, both of them!" she said.

He showed them, palms up, then on her signal, turned them so she could see the backs.

She slid her cupped hands beneath them. Whipping around, she glared balefully at Martha. "This boy would be better in college."

"Yes, Zusane," Martha said. "He is in college."

She turned back to Aleksandr. "Where? What are you studying?"

"Fordham. Engineering."

Aaron didn't have to be a psychic to know what Zusane was thinking. The kid was no dummy.

"Good." She nodded. "Sometimes life doesn't turn out like we wish, and we need something to fall back on."

"So you don't see a gift?" Aleksandr whispered.

"No. But there's something here. . . ." She slid her gaze from Aleksandr's left shoulder and across his chest. "The tattoo?"

"It's there."

"It came at adolescence." She sounded certain. "Does it resemble your father's? Your grandfather's?"

"The colors, yes, but the pattern has never been seen before." Aleksandr shifted awkwardly. "Or so my grandfather says."

"He would know." Zusane patted his cheek. "All right. Don't worry. Study hard. Make your family proud."

"I always do," Aleksandr said.

Zusane smiled at him and headed toward the others in the circle.

In an undertone, Aaron asked Charisma, "Zusane is the most famous *what*?"

"Psychic." Charisma really did know everything. "She's the current psychic for the Gypsy Travel Agency."

"And the psychic is always a woman?" Aaron watched as Zusane approved Isabelle Mason.

"Not always, but the guys never seem to quite get it right." Charisma watched, too, all her attention focused on the drama playing out before them. "The guy who's here—Tyler Settles—calls himself a psychic. Zusane has always been very vocal about her disapproval of male seers. This is the first time the directors have tried to bring one in."

Zusane waved her hands around Tyler, close to his skin, but never touching.

Tyler preened, flattered by her attention.

She frowned.

He spoke to her, smiling all the while. Brought her gaze up to his.

And after a tense pause, she laughed and relaxed.

"Martha would tell us that because of the lack of talent this year, they had to stoop to trying out a male seer," Aaron said to Charisma.

"Yes. I think you're right." Charisma shivered. "Spooky, isn't it, to think we're the weakest group since the Chosen Ones were formed."

"I don't really know what difference it makes," Aaron said indifferently. "It's not like we have to do anything but what we're good at."

Charisma shot him a cautious, sideways glance.

Remembering the directors' slick description of his duties, he mulled and realized—they were paying him well, promising him protection, and if they were telling the truth, they asked very little in return. "What can go wrong?"

"In ordinary times, a job at the Gypsy Travel Agency is dull." Charisma positively sparkled with reassurance.

He wasn't buying it. "In extraordinary times?"

"Ohhh . . . I suppose you could say that in the past, extraordinary times have been . . . exciting."

"Is that a euphemism for 'dangerous'?" He'd joined up to get away from "dangerous."

"You really ought to read that book," she told him.

"As soon as I get out of this circle," he promised.

Zusane stood between Isabelle Mason and Samuel Faa, and her frown returned and deepened. She threw her arms out in a wide, encompassing gesture. Her sequins shimmered in the fluorescent light. Her fingers, manicured with red, formed wide stars. "Never in my experience have I sensed something like this."

From outside the circle, Aaron heard a ripple of amusement.

Zusane paid no attention. "There is something very wrong with this combination, a whiff of something rotten, and until I can discover what is wrong, I cannot release this team."

The laughter in the subway grew, and Aaron did a quick check. The New Yorkers were pointing at this suit-wearing, dangerous-looking Italian guy carrying a long-legged jean-clad blond girl. He had her in a fireman's lift, she was kicking and shrieking, and the odd couple was headed straight for them.

Didn't that just figure? Because right now, this subway station was the epicenter of oddness.

Relentlessly, Zusane plowed on. "Each of you, come close so I can discover the discordance. . . ." She caught sight of the Italian and the girl. Her voice trailed off. Melodrama fell away from her like a discarded cloak. She tapped her toe. She narrowed her eyes. She looked like a shrewish wife—or a disapproving mother.

The Italian strode forward, ignoring the laughter, ignoring the blonde's kicks to his ribs. He kept his gaze fixed on the circle.

Just outside the chalk line, he dropped the girl to her feet, steadied her with his hands on her arms, and looked down at her, demanding . . . something.

The girl almost flamed with fury. "I won't!" she shouted at the guy.

The guy didn't move. He simply stared at her.

Zusane glared at her.

The girl set her jaw and said, "I won't!" again. But the words were softer now, almost dreamy. Perspiration popped out on her forehead, and she lifted her hair off her neck. Her chest rose and fell with her breathing, a slow, hypnotic motion, and Aaron could almost see her consciousness fade.

Everyone in the circle, everyone outside it, watched, spellbound by anticipation.

Drawn by a certainty he couldn't explain, Aaron looked at Zusane. She leaned forward, hand on her chest, yearning etched on her face.

She loved the girl, but she wanted something from her. Or maybe . . . she wanted something for her.

In that instant, the girl snapped back to place, to the moment. She pushed at the Italian's chest, said, "All *right*," and moving like a dancer, she leaped into the circle.

In that second, Aaron fell in love. Whoever she was,

she was built, she was blond, she was graceful, and she had a radiance that reminded him of Zusane at her best.

Zusane's mask of beauty cracked with disappointment. For the first time, her voice lost its husky warmth. "At last. Our seventh member has arrived. She could have been on time. She could be dedicated. She could be organized. She could wear something more respectful of this momentous event. She could *occasionally* clean her room."

The girl glanced around at the Chosen in the circle. She rolled her eyes, and with a gesture at Zusane, she mouthed, *Sorry*.

With a shrill edge, Zusane continued. "She could at least do as well as the Wilder boy and attend college when her mother pulls every string to get her admitted to Harvard even though her grades weren't good enough to—" Zusane stopped and gathered her composure.

The girl waved at the others, one of those tiny, embarrassed waves. "Hi, everybody. I'm Zusane's daughter, Jacqueline."

So Zusane was a mother, Jacqueline's mother, and no matter how glamorous Zusane appeared, she was just like any other mother—frustrated as hell with her rebellious daughter.

Beside him, Charisma waved back at Jacqueline, and pointed. "Aleksandr Wilder. Isabelle Mason. Samuel Faa. Aaron Eagle. Tyler Settles." With another little wave, she said, "I'm Charisma."

Zusane glared, and her voice swelled majestically. "Are we *done*?"

"Yes. Sorry." Charisma's voice squeaked.

"Mother. Don't be rude," Jacqueline said.

But Charisma sounded unrepentant when she murmured to Aaron, "But Zusane can't be her real mother. It's not possible if she's one of the Abandoned Ones."

"Maybe she's like Aleksandr—an experiment the directors are trying," Aaron replied.

"Hm. Maybe." Charisma indicated the guy who'd carried Zusane's daughter to the site. "Look at *him*."

He remained immobile where the girl had left him, staring blindly, waiting.

Charisma shook her bracelets at him. "He's involved with Jacqueline."

"Obviously." Aaron didn't need singing rocks to see that.

"He's not gifted, because he knows we're in here, but he can't see us," Charisma said.

"Right." This was one weird situation Aaron had gotten himself into.

Taking Jacqueline's left wrist in her hand, Zusane turned her palm up and looked at it. She expressed her disgust eloquently, Aaron thought, although he didn't understand a word of the language she was speaking.

Jacqueline wore fingerless gloves in a leather that almost matched her skin tone.

"So it's come to this," Zusane said. "You contain your power behind a shield."

"A glove is hardly a shield." Quickly Jacqueline added, "And I don't have any power."

Zusane smiled triumphantly. "Then take it off."

"Fine." Jacqueline stripped away her glove.

"Look." Zusane held Jacqueline's palm up to Jacqueline's face. "The most powerful sign, one not seen since the first two Abandoned Ones."

In an undertone, Charisma explained, "The mark on her hand must be a stylized eye, done in black lines."

Aaron craned his neck, but couldn't see the mark.

"The bad twin," Jacqueline said to Zusane. "Remember, Mother. She was the *bad* twin."

Zusane rolled on, ignoring her daughter's fierce objection. "You push your gift aside, deny it, claim that you can't take my place!"

"I can't!" Jacqueline leaned closer to Zusane and sniffed. "Have you been smoking?"

"Certainly not!"

"Hanging around in a cigar bar again?"

"No."

Jacqueline sniffed the air around her. "Can you smell that?"

"You are trying to distract me."

"No, I'm not. Something's burning," Jacqueline said with assurance.

"I don't care if something's burning. I only care about what I've seen . . . I've seen . . ." Zusane tilted her head. Her eyes became unfocused. Her body remained, but Zusane—her personality, her *self*—was no longer here. Beneath the expertly applied cosmetics, her complexion changed from pale to a light green, and her mouth worked helplessly.

"What's wrong with her?" Charisma whispered.

"I don't like this," Aleksandr muttered.

"Mother?" Jacqueline gripped Zusane's hand. When she did, her eyes fluttered closed and she paled, too.

Zusane shrieked. Shrieked so loudly, Jacqueline jumped, opened her eyes, and shook her head as if waking from a trance.

"Look out!" Zusane screamed. She writhed. She flung out her arms. "Look out! It's going to blow! There's a bomb! *Run!*"

Chapter 8

———◈———

In Zusane's whole lifetime of convenient visions and relentless overacting, Jacqueline had never seen her behave like this.

"Oh, God. Oh, God!" Zusane's gaze was fixed, her eyes wide and horrified. "Look. Look! It's blown up!"

"Mother!" Zusane was scaring Jacqueline, scaring her to death. "This bomb. Where is it?"

Zusane shouted, "Fire! Fire! Oh, my God! The relics. They're gone. The carnage! Look at the bodies. Blood. So much blood!"

Jacqueline tried again. "Is it *here*?"

"It's gone. It's—fire! *Fire!*" Zusane broke into a sweat and whimpered as if the flames burned her skin.

"Mama, please. You're going to hurt yourself." Jacqueline wrapped her arms around Zusane, trying to contain her violent gestures, her wild thrashing.

Nothing stopped Zusane. Nothing—no consoling murmurs, no reassuring pats—comforted her. Although Zusane was shorter than Jacqueline, she was solidly built and strong, and her struggles would leave bruises. But Jacqueline couldn't leave her alone. She might hurt herself. She might break the circle, and Jacqueline knew all too well how dangerous that was.

The other Chosen looked as if they didn't know whether to lend a hand or run away.

Desperately, Jacqueline glanced toward Caleb.

Zusane's shrieks had penetrated outside the circle, for he'd discarded his thin veneer of civilization. His eyes were fierce slits, his mouth compressed and his nostrils flared. The bodyguards had their weapons drawn, and Caleb gave orders that put them into high alert. Turning, he prepared to leap into the circle.

Martha body-tackled him.

Caleb threw a punch, realized at the last second who had brought him down, and barely avoided breaking Martha's face.

Martha held Caleb, talked fast, while Caleb stared into the circle. He wasn't really listening, Jacqueline could tell, but he, too, understood the power of the circle.

Zusane began to sob in deep, wrenching sounds that were all the more painful for lacking tears. "They're all gone. They're gone. Everything is gone. What will we do? What will we do?"

The subway passengers turned and stared, hearing a commotion, but not quite able to see the figures inside the circle.

"Are we safe?" Isabelle asked.

"Inside the circle, we are," Charisma answered. "It's protected by—"

"Chalk?" Isabelle looked remarkably calm, but her voice cracked with strain.

"Enchantment," Charisma whispered doubtfully.

"Fire . . . gone, all gone . . ." Zusane's voice was fading.

"Mother. Talk to me. Where's the fire? Who's gone? *What's happened?*" Frantic to get through, Jacqueline shook her.

Zusane blinked once. Twice. Like a marionette on strings, she turned her head in little jerks. She looked at her daughter. She saw her—and collapsed into her arms.

Beneath her mother's limp weight, Jacqueline staggered and went down.

The men leaped forward. Tyler clutched at them; then under the combined load, his grip failed. Aaron and Samuel caught them a split second before their heads hit the concrete floor.

Jacqueline freed herself from Zusane's clutches, then ordered, "Lay her down."

Gently, the men placed Zusane, pale and unconscious, on the floor. They knelt there, waiting and anxious.

Charisma joined them and sat at Zusane's head, brushing at Zusane's aura . . . or something.

It must have worked, because Zusane groaned—not an attractive, breathless moan, but a full-bodied, despairing moan. She opened her eyes, and with relief, Jacqueline realized her mother was back from wherever she'd gone. Zusane clung to Jacqueline with desperate hands, almost childish in her despair. "It's the worst thing that could have happened. The end of the world."

"Tell me," Jacqueline coaxed, and stroked Zusane's hair off her sweaty forehead.

"I never in my worst nightmares foretold this, but now . . . now . . . now I have seen it. I have felt it. The explosion rumbled the ground beneath my feet. The fire burned my hands and face. I wanted to run, but couldn't." Zusane gave a sob, all the more heartrending for being harsh and agonized. "The Gypsy Travel Agency is no more."

The guys glanced at each other.

Samuel said, "The Gypsy Travel Agency's building is old, but solid. What could have happened?"

Zusane replied with conviction. "Sabotage. Sabotage! Now, when everyone has gathered for the Choosing. The offices, the library, the sleeping quarters, all of it— blew up. It's burning. Everyone inside is dead. Dead. The directors are gone. The Chosen Ones are gone." In a trembling whisper, she said, "They're all gone."

Charisma continued to brush at Zusane's aura. "Don't worry. *We're* still here."

"Oh, God." Zusane staggered to her feet. Putting her manicured fingers to her forehead, she muttered, "The world is lost."

"Mother!" Once again, Zusane's rudeness left Jacqueline speechless. And embarrassed. And wondering why everyone looked at her as if *she* was the crazy one. "I'm sorry," she said to Charisma. "When she comes out of a vision, she's—"

"Truthful?" The girl seemed unruffled.

"That, too." Personally, Jacqueline thought her mother used the truth as a weapon and a tool, and could twist it to her purposes at any time.

Zusane swayed on her feet, then visibly gained control of herself. "One good thing will come out of this disaster." She took a snowy handkerchief from her purse and blotted her damp forehead and upper lip. "At last, *you'll* have to face up to responsibilities."

She was talking to Jacqueline. "What are you talking about?" Familiar panic began to rise in Jacqueline's throat.

Zusane dropped the handkerchief to the floor. "I mean I have a party to attend. In Turkey."

Jacqueline picked it up. "You can't be serious." Not even Zusane could scream like a woman seeing bloody murder, announce that her own company had been blown to smithereens. . . . Not even she could be selfish enough to then breeze away to attend a party.

"You'll have to take the reins for your little group. They will be lost without a psychic." Zusane glanced at Tyler, frowned as if puzzled, then lowered her voice. "A competent psychic."

"Not me," Jacqueline protested frantically.

Zusane took Jacqueline's wrist and once again showed her her palm. "You *know* what that means."

Jacqueline stared at the eye, etched into the skin, black and emphatic, and drawn with the skill of da Vinci for the *Mona Lisa*.

She didn't care. She hated the mark. "It means I'm a freak."

"A freak, yes. But a prescient freak." Zusane dropped Jacqueline's hand and collected her black satin opera-length gloves out of her purse and pulled them on, a slow, intricate process with which Jacqueline was far too familiar.

For all that Jacqueline had been raised on the legend and the traditions of the Chosen Ones, she had never wanted to be one of them, if for no other reason than her mother wanted her there. Now, because of a fatal moment of weakness, she had stepped into the circle. She figured that had all the weight of a Girl Scout bridging ceremony, a trivial moment of childish swearing.

Yet . . . she *did* still get the Girl Scouts' magazine, and she'd kept her badge vest wrapped in tissue paper in her cedar chest, so maybe the oath she had sworn at the age of eight had been exactly that—an oath on which she could stake her soul.

And maybe stepping into a chalk circle drawn with precision on the floor of a New York City subway station had been an unspoken vow of equal importance.

Because it wasn't the oath or the gesture that was important, but whether or not she chose to honor it.

She wasn't one of the Chosen Ones. Because she had walked into the circle of her volition, she *had* chosen.

Now she watched miserably as Martha took the whisk brush from the pocket in her skirt and started dusting the chalk off the floor.

As if a great barrier had been removed, the sound of the subway station increased and Caleb locked his gaze on her again.

Of course. Until she'd stepped into the circle, he hadn't let her out of his sight since San Michael. Somehow, she suspected she might never escape him again.

"Darling." Zusane pinched Jacqueline's chin to get her attention. "On the day I took you in, I foresaw a time when you would take my place among the Chosen Ones."

"You adopted me because you wanted a clone." Jacqueline lowered her voice, wanting desperately to keep this confrontation private.

Zusane raised her voice, because she loved nothing as much as melodrama played to the crowd. "I adopted you because I saw you and knew you were mine. Is that so impossible?"

Jacqueline jerked her head away. "Considering that I spent my entire childhood waiting for you to come home from a party, I'd say yes."

"I had no one to depend on except myself. If we were to live in the manner I desired, I had to stay on top of things."

"You could have gotten an education. You're smart enough." Of that Jacqueline was certain. Zusane had an IQ off the charts, and a sense about others that had nothing to do with telepathy and everything to do with an earthy knowledge of the human race.

"My dear. What a lovely tribute. But look at me!" Zusane spread her hands wide to indicate her Marilyn Monroe body covered by glittering sequins. "This is not the form of an accountant, and I used it for us. For *you*. So you would have a good life."

"Mother. This is not the time for this discussion. We, all of us, need to go to the Gypsy Travel Agency and—"

Zusane talked louder still, talked over the top of Jacqueline. "I wanted you to have the childhood I never had, so I kept you innocent and untouched until—"

Jacqueline's patience snapped. "Until your body-guard seduced me."

Zusane stopped talking. Her gaze dropped. "Yes." She looked up again. "But I took steps to correct the matter."

"Did you?" Jacqueline had wondered. Now she knew.

Not that that made it any better. On Zusane's command, Caleb had dropped Jacqueline like a hot potato.

What a guy.

"You sent him to get me in California." Remembering the day and night before he dragged her to the private jet at the Napa Valley airport, the hours of passion, the flight—and fight—that followed, Jacqueline asked, "What were you thinking?"

Zusane's blue eyes got soft and dreamy, the way they did when she knew something no one else did. Then she drilled a look into Jacqueline's eyes, and her voice was brisk. "I had to use him. He was the only man who could get you here."

Jacqueline's bitter cup overflowed as she turned to look at Caleb. "Your own personal Rottweiler. Don't bother to pay him a bonus. I already reimbursed him."

Zusane considered the two of them, and Jacqueline remembered she was an expert on what made men and women tick. "Did you."

Even Jacqueline heard the similarity in their voices, in their tones. No matter that Zusane wasn't her birth mother, or that she didn't want to be like her—Zusane had been her role model, and they were alike.

Taking Jacqueline in her embrace, Zusane pressed her cheek to Jacqueline's. "All right, darling, I've got an important assignation that is more imperative than ever. So I'm off." She blew kisses at the Chosen.

Caleb directed the bodyguards into place.

Aggravated and embarrassed, Jacqueline stood stiff and cold.

Seeing her expression, Zusane stopped her diva imitation and pleaded, "Don't be that way, darling."

Jacqueline began, "If you would only stay—"

Zusane pulled a pocket watch from between her breasts and studied it. "I'm going to be late. I can't be late. Now . . . you be good and make me proud." She hugged Jacqueline again, stepped into the circle of bodyguards, and started toward the subway stairs. "I know you'll be a wonderful seer for the Gypsy Travel Agency—"

"You said it was blown up," Jacqueline answered.

Zusane stopped short.

Martha straightened, whisk broom in hand.

Zusane turned to face the small group of seven huddled in what remained of the circle. "Yes, but the Chosen Ones are not vanquished!" She sounded incredulous.

The Chosen Ones stared as if she were speaking her native language.

Zusane blew her breath out and up, trying to cool her forehead. "Darlings. Charisma is right. The building is gone. The experienced fighters are gone. But you *are* the Chosen Ones. By stepping into the circle, you accepted your fate, and that is to vanquish evil. As long as you are alive, the Chosen Ones live."

Samuel spoke for all of them. "I signed a contract with the board of directors of the Gypsy Travel Agency. If that contract has been blown up, what binds me to my agreement?"

For the first time in her life, Jacqueline saw Zusane throw off her frivolous persona and become what she could always have been—a noble, clear-sighted creature. "I don't know, Mr. Faa. You're a lawyer. What *does* bind you to your agreement with the Gypsy Travel Agency?"

No one answered. They looked at each other, then at Zusane, and even Mr. Faa looked embarrassed at her forthright question.

"Yes," she said. "Whether or not the paper is burned, you put your signature there with full knowledge of what it meant. You gave your word. Does it stand for less—or more—because the contract is gone forever?"

The seven of them squirmed like kids caught lying.

"We're stuck with each other," Aleksandr said.

"Aleksandr, darling, you are so smart. I don't know how, but someday, what an asset you'll be!" Zusane blew another air kiss toward Jacqueline, and with a jaunty wave of her hand, she again started toward the exit.

Caleb urged her bodyguards to run, to keep their pistols close at hand.

Zusane might have already airily dismissed the explosion at the Gypsy Travel Agency, but Caleb had not. He shot Jacqueline a grim look, then hurried toward Zusane. He stopped her, spoke quietly and urgently.

She took him by the hand and, in a voice that projected clearly across the distance, said, "No, darling, you stay. I depend on you to protect Jacqueline."

Jacqueline thought he would object.

But he stood still, leaned down so Zusane could kiss him on both cheeks, then watched her walk away.

Chapter 9

❧

Caleb took a moment to observe the expressions that hurried across Jacqueline's face: surprise, suspicion, horror, and possibly . . . pleasure. Hopefully, pleasure. But fear drove him like a prod. "Hurry, Martha. Finish your duty. We've got to get away from here."

He felt like a shepherd defending his helpless sheep against some unknown peril.

The fledgling Chosen looked at him with varying reactions. One by one he checked them off in his mind: The thief, Aaron Eagle. The lawyer, Samuel Faa. The lady, Isabelle Mason. The boy, Aleksandr Wilder. The boy-psychic, Tyler Settles. Charisma Fangorn, the girl with the tattoos and the crystals. And Jacqueline, the unwilling seer.

He knew them all; he'd been present when Zusane and the board of directors had argued about who held the right gifts for this cycle. He'd watched as they were interviewed, and more than once, Zusane had asked his opinion. Yet he didn't know how the new Chosen would react to this kind of pressure; they were untested, and he didn't have to be clairvoyant to know this was a disaster of untold proportions, or that he had to step carefully or he would lose them all.

The men were aware of the danger, but jockeying for lead position. The boy stood morosely, hands in his pockets, waiting for someone to tell him what to do. The women were not worried about their places in the pecking order, for better than the men, they understood the ramifications of Zusane's vision.

Caleb spoke to the group, low and intense. "We need to stick together. For now, follow me"—he acknowledged the men and women, their intelligence and their wills—"and when we're safe, we'll sort out who's in charge."

"Why should we follow you?" Faa fixed his dark eyes on Caleb. "For all we know, this could be a hoax. This could be a test for us. You could be in league with the devil."

Martha straightened. "Mr. D'Angelo is the longtime head of Miss Vargha's bodyguards. He is a trustworthy gentleman."

"Thank you, Martha." Caleb waited for Faa and the other men to make their judgment. Waited for Jacqueline to speak for him, too.

From her expression, it was clear he could wait forever.

"You gentlemen can do as you like. I'm going with Miss Vargha's bodyguard." Isabelle stepped forward to join Caleb.

Charisma followed suit. "I'm good with that."

Aleksandr moved to join them.

Faa and the other two nodded. The Chosen Ones were on board; all except Jacqueline, who stood staring toward the subway stairs.

Caleb had conquered, for the moment. "Martha, hurry!" he said.

Martha finished, tucked away her whisk broom, and joined Caleb. "Where to, sir?"

"First we'll go to Zusane's apartment—that's safe; then—"

"Sir?" Martha indicated a figure stalking away from them.

"Jacqueline!" Caleb leaped after her.

At his voice, she broke into a run, up the stairs and into the street.

He followed, and behind him he heard Martha calling to the Chosen Ones, "Keep up with them. Stay together and keep up!"

It was early evening, but still light. The street was thronged with people from the neighborhood, Italians and Asians, mostly. Emergency vehicles, loud with sirens, inched through the traffic. Ahead of Caleb, Jacqueline dodged through the crowd, heading up two blocks to the street where the Gypsy Travel Agency was housed. She was thin, long-legged, fast, and determined, and he caught up with her as she turned the corner into the heart of the excitement.

He grabbed her arms, wanting to stop her before she rushed past the police barriers.

But she stopped on her own, held stock-still by horror.

The cast-iron buildings stood like a row of teeth rising above the sidewalk—and right in the middle of the block, one of the teeth had been knocked out. The building was gone, nothing left but a black hole in the ground.

More important and even more strange—none of the buildings around it had been touched. There was no debris on the street; the building seemed to have imploded. The fire still burned, contained within the vanished building.

"Even the smoke is rising straight up into the sky like there's a chimney holding it in place. . . ." Isabelle murmured incredulously.

In a low voice, Charisma said, "The enchantments that protect the outer skin of the building are still in place."

"Oh." Isabelle stood quiet and thoughtful. "Oh."

Only when the smoke had passed the barriers of where the building walls had once stood did the wind catch it and carry it away.

The people who stood with them, the people off the streets, the police and firemen, were as stunned, speaking in whispers. "Weird." "How is that possible?" "How could terrorists do that?"

"I had to see. . . . I hoped she was wrong. But she was right. Mother was right. The explosion obliterated . . . them. The rooms. The papers. The library. The . . . friends." Jacqueline shivered in shock.

Caleb wrapped his arms around her, pulled her chilled body into his, and she leaned against him as if standing alone was more than she could bear. He spoke into her hair. "It looks fake."

Behind him, Martha said, "A horror movie."

The Chosen Ones crowded around Caleb and Jacqueline. They gaped, transfixed by the impossible.

Beside the barrier, the police gestured and shouted, "Move back. Move back! We've got more fire engines coming in. Move back!"

Tyler and Samuel whipped out their cell phones and took photos.

Everyone was taking photos.

Worse, twenty-five feet away, a television news crew was setting up their cameras.

Recovering his wits, Caleb said, "Turn those off and put them away."

"Excuse me?" Samuel said in chilly astonishment.

"If we're lucky, none of the Others know you're alive. But if they're watching for your GPS—"

Tyler snapped the phone off and put it in his pocket.

Caleb had to give him credit. He was a smart man.

Samuel followed suit, more reluctantly and with a great deal more suspicion.

"Pass the word," Caleb said. "Turn them off."

Jacqueline paid no heed; she still stared at the wreck of the Gypsy Travel Agency building.

"We've got to get away." Forcibly Caleb turned her around, and picked her pocket as he did. He turned off her phone and slipped it back into place. Then he said, "Come on," and headed up the street away from the disaster, from the cameras, from the onlookers who might recognize him, or Jacqueline, or any of the other new Chosen.

One quick inspection proved they followed close on Caleb's heels.

Aaron walked at the back, herding them like a sheep-dog. Tyler held Isabelle's arm. Samuel walked briskly, brow furrowed, being a lawyer, no doubt, and sifting through the evidence. Aleksandr shambled along at Charisma's side, and both kids were wide-eyed and scared.

They probably had a better sense of smell than the others, for the stink of danger was thick in Caleb's nostrils. The skin crawled on the back of his neck, and he watched for anyone out of place, anyone who showed an undue interest in the new Chosen. Whoever or whatever had managed to get past the safeguards at the Gypsy Travel Agency demonstrated an evil skill unsurpassed in all the centuries that had gone before. If he . . . they . . . *it* realized these callow Chosen had been spared, Jacqueline, Faa, Aleksandr, Charisma, and the others would be taken, tortured, killed. . . .

People rushed past them, heading toward the disaster. Fire engines screamed along the street. But as the Chosen Ones passed from one block to another, traffic thinned, became New York City–normal. Caleb began to plan transportation to get nine people to Zusane's apartment. Cabs, yes, or he could call on Zusane's connections. Whom did he distrust more? As he scrutinized the street, making his decision, he became aware of a situation.

A 1952 classic Rolls-Royce Silver Wraith limousine with dark-tinted windows tracked them at walking pace.

Charisma tugged at his sleeve. "There is an *excellent* limousine following us."

"So I see." Good news? God, he hoped so. They could use some luck.

Caleb watched the Rolls slide to a stop at the curb beside him.

Jacqueline recognized the limo. Her eyes lit up, and she tried to leap forward. "Irving!"

Caleb held her back. He pulled his pistol. "Wait. If they could blow the Agency building like that . . ."

She froze in place.

The chauffeur leaped out of the driver's door, his hat askew, his coat buttoned crooked.

"It's McKenna." Jacqueline sounded so relieved, Caleb hated to crush her hopes.

Still he said, "Wait." Because right now, he didn't trust anyone.

The short, stocky Celt rushed around the car, opened the back door, and Irving Shea, ninety-three and sharper than the thirty-year-olds who had replaced him, leaned out and snapped, "Hurry up. Get in!"

For the third time, Caleb said, "Wait." With a gentle hand, he moved Irving back and looked into the interior of the limo.

It was empty.

"It's safe." Irving put his shaky, age-spotted hand on Caleb's wrist. "They haven't got me—yet."

"All right." Caleb gestured to the Chosen Ones. "Get in."

Chivalry was not dead. The men pushed the women ahead of them into the roomy interior, then followed close on their heels.

"Get ready to drive," Caleb said to McKenna, who scuttled around to the driver's seat.

Caleb stood guard, pistol held unabashedly in his grasp, observing the street, the traffic, the pedestrians, the buildings.

He saw nothing. No one. Had they really been lucky enough to escape?

"Caleb!"

Jacqueline called him. Her voice was rough and impatient, but at least she called him. She cared. Whether she acknowledged it or not, she did care.

He slid into the limousine, shut the door behind him, and counted heads. Even with two bench seats, one facing forward and one back, they were packed into the luxurious Rolls. On the seat facing Caleb, Aleksandr had squished his narrow rear into the corner. Jacqueline sat next to him, and Irving was beside her, tall, dark-skinned, white-haired, healthy, yet fragile with the constantly increasing burden of years. Isabelle was wedged into the other corner, and for a woman who had just hiked five blocks in heels, she looked cool, calm, and reasonable.

Martha sat on the floor, her back against the far door, her knees drawn up and her head bent. She held the whisk broom in her hand and waved it in a slow circle, watching the movement as if fascinated—or frightened.

Charisma sat on the floor on the other side, eyes closed, holding her bracelets and taking deep breaths.

The four guys sat facing forward, their shoulders bumping.

McKenna released the brake and glided away at a dignified pace, heading north toward Central Park and Irving's nineteenth-century Upper East Side mansion.

Next to Caleb, Aaron Eagle said, "I hope we aren't chased."

Caleb faced him. "You would not believe the engine in this car. It *moves*."

"I know about this car." Aaron's mouth quirked; obviously, he recognized what a Silver Wraith could do. "But what about the driver?"

Caleb laughed, a brief explosion of misplaced mirth that brought a glare from Jacqueline. "If necessary, I can drive."

Tyler leaned around the other two men, looked at Caleb, and said, "I'd love to see what her speed would be with one of us at the wheel."

"*Now* would be great." The plodding pace had clearly irritated an already edgy Samuel Faa.

"New York's finest tend to get a little twitchy when buildings blow up, Mr. Faa, and the last thing we want now is to attract their attention." Irving smiled serenely at the man across from him, proving not only that his intelligence was sharp as ever, but also that the batteries in his hearing aids were charged.

Caleb scrutinized Samuel and made a decision. "I want your cell phones. All of them."

Every pair of eyes fixed on him in horror.

"Come on," he coaxed. "I know they're hard to give up. That's why I want them. But you can do it. I want to be damned good and sure those GPSs are not functioning."

Isabelle plunged her hand into her purse and handed

hers over. "I want that, too, Mr. D'Angelo. Wherever we are going to hide, I want no one to know."

"Are we going to Irving's?" Jacqueline asked with open hostility. "Because I know and you know the Others will consider his home as our first refuge."

"The longer they don't know we're alive, the easier it will be to survive," Aaron told her, and slid his cell phone into Caleb's hand.

One by one the cell phones came his way. He checked each one to make sure it was off, then slid each one into his jacket pocket. At last, only Jacqueline's remained to confiscate. "This isn't the time to take a last stand," he told her softly. "There are too many lives at stake."

With a flounce, she tossed him her phone.

McKenna used the car's size to muscle his way smoothly through the crippling traffic.

Caleb watched out the window for anything that could be construed as a danger. The odd thing was—everything looked normal. New Yorkers walked briskly, heading for the theater or the restaurants. Tourists gawked or consulted maps. Cabs raced each other through the intersections. As dusk settled over the city, lights came on in store windows and on signs.

Yet Caleb knew nothing would ever be normal again. He had left his duty to Zusane . . . and now cared exclusively for her daughter.

Jacqueline . . . she resented him so much. Yet never had she needed him more.

She held Irving's arthritis-twisted hand, and one by one she introduced the Chosen Ones to him. Then in slow, precise tones, she said, "Our rescuer is Mr. Irving Shea, the retired director of the Gypsy Travel Agency. He still sits on the board, and goes to work there every day. They ask him for advice—"

"And sometimes even take it," Irving said.

The Chosen Ones, seven men and women flung unprepared into the front lines in the ancient battle between good and evil, chuckled and visibly relaxed.

McKenna drove beside Central Park, then turned east, then north again, maintaining a constant, decorous speed as they glided past museums, hotels and universities, through some of the most expensive real estate in the world.

"How did you escape, sir?" Caleb asked.

"I went home for my nap. I merely went home for my nap, and on my way back, I heard the report on the radio. My whole world has gone up in flames." Irving started strong; then his voice got shaky, old, and feeble, and tears trembled on the ends of his sparse eyelashes. He closed his eyes and fought for control. Squaring his shoulders, he discarded the burden of age. He looked up at Caleb, and his dark eyes pierced the midnight corners of Caleb's mind. His voice changed, became the commanding tone of a director of men, and he asked, "What do you know?"

"I know only one thing for sure." Caleb took a breath, then told the unvarnished truth. "The Gypsy Travel Agency was sabotaged by someone . . . on the inside."

Chapter 10

———— ❧ ————

Later, much later, that night, Caleb stepped in from the darkness and the rain. He put down his gym bag, handed Martha his jacket, shook the water out of his hair, and asked, "How are they?"

"The Chosen Ones are fine, sir. No injuries, although their spirits are depressed." Martha walked to the security panel and set the alarm, then faced Caleb again. "But I suppose that is to be expected."

Martha had always been a tight-ass about Caleb and his privileged place in the Chosen Ones' world, looking down her noble gypsy nose at Zusane's bodyguard. But now she stood holding Caleb's jacket and looking so pitiful, Caleb had to ask, "What is it, Martha? Has something happened I should know about?"

"No, sir."

Caleb's anxiety took a sudden jump. "Jacqueline is still here?"

"Yes, sir."

He relaxed a little. "Have you heard from Zusane? Is she all right?"

"I haven't heard, but as far as I know, she's fine. Everyone here is fine." Martha glanced around and lowered her voice. "I made an assumption that you'd gone out to scout the city for information."

"Yes." This afternoon, Caleb had walked into Irving's mansion, made sure Jacqueline was settled, then walked out again. He'd briefly checked in with his mother, then spent the last hours riding in cabs, drinking in bars, chatting casually about the explosion at the Gypsy Travel Agency, listening to opinions and theories, and seething with anger and frustration.

How had this happened? How had someone gotten past the safeguards the Gypsy Travel Agency put in place? Would the Others seek them here, or would they assume the fledgling Chosen Ones had been killed in the blast?

Martha continued. "I was wondering if you found . . . anything or anybody from the Gypsy Travel Agency?"

Martha was anywhere between sixty and ninety, had been a part of the Gypsy Travel Agency for as long as anyone could remember, yet she was not and had never been one of the Chosen Ones. The Romany had secured her job, and she had worked as a servant all the years of her life. She was always present when the seer approved the new slate of the Chosen Ones, and as a sign of their trust and with their help, she had been allowed to create the spell that hid them from the subway passengers. She had no gift, but she knew everybody. She knew everything. She never gossiped. And now she was breaking her own immutable rule.

Caleb supposed it was to be expected. Martha was such an integral part of the Gypsy Travel Agency; she would desperately want to know what had happened to cause the explosion . . . or perhaps she wanted to know if her own treachery had been exposed.

Because after all, who better to betray the Gypsy Travel Agency than an ungifted, resentful, and trusted servant?

Caleb watched her closely as he said, "It's quiet out there. I didn't find any Chosen. That's not to say some of them didn't escape, but if they did, they've gone underground. I had hoped some would show up here."

"No, sir, but you know they gather at headquarters to wait for Zusane's confirmation after she has met the new recruits. I don't expect that any have survived." Martha's voice trembled, and she cleared her throat. She certainly looked devastated, but after all, if she had been the faithful servant, she had lost the people she'd known and with whom she'd worked. On the other hand, if she had opted to betray them all, a little acting would be required . . . and not worth mentioning. "Did you find any of . . . the Others?"

"Not a sign of them." Which was not strictly true, but he wasn't saying more right now, at least not to Martha. "Maybe they were watching me from behind their enchantments and laughing. But they won today. Why hide?"

"May they all burn in hell."

"We can be sure of that." He loosened his tie. "But how soon? That's the question."

Martha roused herself from her apparent misery. "The company is at the table. They asked that you join them when you arrived."

"Thank you. I will. I'm starving." And a variety of succulent odors called to Caleb. Picking up his bag, he strode into the dining room, a cavernous space of dark-paneled walls, a cherub-painted ceiling, and gilt-edged mirrors. The long table could easily seat thirty, and the Chosen Ones huddled there, seven unwilling strangers brought together by disaster. Irving sat at the head, Jacqueline at his right hand, and the burning look of scorn she shot Caleb worried him not at all. She was still here and safe. That was all he cared about.

But while he put up with whatever crap Jacqueline handed out, he wasn't ready to listen to the rest of them dish it out—and they started in right away.

"Why did you leave without asking?" From Samuel Faa, an arrogant son of a bitch who needed to be brought down a few notches.

"He does whatever he wants whenever he wants to." From Jacqueline, always willing to stab him with a sharp comment.

"What did you find out?" From the golden boy, Tyler Settles, another man far too used to getting whatever he wanted.

"I would not think, Mr. D'Angelo, that you'd indulge in this kind of suspicious behavior without a reason." A softly voiced yet stern comment from Isabelle Mason.

Irving tapped his wineglass with his spoon. "Gentlemen! Ladies! Mr. D'Angelo is no doubt tired and hungry. Let's finish our meal, let him eat, and then we'll hear what he has to say."

"Thank you, Irving." Caleb inclined his head. "And for the rest of you—it's worth noting that while I am employed by Zusane and take orders from her, I am not answerable to any of you for any reason. In the future, please remember that."

Samuel started to speak.

Caleb held his gaze.

Samuel subsided.

Caleb seated himself at the empty place next to Tyler and across from Charisma and Aaron, two people who seemed to have quickly formed an unlikely friendship. He stashed the bag under the table, and at once McKenna appeared at Caleb's elbow offering two kinds of wine, a white and a red, and a variety of dishes kept warm in the kitchen. As always at Irving's home, the food was exquisite: a garlic-crusted rack of lamb on a bed of ratatouille, and twice-baked potatoes. With an Italian's appreciation for a good meal, Caleb told McKenna, "Give my regards to the chef."

"I had to order out, sir. I wasn't prepared for such a crowd. But thank you for your compliments; I will certainly use the restaurant again." McKenna was probably forty-five, an accomplished butler and Irving's trusted aide in every matter.

Another suspect.

The Chosen Ones finished their dinner with varying amounts of enthusiasm; apparently nothing kept Charisma or Aleksandr from a good meal, while Tyler cupped his cheek in his hand and picked at his food. Isabelle kept her gaze on her plate, while Samuel's gaze wandered far too frequently to her face.

Jacqueline had apparently finished. Perhaps she wasn't hungry. Perhaps she was grieving for the dead, or because her mother had once again left her alone. In either case, she sat holding her knife clutched in her gloved hand. Caleb picked up his own knife. Perhaps she was contemplating murder—his.

If that was the case, he would enjoy the final battle.

He ate with the appetite of a man who knew what

it was like to be hungry, who knew that the next meal might never be forthcoming. When he put down his fork, he found himself facing eight pairs of eyes. He smiled a tight-lipped smile. "What's for dessert?"

Samuel exploded, "Oh, for God's sake!"

McKenna appeared at Caleb's side at once. "I threw together an English trifle. I hope that's acceptable."

"It sounds wonderful, McKenna." Caleb watched him hurry toward the kitchen on the lower level, watched Martha walk from person to person to clear away the dirty dishes. Then he turned to face Samuel. "To answer your question—I went out because I'm the only one here who is expendable."

Samuel slapped his palm on the table, stood, and leaned forward. "Or because you're making plans with the enemy to blow us up, too?"

"Sit down, Mr. Faa," Irving said. When Samuel ignored him, Irving's voice became a whip. "Sit *down*!"

Samuel sat.

A brief smile slipped across Isabelle's lips—a smile Samuel noted with resentment.

"If Mr. D'Angelo were to try to blow us up, he would be disappointed." Irving looked around the table, warning them all. "Since the explosion at the Gypsy Travel Agency, I changed the security that protects my home."

"The security?" Tyler ruffled his golden hair in bewilderment.

"The enchantments, if you would. I am now the only one who knows them."

Dangerous. Caleb met Jacqueline's gaze. If anything happened to Irving, they would have no way in or out—and a ninety-three-year-old man didn't need to be murdered, didn't need to meet with an accident. He could just . . . die of old age.

Yet Irving knew the risks better than anyone, and had made his decision. Meeting Caleb's gaze, he said, "Desperate times require desperate measures."

"Yes." Caleb interceded before the Chosen Ones could make their own deductions. "The confirmation of the Chosen Ones is a time-honored celebration. Almost every one of the Chosen Ones from years past attends. According to my records, Zusane arrived at the Gypsy Travel Agency at two p.m. She had a drink, met Chosen from twelve cycles ago—"

"Twelve cycles ago? That's eighty-four years." Tyler gaped at Caleb. "That's impossible!"

"It is not," Irving said. "In the past, the Chosen Ones came to us as youths as young as thirteen. In the past, when they achieved adolescence, the gifts were at the height of their power. Those Chosen were mighty indeed, and only the advent of middle age caused their abilities to fade. In addition, the gifts seem to lend long life to those so blessed. So at the Choosing today, I met men and women who far surpassed me in age and wisdom."

"They're gone. Dead. At rest at last." Caleb didn't have a doubt. "Zusane left the Gypsy Travel Agency at four forty-five. She greeted fans on the streets—"

"Wait a minute. You weren't with Zusane." Jacqueline glared at him. "You were with me."

"You saw me on my phone. What did you think I was doing?" She didn't answer, and he didn't wait. "I was supervising Zusane's bodyguard. I am in charge of her safety."

"What are you doing here, then?" Aaron asked.

"I am now in charge of her successor's safety." Caleb explained himself not because he felt the need, but because these people were uncertain and afraid. Because the events of the day had ushered in a new age of the world, and somehow, he knew he was an integral part of its success.

McKenna arrived with the trifle and with a flourish placed the glass bowl before Irving. Red berries, white whipped cream, and pale golden ladyfingers had been lovingly arranged into a work of art—a work no one had the time or patience to admire.

"Lovely. Serve it," Irving instructed.

"Louts!" McKenna sniffed in disdain.

"McKenna," Irving said in warning.

"Yes, sir." With the care of a Michelangelo dismantling his *David*, McKenna took the trifle to the sideboard, divided it into nine equal parts, and placed the servings on vintage Meissen dessert plates.

He might consider them louts, but that didn't mean he should lower his own serving standards.

As he placed the trifle before each person, Caleb said, "Zusane arrived at the chalk circle at five thirty, at the height of rush hour, and I arrived with Jacqueline at five forty-five."

Heads nodded around the table.

"During the time Zusane was gone, no Chosen left the building. No board members left the building." The search for the facts led to an immutable, grim picture, no matter how many times Caleb reviewed them. "Yet five more Chosen arrived and rushed into the building."

"Why were they in a hurry?" Aleksandr picked up his fork and dug in. "This is good!"

"Thank you, young sir," McKenna said in a deadly tone of appreciation. "Shall I pour the port, Mr. Shea?"

"Port or brandy or coffee, whatever they want." Irving lifted his hand in blessing.

Caleb asked for coffee, toyed with his fork, and waited—waited to see if Aleksandr would keel over from poison or drugs.

The young man plowed right through the serving and glanced around for more.

Jacqueline pushed hers toward him. With a grin, he thanked her and, while everyone watched, polished it off, then asked McKenna if he could have a shot of vodka.

"You have an iron gut," Tyler said in awe.

Aleksandr shrugged.

"That goes without saying," Irving said. "He is young, male, and Ukrainian."

"I'm American," Aleksandr said proudly.

Irving inclined his head, and rephrased his comment. "Aleksandr is young, male, and of Ukrainian origin."

"Thank you." Aleksandr inclined his head in return.

Caleb picked up his fork and tasted the trifle, found it good enough to risk a slow-acting poison for, and went to work on it.

"Why were they in a hurry?" Aleksandr glanced around the table, then patiently dragged the conversation back to the topic at hand. "Caleb said five more Chosen rushed into the Gypsy Travel Agency. Why were they rushing?"

"Because if the Chosen Ones didn't arrive by five thirty, when the cocktail party began, they wouldn't be allowed in. Those were the rules." Caleb examined the faces around the table. One by one, Samuel, Aaron, Tyler, Charisma and Isabelle picked up their forks and ate their desserts with varying degrees of gusto and murmured appreciation.

None of them looked ill, and none of them looked brokenhearted. They had accepted the deaths this afternoon as a tragedy, but their real concern was for themselves and how the situation would impact them.

But then . . . only one of the Chosen Ones had known the victims; that was Jacqueline, and she had never pretended a fondness for the people who had so often taken her mother away from her.

For all that he suspected everyone, he could not see how any of the other six, so new to this world of protection and heroics, could have the knowledge and the control to bring about such a hideous offense. "Those have been the rules since the Gypsy Travel Agency incorporated forty-nine years ago."

"This trifle is most excellent, McKenna. Thank you for your efforts in such a difficult situation, and you, too, Martha." Irving put down his fork after a few small bites and addressed the group. "When I was the director, I always demanded a prompt arrival, and that tradition has thankfully continued."

Jacqueline explained to the table, "Until Irving arrived, the Gypsy Travel Agency was run by the Chosen Ones themselves. It teetered on the brink of bankruptcy and disaster, and Irving gave them—us—financial solvency."

"And a few badly needed rules," Irving said. "They were mavericks, all of them."

The new Chosen examined Irving, in his dark suit and red power tie, and none of them seemed surprised.

Irving turned back to Caleb. "How do you know who left and who arrived?"

"I accessed the records, which are kept off-site. You can see the video, Irving. You can see multiple views of every entrance and exit." Caleb held Irving's gaze.

Irving nodded reluctantly. He knew technology well enough to know that video could be tampered with, but probably not so quickly and/or so thoroughly, and he was a smart old guy. Like Caleb, he had confidence in no one, but he had met Caleb the first day the young man landed in New York City. If there was trust to be had, Caleb had his.

"The explosion occurred at six p.m., a half hour after the cocktail party had begun." Caleb looked around the table. "An ominous hour, six."

"Why?" Aaron asked.

Like a college girl, Charisma waved her hand in the air. Her bracelets jangled and her tattoos were vibrant with color. "I know! I know! I read it in *When the World Was Young: A History of the Chosen Ones*. Am I the only one who did the required reading?"

Depending on their characters, the Chosen Ones looked guilty or aggravated.

Charisma finished, "Because six is the devil's number."

Tight-lipped with irritation, Samuel said, "I sincerely doubt the devil had anything to do with this disaster."

Caleb was startled to discover Charisma could do irritation at least as impressively as Samuel. Her black and purple hair stood up like a wolf's ruff, and she rapped on the table with her knuckles. "Mr. Faa, do you not understand what and who we are? We are the bulwark between the darkness and the light, and the devil is exactly who we stand against."

"If the devil is behind this, then why wasn't it completely successful? Why aren't we dead? And in fact, why doesn't the devil just take us out himself?" Samuel was angry as only a man trapped in an untenable situation can be.

Charisma showed no patience with his interrogation. "Because Lucifer isn't allowed to intervene personally. It's against the rules."

"Whose rules?" Samuel demanded.

She put her fists on her waist. "Whose do you think?"

Aaron gave a laugh that quickly changed to a cough.

Caleb glanced at Jacqueline and found her eyes full of amusement, an amusement she shared with him for one golden moment before she remembered her hostility and turned away.

"Lucifer is a fallen angel, and that is a powerful being. But he is not in charge of this world or any other." Irving spoke slowly, weighing each word as if it were gold. "Mr. Faa, unless you accept that, you're going to have a difficult time with your role in the organization. The Chosen Ones who succumb to hopelessness are those who succumb to the blandishments of the enemy."

Samuel was a lawyer. He exuded power in the way he dressed, the way he talked, and in his person. He did *not* appreciate their amusement, or having the matter spelled out by a ninety-three-year-old man. His dark eyes flashed with resentment, and Caleb made a note to keep an eye on him, too.

In this room, the only people he trusted were Jacqueline and himself, and he knew given the chance, Jacqueline would put a knife through his heart.

But at least she had good reasons. Personal reasons.

Aleksandr cleared his throat twice before he managed to croak out, "Are you saying the Chosen Ones can switch sides?"

"Yes, indeed." As if pained, Irving placed his hand on his chest. He looked down toward the table, and whispered, "Any of you can break your word and betray us."

"Has it happened before?" Jacqueline asked softly.

He looked up as if surprised to see her there. "Not often." His voice was slow and soft. "Not often, but it does happen, and whenever it does . . . it is a failure for which I pay, and pay, and pay."

A chill crawled over Caleb's skin. For the first time in Caleb's memory, Irving's mind seemed to be wandering. He was old, but he had always seemed so sharp, so intelligent. Had he been fooling them all?

Or . . . had Caleb been seeing what he wanted, an infallible leader of the Chosen Ones?

In fact, was the old man in the early stages of dementia? Of Alzheimer's?

Was he the one who had somehow given up the security of the Gypsy Travel Agency to the enemy? Had he caused the murder of so many gifted men and women?

Chapter 11

———◆———

In all the time Jacqueline had known Irving, she'd never thought of him as old. But right now, his voice was low and shaky, his hands had a tremor, and the skin under his eyes drooped as if he was sad and weary. "Irving, you can't assume that responsibility for all time. You can't protect everyone. Besides . . . that means the Others can come to *our* side, also."

"Yes. It has happened. But seldom, so seldom, and we don't ever really trust them, do we?" Irving stared into Jacqueline's face, pleading for something. For insight or kindness or . . . understanding.

She glanced at Caleb, at McKenna, at Martha, not comprehending this sorrow that seemed to weigh so heavily on Irving.

Caleb shook his head slightly. He didn't know, either, and for all that she wore her dislike of Caleb and his methods like a badge of honor, she believed him.

But McKenna stepped forward. "Sir, I hate to interrupt so lively a discourse, but should I serve the after-dinner refreshments here? Or would you prefer to take them in the comfort of the library? The library is warm and cheerful; I've lit a fire, and there's the pool table should the young people wish to play, and of course, there is a table for poker and other gaming indulgences."

Jacqueline fought the tug of amusement. McKenna was ever the stern Celt, disapproving of gambling in any form. Yet tonight, he was willing to suggest "gaming indulgences" to lift Irving's spirits. Grasping Irving's hand, she said, "McKenna is right. Let's go to the library. On such a night, this room is too large and gloomy."

Irving tottered to his feet. "Those of you who work out on a regular basis should know that I have a thoroughly equipped gym down in the basement. I keep towels and workout garments. Just ask McKenna should you wish to indulge."

"Thank God," Samuel pronounced. "I'm going to go nuts stuck in here if I don't do something."

Jacqueline tucked her hand through Irving's arm and allowed him to lead her into the foyer.

With a scraping of chairs, the Chosen Ones stood and followed.

The library was as warm and cheerful as McKenna had promised, with walls painted the color of mustard, mahogany shelves filled with leather-bound books, and wide sweeps of antique Aubusson rugs on the floor. A massive fireplace, with an opening as tall as Caleb and as wide as his outstretched arms, blazed merrily. Comfortable seating clustered around it, the gaming and pool tables dominated the center of the room, and heavy blue velvet curtains kept out night's menace.

Aleksandr spoke for them all when he picked up a pool cue, weighed it in his hand, and said, "Very . . . cool."

Even the dour McKenna looked pleased at the approbation. He and Martha hustled around, filling their drink orders, and when that was done, the two servants disappeared.

The group quickly divided into the players and the watchers. Isabelle selected a cue and Tyler as her partner. Aleksandr waited for someone to partner him, and when Samuel took up a cue, the teams were formed.

The others settled down to watch, drinks in hand, and Jacqueline surveyed them all.

Charisma sat on the floor beside the fire, brandy snifter hanging carelessly from her fingers.

Aaron stretched out on a love seat, a mug of coffee clasped between his palms.

Irving sank into his worn leather easy chair and accepted a small Waterford glass of tawny port.

Caleb . . . had vanished on his way to the library. Potty break, Jacquelilne supposed.

So these people were all that were left of the Chosen Ones.

Was that good? Was that bad? Jacqueline didn't know. She had visited the Gypsy Travel Agency many times in her life. The company had been a constant in her life. The board of directors employed her mother, sent her on trips, encouraged her romances, all in the name of keeping the world safe from the devil's machinations. Except for Irving, Jacqueline had never liked any of them . . . and occasionally, she suspected that if she'd known Irving during his heyday, she would have disliked him, too. To her, the directors seemed to be cold, self-absorbed men who directed the moneymaking part of the business with enthusiasm while maintaining their saintly reputation for protecting the Chosen Ones.

She sank down on the cushions thrown in careful disarray against the window seat and sipped from a glass of Grand Marnier.

She knew the traditions of the Chosen Ones. Ideally they would first struggle and argue, then find a natural leader, then settle down to the job at hand. Usually that job was finding and rescuing others like themselves . . . the Abandoned Ones. If they found the babies in time, the children would be adopted into families and disappear into the real world to live out their lives in obscurity. If they failed to retrieve the babies, the Others would take them. Sometimes they sacrificed them. Sometimes they raised them to be steeped in evil. Always they reminded the children that the Chosen Ones had not cared to rescue them. Always they cultivated resentment against the Chosen Ones.

Sometimes the mix of the Chosen was less than ideal. Sometimes there were two leaders, or three, or four, and the group fought fruitlessly, never establishing a rapport. Sometimes the Chosen were born into a time that required physical strength and acts of heroics, and they had become bulwarks in the struggle against evil.

Right now, with the strife and the arguments, it seemed this group would be one of the insignificant Chosen.

Yet . . . they needed to be so much more.

The pool players racked up the balls. Isabelle broke, and ran five balls before giving over to the other team. She watched and chalked as Aleksandr placed three balls in three pockets, then turned to face Irving. "I need to call my mother, let her know where I am, what I'm doing," she said.

"This is a delicate situation. You can't call her," Irving said.

Samuel crossed his arms over his chest and leaned a

hip against the table. "God forbid your mother should worry."

For all the attention Isabelle paid to Samuel, he might not have existed. "I can't not call her. If she doesn't hear from me sometime tomorrow, she'll call the FBI. And the FBI will listen to her."

Samuel sighed loudly.

Isabelle continued. "My fiancé works in DC as a lobbyist." Samuel snorted so loudly, Isabelle snatched the handkerchief out of his pocket and pressed it over his mouth. Pressed it hard, like she wanted to cut off his air. "After that snort, you're unattractively moist. And don't tell me you don't have someone *you* want to know that you're alive."

With his dark eyes focused on her, he pushed her hand away. "My secretary."

"You're sleeping with your secretary?" Isabelle's voice rose. "Again?"

Jacqueline squeezed her spine against the window seat and wished she could turn away from the scene. But they were both so passionate, so angry, sparks flew between them, riveting the attention of every person in the room.

"I am not sleeping with anybody. And I resigned from my law firm to take this job."

"Then you don't need to talk to anybody, do you?" Isabelle asked.

Samuel drew a breath. "I have to notify my parole officer."

Isabelle looked as if he'd struck her in the face.

She stared at him, her eyes so wide and horrified, he taunted, "You always knew I would come to this. Or at least—your mother did."

She turned her back to him and thumped her cue to the rug hard enough to create a vibration through the hardwood floor. "What did you do?"

"Another attorney claimed I used coercion to extract a confession from his client. The judge agreed."

"Because you did."

"No one could prove that, but it was enough. . . . It doesn't matter. They convicted me."

Isabelle stood with her head bent, breathing hard.

"Ma belle . . ." Samuel used a voice deep and warm, so reassuring that Jacqueline put her hand over her heart.

But when he would have cupped Isabelle's shoulders, her hand slashed out in a gesture that clearly said *Halt. "Don't* touch me."

His usual cynical sneer snapped back in place. "Of course not, Miss Mason. I wouldn't dream of dirtying your noble self."

Whew. Bad blood between those two.

To Jacqueline's surprise, Aleksandr stepped into the breach with the assurance of a man twice his age. "Mr. Shea, I have to call my mother, too. If I don't, there will be a very large and angry clan of former shape-shifters descending on your house."

"If my mother heard about the explosion at the Gypsy Travel Agency, then she's having a fit right now," Charisma said.

Irving nodded. "In that case, you're right, Miss Mason, Mr. Wilder, Miss Fangorn. Not calling your contacts would create a greater danger than calling. We'll arrange for everyone to contact family or . . . whomever they need to tomorrow."

"Thank you." Isabelle turned back to the table in time to see Samuel finish the game. Without a word, she walked over, handed her cue to Aaron, and said, "Your turn."

He wasn't fool enough to say he preferred to remain stretched out on the love seat. Instead, he took the cue, headed for the pool table, and warned Aleksandr, "You're going to be sorry. Pool is not my game."

Jacqueline noticed Caleb even before he stepped into the room. He moved without sound, but sometime in the last few days she'd picked up an awareness of his vibration, his scent, his presence.

Irritating.

He swooped over, snatched a pillow from under her arm, seated himself close against her side, and braced his shoulder against hers.

She moved away.

He moved close.

She glared at him.

He smiled at her.

She contemplated kicking him, but she'd tried that before, unsuccessfully, and she didn't intend to face that kind of humiliation here and now.

Irving watched the two of them jockey for position; then with more cheer, he said, "Do you know, the last time a disaster of this magnitude occurred, the Dark Ages followed."

"Great." Tyler chalked his cue and proved the players were listening. "We've got something to look forward to."

Irving continued. "But you, dear Jacqueline, you have given me hope."

"Hope? Me?" She didn't mind giving him hope. She simply didn't enjoy the attention that went with it.

"At last . . . at last, you've agreed to become the seer of the Chosen Ones."

She shrugged carelessly, dismissing her gesture as inconsequential. "For this group of the Chosen Ones."

"My dear." Irving smiled so warmly, all shadow of sorrow was banished from his face. "All your life, you've heard that there is only one seer."

Tension crept over Jacqueline. "Every *cycle*. There's one seer every seven years."

The players stalled; everyone grew still and silent.

Charisma covered her head with both hands; clearly, she knew what was coming.

"No," Irving said gently. "Our seer is our most precious commodity, and we are blessed with only one at a time."

He didn't mean what she thought he meant. He *couldn't*. "But my mother is still psychic. She proved that without a doubt."

"When you stepped into the circle, the transfer of power began. When she stepped out, she was no longer our oracle. She was Zusane Vargha, a lovely lady to whom we are grateful." Irving's adoration for Zusane couldn't have been more clear.

Jacqueline grabbed Caleb by the shoulder and turned him to face her.

He gazed at her, his pale blue eyes cool and interested, as if she were a bug under a microscope. He said, "There always has to be one. Her term extends for as much time or as little as she likes, she picks her successor, and every seven years, she has to approve the new Chosen."

The bastard. He'd known this all along.

"So the fate of the world depends on me and my visions?" Jacqueline spoke to Irving, but she stared into Caleb's eyes. "Then the Chosen Ones are in trouble, because I've *never* had a vision."

Chapter 12

———————◆◆———————

"What?" Aaron Eagle swung away from his shot.

"Great. Just great. This seems like a good time to take a"—Samuel stopped, looked at Isabelle, and finished in a sarcastic tone— "a powder room break."

"Why don't you do just that?" Isabelle said. He strode from the room, and she muttered, "Run away. That's all you're good for."

"How could you have never had a vision?" Aaron asked.

"I just never have." Jacqueline didn't like the way the American Indian fixed his dark eyes on her and demanded an explanation as if he had the right.

"Wow. I'm not the only one without a gift." Aleksandr Wilder seemed less morose, more relaxed.

"Jacqueline, you have the mark," Irving insisted.

"I *know* I have the mark." Jacqueline tried to be quiet, but when she got defensive—and that happened a lot around the Chosen Ones, past and present—her voice rose. "I've never been allowed to *forget* I have the mark. That doesn't mean the mark has ever done anything to me. Meant anything to me. I mean, what if it's just a birthmark?"

Naturally, Irving paid no heed. "Have you gone underground? The earth always sheltered your mother, gave her the cradle she needed to access her talent."

"It doesn't work." Jacqueline scooted into the mound of pillows, crossed her arms, and wished she didn't feel like a sulky kid. She wished she didn't feel as if she'd just failed the Chosen Ones. She wished Caleb would stop watching her so knowingly.

She wished . . . she wished that sepia-colored world would recede from the edges of her sight.

"If you're not a psychic, why did you step into the circle?" Isabelle asked, her voice cool, aristocratic, and yet somehow comforting. Maybe she wasn't so thrilled with her gift, either.

"It seemed the thing to do at the time. I didn't know the building was going to blow up—" As Jacqueline remembered that blackened crater, her voice shook. "And I really didn't realize there could be only one. I figured my mother would be around to pick up the slack." Which was the truth, but not all the truth.

Caleb took her hand and toyed with the Velcro that

held her glove in place. "Do you ever say something unintentionally? Something you never really thought about, but that comes out of your mouth and turns out to be true?"

Damn him. He knew the trouble she'd gotten in as a child, blithely predicting divorces and new siblings and Christmas presents.

"Yes. I did. But those aren't visions. Those are premonitions. If you want me to tell you that your computer's going to fry, I'm your woman. But if you want to know who blew up the Gypsy Travel Agency, or why, I haven't got a clue." Jacqueline had learned to close her mind to her premonitions, too. If she hadn't, Caleb wouldn't have found her in California. She would have hauled ass out of the country—for all the good that would have done her. She might have premonitions on her side, but he had her mother's money on his.

"Look. It's okay. You guys are forgetting—I'm a psychic." Tyler sounded more than a little irritated at being ignored.

"That's right," Charisma said in relief. "He's a psychic. We've got one." She glanced apologetically at Jacqueline. "More than one."

So there, Jacqueline mouthed at Caleb.

Irving tapped his long finger on his lips and examined Tyler. "It's unusual for males to have an intuitive gift. Usually the sensitive gifts are the arena of females. . . . Interesting." Irving looked as if he were trying to remember something of importance. "What kind of visions do you see?"

"It depends on what happens and what I'm looking for." Tyler was a handsome man in his late twenties, tanned, with shoulder-length golden hair and the greenest eyes Jacqueline had ever seen.

"So you have control over your visions?" Irving asked.

Tyler shook his head. "I didn't foresee the explosion at all, but I think we can safely assume Zusane didn't, either, or she would have stopped it."

"But she *did* see the explosion," Aaron said.

"She was very connected to the site and the people. I had only been in the building a few hours when they brought us down to the subway station. And unlike Zusane, I don't receive well underground." Tyler shrugged ruefully. "To tell you the truth, I don't understand my gift or how it is given to me. I merely know I'm blessed to have it."

"All of you gentlemen have done very well for yourself with your gifts." Irving leaned toward Aleksandr and said kindly, "And I'm sure your gift will arrive in due time."

"I hope so. It's not easy being the untalented, unremarkable Wilder."

Jacqueline really did like the boy. His youth hid a wry humor and an acceptance she wished she could claim.

"There are a few points about today's explosion I don't understand," Charisma said.

Samuel walked in and proved he'd heard when he said, "Only a few points?"

"More than a few, but . . ." Charisma slid the bracelets around and around her wrists. "Did the perpetrators know we would be out of the building?"

No one answered. Finally Isabelle said, "We didn't know what time we would leave to go to be confirmed. We were sent into that subway when a call came through."

"From me," Caleb told them.

Isabelle continued. "How would an enemy judge the right moment to eliminate us? I think it's possible that they don't know we're still alive."

"That's a hopeful view of the matter." Samuel watched her as if he were sorry for his previous cutting comments, as if he cared for her more than he could say.

Yes, you jerk, you hurt her when you behave like a jackass. Jacqueline's gaze shifted to Caleb. Oh, she knew about jackasses. And she knew about hurt. Luckily, she wasn't as delicate as Isabelle. With a mother like Zusane, she had learned to be tough. It was the only way to survive.

"Do you think the perpetrators died in the explosion? Are we talking suicide bombers?" Tyler looked intensely at Caleb, wanting an answer from the man who, because of his experience, had assumed leadership of the investigation.

"That's what I *think*," Caleb answered. "Ask me what I *know*."

In the doorway, someone cleared her throat, and everyone in the room swung around.

"If I could be allowed to speak . . ." Martha sounded, and looked, sarcastically polite.

"Of course, Martha," Irving said.

"Someone should be sent to protect Gary." Martha's eyes kindled with anger. Her shock at the day's events had curdled into bitterness; she sought to blame someone for the tragedy.

In a way, that removed her from the list of suspects.

"Who?" Irving asked. "There's no one to do it."

"Who's Gary?" Charisma asked.

"Something you don't know!" Samuel said in pretend shock.

In a smooth, cool, aristocratic voice, Isabelle said, "Samuel, you've already won the award as the nastiest person in the Chosen Ones. You don't need to try and cement that honor."

Jacqueline was starting to like Isabelle.

"Gary White. He was a team leader, one of our most talented, most trusted Chosen. Four years ago, he led his team into a dangerous situation. He lost almost every one. He returned—in a coma. There's been no sign of recovery. He's in a nursing home. . . ." Irving shook his head. "Forty-two years old. He could live like that for another fifty years."

"Wow. When they recruited us, they never told us stuff like *that*." Tyler was clearly displeased.

"Only a fool would imagine anything different." The words escaped Jacqueline without forethought. Then she wanted to clap her hands over her mouth.

But it was too late.

Tyler glared and said, "If I'm such a fool, you'll be relieved if I leave."

"You can't leave. This is more than a job. It's a destiny. It's your fate, and you cannot escape your fate. Tomorrow, we'll begin to plan what we must do, but for tonight"—Irving gestured to the servants at the door—"Martha, McKenna, if you would fill everyone's glasses again? And fill your own."

When each of the Chosen Ones and the servants held a drink, Irving came to his feet.

Jacqueline stood. Caleb did also. Charisma and Isabelle rose. Everyone stepped forward, sensing the gravity of Irving's intent.

Irving lifted his glass and began the traditional toast, the toast that had ended every evening at the Gypsy Travel Agency for as long as Jacqueline could remember. "To our fallen heroes, the Chosen Ones of days past."

Jacqueline and Caleb, Martha and McKenna, lifted

their glasses, and the Chosen Ones followed suit. "To our fallen heroes," they echoed, and drank.

"And to the saviors of the world, our newest Chosen. May God bless our righteous endeavors and illuminate the right path." Irving looked around. "Even if the path leads to darkness. Even if the path leads to death."

The Chosen Ones froze with the glasses upraised.

"I never signed on for this." Samuel looked around at them critically. Suspiciously.

To Jacqueline's surprise, Charisma agreed. "I never wanted to be a hero."

Chapter 13

As the others drifted out, Caleb caught Jacqueline's hand and held her in place.

Irving looked up inquiringly. "What can I do for you two?"

"I forgot to mention—on my trip out tonight, I did see something of interest." Caleb's voice was offhand.

But Jacqueline knew him too well. She read his mood, identified his posture, and recognized that this was important. Her hand convulsively tightened on his.

"It was probably nothing," he continued. "It didn't seem worth reporting to the rest of the group."

Irving's gaze grew sharp. "Yes?"

"I saw a woman. An older woman, handsome, in her sixties. She was having a drink at one of the bars I visited, and I wouldn't have noticed her, but her nose had been slit down the middle."

Jacqueline sucked in her breath.

"She's had work done." Caleb bent toward Irving. "But my mother told me that years ago in the Mediterranean basin, they would do that to women for infidelity. To see a mutilation like that here and now seems so barbaric that I wondered . . ."

Irving blinked in wide-eyed confusion. "Poor woman. I can't imagine who she is."

Jacqueline didn't believe him.

Neither did Caleb, but he said, "No. I don't suppose you can. But I thought I'd check." Turning to Jacqueline, he kissed her fingers, intertwined as they were with his. "Shall we?"

"No, we shall not." But he'd hooked her with that last too-casual query to Irving, and she followed him.

Before they stepped out the door, Caleb stopped and turned. "Irving, I forgot. When I left the bar, I heard a woman's voice whisper, 'Give Irving my regards.' "

Irving stared back at Caleb. "You must have imagined it."

Caleb bent his head in sardonic agreement, then tugged Jacqueline out the door.

She went because Caleb had asked a loaded question, and Irving had lied when he answered. "Who was the woman?"

"I don't know."

"But she said something to you?"

"Without speaking a word or standing close." He

stopped on the stairs and turned to look at Jacqueline. "She smiled at me."

Jacqueline contained her amusement. "Caleb, a lot of women smile at you. You're a man worth smiling at."

He stepped down so his head was level with hers, and leaned his forehead against hers. "Thank you. But it was the smile that made me run to the next bar."

"She scared you?" Jacqueline asked incredulously.

"Yes."

Jacqueline tried the words again with a different cadence. "*She* scared *you*?"

"I heard her in my head." His pale blue eyes were troubled. "And that smile . . . like she knew me. All my secrets, all the things I've done wrong, all the things I've done right. All my plans for the future."

"Okay. I understand that." Jacqueline hunched her shoulders. "That would creep me out, too."

He put his arm around her and together they started back up the stairs. "I went to work for Zusane the day I graduated from college. That was nine years ago. I've met the Chosen Ones, and I've met their adversaries, and I have never had anything like that happen before."

She'd never seen him like this. She didn't think he'd ever been like this. Troubled, she tried to put her half-formed thoughts into words. "I think today marks the end of the Chosen Ones as we knew them. Everything's different now, and I don't know what kind of changes we're facing. But I know I'm frightened, too. I think anyone who knows about the Chosen Ones, and the Others, and the battle between good and evil, would be a fool not to be frightened."

"You're good with a left-handed compliment." He laughed. "But you're right. No one would ever call me a fool."

"Exactly."

The corridor upstairs retained the appearance of a nineteenth-century mansion: wide, tall, and lined with dark oil paintings in ornate gilded frames. The doors that opened off led to lavish, chilly bedrooms heated by registers that puffed and groaned. McKenna had put the women to the right of the stairs, the men to the left, but without hesitation, Caleb headed right.

Jacqueline stopped. "Where do you think you're going?"

Caleb stopped. "With you."

"How do you know where I'm sleeping?"

"I took my bag up after dinner." With a confidence that set her teeth on edge, he said, "I bought you a few things. Underwear. Toothbrush."

"That is low."

"What?"

"As if you don't know. Enticing me with clean underwear!"

"Are you enticed?"

Of course she was. "Irving isn't going to allow this.

It's his house and he has old-fashioned views about a man and a woman sharing a room."

Caleb's face got flat and cold. "Irving doesn't have a choice. I took on the job of making sure you're safe, and I intend to do it."

"You weren't worried this afternoon. You left as soon as we arrived." *Wrong! That sounded whiny and far too aware of him.*

"You're wrong. I was worried. But you were awake and, as I'm well aware, able to protect yourself."

She recalled all the ways he'd taught her to fight. And she recalled her struggle—and surrender—in the bathroom in Napa Valley. "Not able enough, apparently," she said bitterly.

He smiled, a slow, wanton smile that warmed with memories and shimmered with sexual tension. "If you really want to win, I would bet on you every time."

He was saying she'd given in because she wanted him.

Her fists curled at her sides.

She hated him. Hated him and wanted him, and cursed herself for the ambiguity.

"I'm not leaving you alone at night." He took her gloved fist in his hand. He kissed it. "Resign yourself to that."

She turned her back and headed for her room. "You can sleep on the floor."

He followed. "*You* can sleep on the floor."

The room was nice, clean, well-tended, with antique furnishings and a girlishly flowered bedspread on a queen-sized bed. The trouble was—the room was small, and when Caleb stepped in, it got smaller. And warmer. Distinctly warmer.

He shut the door behind him. "You should call your mother."

She threw up her arms. "To think I was worried you'd want sex!" Damn. She shouldn't have said that, either.

"I do want sex. I always want sex." He waited a significant beat. "With you. But I'm not going to wrestle with you again. It's up to you now."

"What does that mean?"

"Just what I said." He stripped off his tie. "You should call your mother."

He was a remarkable man. He managed to change the subject from sex—the one she thought she least wanted to discuss with him—to the one she wanted even less to discuss. With her hands on her hips, she demanded, "Why? She ran off and abandoned me to this mess."

He dug into the bag on the bed and threw a voluminous nightgown at her. "Because she went Dumpster diving for you."

"What?"

"When you were an infant. When she rescued you. She climbed in a Dumpster and found you."

Jacqueline let the garment drop at her feet. "You know that? For sure?"

He faced her full-on. "She never told you?"

"No . . ." No one had ever told Jacqueline where she'd come from or how she'd ended up in Zusane's care. She had just always known she should not ask too many questions about Zusane, or her past, or what she did and why she did it. Mostly, she knew she should be grateful to Zusane for saving her from a fate worse than death.

Yet every time Jacqueline had wondered who her real parents were and why they had given her up, the color washed out of the world, leaving it sepia-toned like an old photo. Her whole life she had instinctively known that to open her mind to that *other* world was dangerous . . . and if she did, she could never go back.

So it seemed safer not to speculate, and she didn't.

Now with relentless precision, Caleb filled her in. "I remember the day clearly. My mother and I hadn't been in this country long, and Zusane was at the house, visiting my mother, asking after her health. All of a sudden, she stood up. Stood up quickly, stiff and straight, and said, 'I can see her, shining like a pure gold nugget lost in filth.' "

The bottom dropped out of Jacqueline's stomach. She wanted to cover her ears. But unexpectedly, the sepia tone that hovered on the fringes of her awareness swamped her. She could hear Caleb, but that other reality called her. . . .

"She walked out. Just walked out." He rummaged

in his bag, and pulled out a shaving kit and a stack of clothes. "My mother sent me after her. Zusane had bodyguards then, too, but she wouldn't let them come with her. She let me. I was nine years old, and I was the only one with her while she scoured the alleys, ignored the people who shouted at her for poking in their garbage cans and the other people who stared at the crazy lady dressed like a goddess. She kept saying she knew the golden child was there somewhere."

Softly Jacqueline said, "It was hot, and I was buried. . . ."

He swung on her so fast, she stumbled backward into the wall. "You *remember*," he said.

"That's impossible." Because she'd been a newborn.

He watched her, waiting for her to talk. It was a method she'd seen him use to great effect. . . . God knew it worked on her.

"I remember something, but it can't be real." She moved her shoulders uneasily, feeling her way through a series of impressions. "The woman who put me in there . . . I knew her. I knew her scent, her heartbeat. I knew she should hold me close inside, but she held me out away from her, like . . . *shit*. She kept calling me *shit*."

"You heard her?"

"I didn't understand the word, but I knew what she meant." All her life, Jacqueline had had this buried in her mind. She'd never told anyone, because . . . well, if people knew she had premonitions, they thought she was crazy. And she feared if anyone knew about this, this bizarre fragment of memory, they would put her away forever.

Yet from the time she was a girl, she could always tell Caleb anything, and she told him now. "This can't be a real memory."

"It *was* the hottest day of the year."

Wrapping her arms around herself, she said, "Funny, because a chill just ran up my spine."

Still he scrutinized her.

Giving herself up to the soft, sad remembrance, Jacqueline said, "I hurt. I was crying, screaming, starving. . . . The woman shook me. Then she threw me. My neck snapped around, but I landed in something soft, and she cursed me again. She wanted to . . . I think she meant to bash my brains out. I remember waving my hand to her as she piled garbage on me. But she didn't see. She didn't care. She slammed the lid and she didn't come back." As anguish built, her voice faded. "How could anyone hate their baby so much?"

"Perhaps she was raped. Or suffered from a mental illness. Or perhaps she saw your mark."

"And rejected me." Jacqueline flexed her hand in its glove.

Caleb went into the bathroom and came out with a glass of water. He wrapped her fingers around it, and helped her lift it to her lips.

To her surprise, her hand was shaking. The glass

rattled against her teeth, but the water wet her dry mouth.

"What happened then?" he asked.

In a low voice, she said, "The darkness was bleak. Then white light flashed. It hurt my eyes. It burned my hand. Burned it all the way up my arm to my brain. Into my heart. I screamed and screamed, but stuff kept falling in my mouth. I was choking and it was so hot. . . ." She was sweating, breathing in loud gasps, the memory overlying the reality of this room, of this time.

Baby could barely whimper now. The dark . . . the heat . . .

"Do you remember Zusane?" Caleb's voice sounded far away. "She opened the Dumpster."

Baby saw light, smelled fresh air.

"She climbed right in," he said.

"Yes . . ." *Baby was covered in filth. Something moved the rubbish around, muttering all the while. Baby tried to call out, but she could barely pant. Hopelessness washed over her. . . . Then something, a hand, touched her head. A voice crooned. The garbage was pushed aside, and Baby blinked at the glittering silhouette of a woman.*

Not the first woman. Not the one who rejected her.

This woman stroked her face, made soft babbling sounds, picked her up and held her as if she were precious, and although Baby's consciousness was fading, she thought the woman was crying, too. . . .

"Jacqueline!" Caleb whispered urgently.

She blinked at him. "I always knew Zusane saved me. I simply couldn't believe I remembered. . . . She was so bright, she hurt my eyes."

"She was wearing sequins." Caleb stood close, his arm against the wall by Jacqueline's head, his body inches from hers, and he anchored her, kept her from drifting back to the place, the smells, the horror. . . .

"Of course she was." She laughed a little. "When doesn't she?" But she knew Zusane never let anything damage one of her precious party gowns, and that she would climb in a Dumpster to rescue Jacqueline . . .

"Call your mother," Caleb said.

Jacqueline snapped back to the present, and to Caleb, with a vengeance. "It's always about Zusane with you, isn't it?"

"No, darling," he said patiently. "It's always about Zusane with *you*."

Jacqueline didn't know what he meant, and she didn't like his tone anyway. "Okay. I'll call her. But I have to shower first." Because she could still smell the garbage on her skin.

Chapter 14

Jacqueline stepped out of the bathroom and spread the edges of the voluminous nightgown like wings. "Where did you get this? From your mother?"

"Yes." Caleb had shed his jacket and belt and placed the clothes he'd brought into drawers in the dresser.

"There's enough material to make all the curtains at Tara." Not to mention lace and white ribbons galore.

"She hoped it would fit you." He glanced at her calves sticking out from beneath the white cotton. "But of course you're tall. She's not."

He didn't seem to want to look at her. Because she was in his mother's nightgown? Because her legs were too long? Because he was mad at her, or mad about her? She hoped it was the latter. She wanted him to suffer. "I've never met your mother."

He smiled a sort of sloppy, sentimental smile Jacqueline didn't associate with a hard-ass like Caleb. "She's lovely."

"Why haven't I met her?" She took a step forward.

He glanced up sharply. "Do you want to?"

"I'd like to thank her for . . . the nightgown." Actually, she wanted to meet the woman who had borne and raised a man like Caleb.

"When it's safe, I'll take you to meet her." He didn't show any emotion.

But Jacqueline thought he was pleased. "What's she like?"

"She's Sicilian down to her bones. She cooks, she cleans and she takes care of her dogs—"

"Dogs?" Jacqueline sidled closer. "I love dogs."

"She has two. One is a retired assistance dog who thinks he's a lapdog, and one is a German shepherd–chow who takes orders from Mama. Only from Mama."

"You put up with a dog who doesn't do what you tell him?" Jacqueline couldn't imagine him putting up with that.

"Her. Lizzie is my mother's dog. I don't get to vote on who, or what, lives in my mother's house." Caleb picked up the receiver on the old-fashioned pink princess phone beside the bed. "Besides, Lizzie is very protective of my mama, and when I'm not around, I like to know she's safe."

"Lizzie is her bodyguard."

"As I am your mother's bodyguard, and now

yours." Caleb dialed a number, Zusane's number, and handed the phone to Jacqueline.

Of course. He would remember. He always remembered her duty to Zusane—and his duty, too.

Resentfully, Jacqueline took it and waited, one bare foot on top of the other. She half hoped Zusane wouldn't answer, because knowing what she now knew, she would have to thank her mother for rescuing her from certain death, and Jacqueline was lousy at those seriously emotional conversations. At the same time, she hoped Zusane did answer, because if she didn't talk to her now, Caleb wouldn't forget, and he'd make her call later. She'd still have to try to thank Zusane, and she didn't need that sword of Damocles hanging over her head.

She waited through six rings, and when Zusane's voice mail picked up, she flashed a grim smile at Caleb. "Hi, Mom, it's Jacqueline. I just wanted to check and see how it was going with you and report in on how it's going with me. If you're interested, I mean."

"Okay, that was unnecessary," Caleb said.

"Also, Caleb told me about—" Caleb's level stare made her break off. His level stare, and the sure knowledge she couldn't live with her cowardice if she didn't thank her mother in real time. "Well. Never mind that. Just call me when you get a chance. Hope you're having fun! Bye!" She slammed down the phone and said, "You don't have to glare like that. I wasn't really going to do it."

He pulled underwear out of the drawer. "I'm going to shower now."

As always, when they spoke of Zusane, Jacqueline felt awkward, resentful, clumsy, like the only freak in the world who didn't worship at the altar of the wonderful Zusane. She did love her mother. She just didn't like her very much, and of that, Caleb made his disapproval clear.

They hadn't settled the question of who would sleep where, and as she watched him stalk away, she considered barricading him into the bathroom. Maybe shoving the dresser in front of the door . . . Of course, since the door opened inward, that wouldn't help much . . . but it would be funny to see the look on his face when he tried to come out.

Then the phone rang. She jumped at it, grabbed it, said, "Mom?"

"Hello, darling." Music played in the background, and the sound of party chatter filtered through the receiver. "I was trying to get to my cell and just missed your call. Are you settling into your new role as psychic for the Chosen Ones?"

In a rush, Jacqueline remembered all her grievances with her mother. "Mom, why didn't you tell me if I was the seer, I was the only one?"

"Didn't I, darling? I thought I had." Zusane's voice was warm, rich, accented . . . amused.

"You know very well you didn't."

"I have such a bad memory for these things." Jacqueline could almost see her patting her well-coiffed blond head. "Have you had a vision yet?"

"No, I have not!"

Zusane's voice sharpened. "You had better try."

"I don't want to try. I don't want this kind of responsibility!"

"I know you don't, Jacqueline Lee, but if you didn't want to be the seer, you should have gone to Harvard." Zusane sounded the way she always did when they discussed Jacqueline's future. Pinched, superior, impatient.

"Or Yale," Jacqueline said sarcastically.

"Or Yale," Zusane agreed. "Or any reputable Ivy League college. I could have gotten you into any of them, and instead, you chose Vanderbilt University."

"That's not exactly a little red schoolhouse. It's ranked in the top twenty universities in the US!"

"But you didn't stay in college. Instead you went tearing off—"

The injustice of that made Jacqueline speak slowly, distinctly. "I had my reasons."

But Zusane was in a full-blown Eastern European rage. "If you'd gone back to school, you would have had an alternative to being a psychic. You could support yourself."

"I *was* supporting myself in California."

"You were wasting time in California!"

"Wasting time? *I* was wasting time?" Jacqueline stammered with indignation. "What about you? You're an intelligent woman who's too lazy to do anything but get married time after time. And when you divorce, you make that stupid joke about what a great house-keeper you were, because when you got a divorce you always kept the house."

"I like that joke." Zusane had the nerve to sound hurt.

Jacqueline seized the advantage. "Now you're at a party somewhere in . . . Where are you?"

"We're having a little gathering here in Manhattan, just a few close friends before I fly off with my new beau to the party in Turkey."

"And who is he?" Jacqueline found herself tapping her toe.

"You wouldn't know him."

"I wouldn't know him?" Jacqueline couldn't believe that. "Why would I not know him? All your beaus are famous."

"Osgood is different. He keeps a low profile."

Jacqueline didn't like the way Zusane's voice got quiet and guarded, as if she had something to hide. "Mother, what are you up to?"

Zusane's tone returned to normal. "I'm divorced. I can do whatever I want, can't I?" To someone at the party, she said, "Thank you, darling. Champagne is ex-actly what I wanted."

"No, you can't do whatever you want." As she scolded, Jacqueline wondered how she always managed to feel like the parent in this relationship.

Whoever it was must have moved away, because Zusane used that quiet, guarded voice again. "Anyway, darling, don't worry about your visions. They're going to come whether you want them to or not."

With a chill, Jacqueline remembered her vivid rescue from the Dumpster, and realized she wasn't supposed to be bickering with Zusane. She was supposed to be thanking her. Awkwardly, she said, "Mother, I talked to Caleb, and he told me about, um, how you saved me when I was a baby—"

"That naughty boy. I told him to keep that to himself." Zusane sounded truly annoyed.

"I'm glad he didn't, because I want to say thank you—"

"Don't be silly, dear. I did it for me as much as for you. I mean, I knew I couldn't be the seer forever!"

"I can always trust you to put things in perspective!" Selfish. Her mother was bone-deep selfish, and Jacqueline should never forget it.

But Zusane truly hated to have her good deeds exposed, and hated more to be thanked, so perhaps Jacqueline should remember that. . . .

The bathroom door opened.

Jacqueline turned to glare at Caleb—and forgot her irritation. In fact, she forgot Zusane altogether.

Because he wore a black T-shirt and black midthigh boxer briefs. He was damp, tanned, and muscled, and looked as tempting as good chocolate.

The sight of him knocked the breath out of Jacqueline, and her *Wow* was soundless and awed.

Meanwhile, Zusane babbled in her ear. "Darling, I have to go. We're taking Osgood's plane to Turkey. He's got an island." She sounded charmed. "Nothing vulgar. Just a little island. He invited a dozen of us to spend some time sunbathing on his beach. We should be there tomorrow sometime. I simply can't wait!"

"Yeah. Have a good time."

"So you're not mad at me anymore for my little memory glitch?"

Reluctantly, Jacqueline brought her attention back to the call. "Mother, I don't want this job."

"You should have thought of that before you stepped into the chalk circle."

"If I had known all the circumstances—"

"This is a case of 'let the buyer beware.' In this case, you're the buyer." Zusane lectured briskly, efficiently. "Now the Chosen Ones are depending on you, and darling, there's never been a time when the fate of the Chosen Ones and everything they stand for was in more jeopardy."

Jacqueline squeezed the phone so hard, her knuckles hurt. "Thanks, Mother. As if I weren't feeling enough pressure."

"Well, darling, ask yourself—*why* did you step into the circle?"

"I don't know!"

"Of course you do. You just don't want to admit it. You have always avoided the hard issues, Jacqueline. It's time to face them." Satisfaction bled into Zusane's voice. "Really. You have no choice."

Jacqueline heard a man asking Zusane a question, although she couldn't quite make out the words. Heard her mother laugh breathlessly and say to him, "It's nobody, darling." Into the phone, she said, "That's all I have time for." A pause, and in a low voice, she said, "Good-bye, good-bye. I love you!"

Jacqueline couldn't believe that her mother had called her a nobody, then dared tell her she loved her. The phone went dead while she held it; then she said, "Yeah. I love you, too." And she flung the receiver on the bed as hard as she could.

Chapter 15

"Looks as if you managed to get hold of your mother." Caleb walked over, picked up the receiver, and put it on the cradle. He wished he'd been in the room for the conversation, but in the end, he couldn't change the outcome of the relationship between mother and daughter. They'd been fighting for as long as he remembered.

"She's impossible."

"She always has been."

"Why have you stayed with her all these years?" she asked explosively. "There are lots of rich people you could protect who aren't as . . . as frustrating as she is."

"You're not the only person whose life she has saved." He watched as Jacqueline digested that comment. "Which side do you want?"

She blinked at him. "What?"

"Which side of the bed do you want?"

He could see her trying to put together an argument about sleeping with him. But she was tired. She couldn't put the words together. And she looked at him, really looked at him, in his briefs and tee, and he saw that spark of appreciation. Then she looked down at herself, enveloped in the yards of white cotton, started laughing, and flopped down on the far side of the bed. "It's not like you could be interested when I'm dressed like this."

The one thing he could always depend on with Jacqueline was an absolute lack of conceit. Part of that was being raised by Zusane, the most glamorous woman in the world. Part of that was his fault. . . . He'd convinced her she was resistible, and someday he was going to have to tell her the truth.

But right now, it was convenient for her to think that the sight of her in his mother's nightgown didn't turn him on—and if she was going to keep that illusion, he'd better get into bed before she noticed he was carrying an unregistered weapon. Lifting the covers on the other side, he climbed in, and waited while she rumbled around, getting under the covers, punching the pillow, sighing deeply.

When she had settled herself, he asked, "Did you thank your mother?"

"I tried!" she flashed.

"Good. You'll be glad."

With a huff, she flipped on her side away from him.

Caleb lay there, propped up on the pillows, his arms behind his head, and listened to Jacqueline's breathing. She wanted to stay irritated with him; instead she went to sleep right away, tired out from the travel, from their fight, from her decision to join the Chosen Ones and witnessing Zusane's dreadful vision. She'd seen the wreckage of the building she'd visited since she was a child, faced the deaths of men and women she'd known her whole life, and confronted a reality she had spent years trying to escape—she had to somehow let loose her psychic talent, or the Others would score a great win. Like a plague of locusts, they would spread their evil and nothing could stop them.

She said she didn't care.

He knew better.

The first time he'd seen Jacqueline, he'd been nine. He'd watched Zusane crawl out of the Dumpster, a skinny, red-faced, filthy, squalling infant in her arms, and knew he and the baby had something in common. Zusane had rescued her, much as she'd rescued him— but he had had his mother to care for him. This child had only Zusane—and Zusane knew one thing. She knew how to love a child.

She clutched the baby to her heart and headed toward her penthouse on Central Park. He ran alongside, fending off street people and baring his teeth at anyone who recognized the already famous Zusane.

When they reached her home, Zusane told him to lock and bar the door.

She acted as if someone was after her—or the child.

She gave him money, told him to be careful, and sent him to buy diapers and formula. When he returned, to his amazement, the glamorous Zusane had bathed the child, wrapped her in a heated blanket, and stood cradling the limp little body against her chest. She coaxed the infant to eat, changed her diaper, fed her again, insisted she be kept warm.

Where had the frivolous, worldly Zusane learned to care for a baby?

She told him she intended to keep the abandoned infant as her own, that her name was Jacqueline Lee, and uncurled the little hand to show him, for the first time, the distinctive mark of the eye.

She told him the baby would need to be protected from people who would do her harm, and that when he grew up, he could be Jacqueline's bodyguard.

Zusane had never kept her promise. Until today.

Oh. And one other time . . .

Chapter 16

❖

Winter, two years ago

Caleb woke with a start. It was still early, just past ten. The warm Bermuda night sang with the wash of waves on the beach and the breeze in the palms. The full moon shone through his window, and the island scents were rich with flowers and sea spray.

Yet something was wrong.

He heard it again, the noise that had brought him out of his first hour of sound sleep—the creak of a floorboard on the lanai.

Pistol at the ready, he was out of the bed in a flash. Clad in his shorts, he opened the door of his bungalow.

Zusane stood there, swaying gracelessly, clutching a bathrobe around her chest.

Caleb had seen the signs before—the unfocused eyes, the strain in her husky voice, the jerky lack of coordination.

She'd had a vision.

Reaching out, he yanked her into his room and shut the door. Hands on her shoulders, he sat her in a chair and poured her a brandy. Shoving it in Zusane's hand, he knelt before her. "What is it? What did you see?" Because if she had managed to fight her way through the post-vision exhaustion and come to him, it must be dire.

"I don't know why, I don't know how, but Jacqueline is in danger."

He came to his feet, flicked on the light by his bed, put a call through to Jacqueline's cell phone. It went right to voice mail. But ever since Jacqueline had gone to college, she had seldom answered calls from her mother and never from him. Not that he'd tried too often, but Zusane occasionally showed her maternal feelings and wanted to check up on her daughter.

He knew the truth, although he never told Zusane. Zusane embarrassed Jacqueline. Jacqueline desperately wanted to be ordinary, and Zusane was too flamboyant for ordinary.

Gathering his black T-shirt, black jeans, and bulletproof vest, he headed into the bathroom. He dressed, shaved, and was back out in five minutes.

Zusane looked better, not as pale, but still drawn with worry. "I've arranged for Peter's corporate jet to take you to Nashville."

"Right." Jacqueline was a freshman at Vanderbilt University.

"I would go with you, but Peter wouldn't understand."

Caleb wrapped his holster around his chest, checked to make sure his pistol was clean and loaded, and slid it inside.

"If it weren't my honeymoon, I would be there for the child."

Caleb hated Zusane's honeymoons. They were boring as hell and embarrassing to watch, and knowing how the marriage would end, he always felt a bit of pity for the guys she married. They were invariably rich, powerful men, the kind who were used to making the decisions and walking away from the relationships.

Not with Zusane.

But the grooms didn't want to hear that. They were always desperately in love, enthralled by whatever acrobatic feats Zusane performed in bed, and they didn't realize that she rather despised the men she captured with such transparent arts. For Zusane, marriage was the beginning of the end.

"Is this danger deadly?" Caleb asked.

"Not yet. But it could be." Zusane clutched the brandy glass in both shaking hands.

"Then you should go to identify the body," he said. It was cruel, but he wanted to shake her out of her self-absorption. Just once, she needed to put her daughter first.

"Don't be silly!" Zusane's voice grew shrill and petulant. "I'm sending you, my best bodyguard. You'll find her. You'll save her. I mean, what else would she want? She always liked you better than she liked me, anyway."

With that, Caleb tuned her out. Put one knife up his sleeve and one in his boot. Grabbed his LED flashlight and mini-GPS locator. Leaned down and kissed Zusane on the forehead, and said, "I'll do what I can."

He left Zusane rambling on, justifying her neglect to an audience of no one.

With the two-hour time change, it was eleven when he landed in Nashville to find some friend of Peter's had a car waiting for him.

Caleb reached the campus in fifteen minutes. Vanderbilt University was steeped in night, quiet . . . tense. Something stalked at the edges of his consciousness.

He could hear fear on the prowl.

So he moved as he'd been trained, silently and always on the alert.

He went to Jacqueline's dorm first, checked in with her roommate, and discovered Jacqueline had been dating Wyatt King, one of the premier frat boys from a respectable family in Buffalo, New York. Her roommate hadn't seen Jacqueline all afternoon, hadn't heard a word from her at all—and it was now eleven fifteen p.m. She said she wasn't worried, but as she talked to him, she bit her fingernails down to the quick. The girl knew something, but he couldn't shake the truth out of her. As far as she was concerned, she was covering for her friend.

So he went out hunting.

First, he checked at Wyatt's frat house. The guys said they weren't concerned, either . . . except they were.

One of them, Richie Haynes, followed Caleb out to the parking lot and told him that, with the downturn, Wyatt had lately had money problems, and he'd been acting strangely. Sort of exuberant, sort of ashamed, and considering how hot

Jacqueline Vargha was, he hadn't been bragging much. In fact, he'd kind of been pretending he wasn't dating her.

When Caleb pinned Richie to the wall and threatened to choke him to death, the guy admitted Wyatt had tried to get him involved in a hinky plot to kidnap this girl with the weird eye tattoo in the palm of her hand, and sell her to white slavers. When Caleb choked him a little more, Richie recalled it hadn't been white slavers, but some spooky guys who sounded like Satanists or something. After that, the dam burst and he babbled freely, telling Caleb that Wyatt had taken the chick into the country to a local sinkhole to deliver the girl and pick up his fee, and before Richie knew it, he was in Caleb's car, giving directions to the sinkhole.

Caleb didn't bother with stealth. It was far too late for that. With his brights on full blast, he drove up the pitted gravel road at seventy miles an hour, ignoring Richie's warnings as he leaped potholes and left a choking cloud of dust behind him. The sinkhole opened right under his tires, and he slammed on the brakes and skidded sideways. Before Richie had even finished screaming, Caleb was out of the car with his pistol drawn. A quick survey with the flashlight located two cars parked off the edge of the road in the trees, and a path leading down into the sinkhole. Yelling for Jacqueline, Caleb ran down the path, sliding past rusting fenders and ruined sofas, through mounds of garbage left by people too cheap or lazy to take it to the dump.

She didn't return his calls; she was unconscious or gagged or . . . or they'd already taken her somewhere else.

He refused to think he'd been too late.

Out of the corner of his eye, he caught a flash of movement. He leaped up onto a battered dryer, grabbed a length of kudzu vine, and swung out over the sinkhole and around behind his attacker. The guy had some kind of power that could have knocked Caleb cold, but his focus was forward; all Caleb had to do was kick him between the shoulder blades and the guy went over the edge and into the abyss.

After that it was easy. The people Richie called the Satanists were some discombobulated branch of the Others, and once their muscle was out of the way, they ran like hell for the rim of the sinkhole. That left the sniveling Wyatt standing on a ledge, the earth crumbling around him. He held the unconscious Jacqueline as a shield, a kitchen knife at her throat, and in a trembling voice, he yelled, "Come close and I'll kill her."

The full moon was rising, slipping through the trees, groping toward the bottom of the sinkhole twenty feet below. The light gave the scene an unearthly cast, and Caleb saw Jacqueline, limp, drugged, gagged, and tied hand and foot.

He wanted to rip that little shit Wyatt from stem to stern.

He knew that the boy clearly saw him slip his pistol into the holster at his side and flex his hands. "Give her to me and I won't kill you."

Wyatt was a stupid, privileged kid who had never faced an adversary in his whole life. Caleb watched the parade of expressions across his face. He was frightened, defiant, angry, frightened again, and finally, like a spoiled little kid, determined to get his own way.

"Let me make myself clear." Caleb spoke softly, but his fists clenched and loosened, clenched and loosened. "If you kill her, if you hurt her in any way, if she slips from your grasp and falls and needs a bandage on her skinned knee, I will spend the next three hours making you pray for mercy as your blood slowly drains into the dirt, and when I'm done, you'll be alive. You'll wish you weren't . . . but you'll have no way to scream in pain. No way to end your own life. No way to even wipe your skinny white ass."

Wyatt may have gotten into Vanderbilt because his father was a paying alumnus, but he wasn't a total moron. Keeping his gaze fixed on Caleb, he let Jacqueline's limp form slowly slide to the ground.

And as soon as she was free of his grip, she came to life and kicked Wyatt's feet out from underneath him.

He toppled over the edge and screamed all the way down.

Chapter 17

One week later

*C*aleb threw Jacqueline to the mat again.

She lay there, panting, exhausted, her white karate gi soaked in sweat.

"Get up," he said. "You're not done yet."

He'd been training her for seven days, teaching her to fall, to kick, to break a man's nose and rip off his testicles. She knew a thousand percent more than she'd known before, but still she didn't know enough.

She staggered to her feet. "I'm tired."

"Oh, please. You slept until eight this morning." He glanced at the sun slanting into the gym at Zusane's Connecticut home. "It's barely three."

"I'm hungry. I'm tired. I'm quitting." Jacqueline stood with her hands on her hips, her elbows akimbo. "For once, just be satisfied with what I've done."

He was never going to be satisfied. Not as long as the

memory of Jacqueline's bound, gagged body remained in his mind. He'd untied her, removed her gag, and carried her to the car while she lolled in his arms, passing in and out of consciousness. At the top, he'd called an ambulance and the cops. She'd gone to the hospital to have her stomach pumped of an almost lethal combination of alcohol and Valium. Wyatt had gone to jail for as long as it took his father's team of lawyers to get him released.

But Caleb didn't tell Jacqueline that. She was so mad—at herself for being a willing dupe, at Wyatt for being a slime bucket—that she focused on the fighting to the exclusion of all else.

Only now . . . she had a funny look on her face. He'd seen that look before, right before his mother started sobbing from sadness or loneliness or memories that weighed too much for her fragile shoulders to bear.

Yeah. Caleb was afraid Jacqueline might have other issues he was ill equipped to deal with, but for now, he knew what to do. Beat her down again and again. Break her. And lift her back into the confident girl she'd been when she had left for college.

Ignoring the first rule he'd taught her, she turned away from him and headed toward the stairs.

He brought her down with a single quick kick to the backs of her knees.

She tumbled face-first onto the mat, and just lay there.

Hands up, he stood waiting for her attack.

She didn't move. Just pressed her face to the floor.

And he realized she was crying.

"No." This was not what he wanted. "No. Fighters don't cry. Black belts don't cry. You don't cry."

She didn't answer. She remained there, shoulders shaking, making no noise at all. But she was definitely miserable, and somehow he had to deal with it.

Warily, still half convinced this was a trick, he knelt beside her.

She didn't knock the shit out of him, so he guessed it wasn't.

"Listen." He placed his hand on her head. "You're a good student. One of the best I've ever taught."

A single loud sob wrenched out of her; it was pure, distilled agony. Then she pressed her arm to her mouth.

He slid his hand down to her back, and rubbed it in a slow circle. "Did he rape you? Is that why you're crying?"

She flipped over so fast, he leaped back. "Is that what you think?" Her eyes were bloodshot, her cheeks wet, and she wiped her nose on her sleeve. "That's all that could be wrong? That Wyatt raped me?"

She wasn't going to distract him. "Did he?"

"No. He was afraid of me." She started to sob again. "He thought—he said—I was a freak."

"You are not a freak." Caleb wiped his sweaty forehead on the sleeve of his gi.

"Really?" She shoved her palm into his face. "Then how do you explain this?"

Caleb stared at the birthmark on her palm. It looked like

a tattoo, a stylized human eye in black ink. The mark was mesmerizing, and in Zusane's world, it meant something very specific—it meant that Jacqueline was a seer of amazing power.

In Wyatt's world, it meant she could be sold for a profit to the Others to be used as a sacrifice to the powers of darkness.

She wasn't likely to forget that.

Taking her hand in his, he said, "There are ignorant people in this world—"

"Like Wyatt? Yeah, I got that. He's ignorant. He's a jackass. And he said he liked me. He said he wanted to date me. He said I was fun and cool and interesting. And I believed him. So if he's an ignorant jackass, what does that make me?" She was red-faced and defiant, yelling at him.

He was a guy, ill equipped to deal with this kind of breakdown. So he offered to do what he'd been itching to do anyway. "Do you want me to take him out? Because I can."

"No, I don't want you to take him out. What I want is to have a normal life, where I date guys who don't want to kill me, and study something dull like accounting, and get married and have normal children—and I'll never get any of that, because Zusane says I have a fate."

"I know."

"I could deal with that. I really could. But here's the question I've been wondering." She thrust her face close to his. "How did you find out I was in danger?"

"Zusane knew. She sent me."

"She sent you? She sent you? She knew I was going to be killed and she sent . . . you? Wow, how maternal of her." Jacqueline's eyes overflowed again, her voice wobbled, and her sobs interrupted every other word. "Did it . . . ever occur . . . to her . . . that I . . . might . . . want . . . my mother?"

"She wanted to come but—"

"But she was . . . on her honeymoon? Do you think I don't . . . get that? Do you think this is the . . . first time she's been too busy for . . . me? My God. My God. I've got nobody. Nobody. Nobody gives a damn about me. Nobody." Jacqueline's voice rose to a shriek.

He couldn't stand it anymore. Tenderness overwhelmed his good sense, and he put his arms around her and whispered, "I care. I care too much."

"You do not." She pushed at him, furious at what she saw as condescending reassurance.

He pulled her closer. "This isn't the time, and I don't have the right, but I don't lie."

"Right. You care about me. Like a brother who watched me grow up. I suppose I should be grateful for that!"

His laughter wavered. "Not like a brother. Are you insane? I've never thought of you like that. Do you think I'm proud of this? I'm nine years older than you and you're nothing but a"—she plunged her hand underneath the elastic at his waist—"child," he finished, and his voice cracked with surprise.

She wrapped her fingers around his erection. Her startled gaze flew to meet his.

"I told you I don't lie." He waited for her to retreat, to run away from the evidence that he did want her.

But one thing he had learned during the days of fighting lessons—Jacqueline didn't retreat. Instead she put her hand on his chest and shoved him to the mat—and the other hand, the one in his pants, squeezed him hard.

He stiffened, torn between glory and anguish. "If you're trying to get revenge on men by using me, you're going at it the right way."

Her grip eased. Her expression was intent, captivated, as she explored him—the length, the breadth, his balls and his belly. Then she came back and gripped him again, and used her thumb to rub the head of his dick in smooth, slow motions.

By now, he could hardly speak, but he managed to ask, "Have you had much experience with this kind of thing?"

"No."

"Because if you don't stop that, I'm going to come in your hand."

Her eyebrows shot up. "Already?"

"There is no already. I've been trying to tell you—you're the only woman I've ever really wanted."

Jacqueline pulled her hand free.

Caleb should have been relieved that she had somehow regained her senses.

But she tugged at the black belt. "I may not have much hands-on experience. But that's not my fault. Before I went out that night with Wyatt, I got myself on the pill, because I *thought I was going to get lucky." She put her face close to his. "I liked him because he looked like you."*

Caleb gazed into her amazing eyes, the color of pure amber, and realized he wasn't the only one enthralled. "Do not compare me with that stinking little brat."

"No, you're not a brat. You're mature and responsible. You never talk about your emotions. I have no idea what you think of me, if you have contempt for me for being so stupid as to get involved with a guy who wanted to sell me because of the mark on my hand."

How could she be uncertain about his feelings for her? He felt as if he wore them on his sleeve. "You're not stupid. You're trusting and fresh and hopeful." He smoothed her bangs off her forehead. "I've seen so much of the world, I haven't been hopeful since I left Italy, yet when I'm with you . . . you make me young again."

The anxiety in her eyes relaxed, and for the first time since he'd rescued her, she looked hopeful again. She looked like Jacqueline again.

Sitting up, she tugged at his belt again. "I'm still on the pill."

Caleb opened his gi top in record time. "Then I guess we're both going to get lucky." Spreading his arms wide, he wordlessly invited her to explore his chest.

She put both her palms on his pecs and smoothed the contours, then worked her way down his ribs to his belly.

He'd been working hard. His blood still galloped in his veins. He was damp with sweat, yet when she leaned close and breathed him as if he were a perfume, he grabbed her arms.

No. You'll scare her.

But it was too late. He flipped her beneath him.

She hit the mat.

He rolled on top of her, thrusting his knee between her legs.

They stared at each other, and he saw the same fire blazing in her that blazed in him. They kissed, openmouthed, tasting each other for the first time. He'd been waiting for this his whole adult life. There had been other women. Of course there had been. But always he'd stood apart, using them to learn his moves, to discover what pleasured them. In the secret depths of his mind, he'd imagined himself showing those moves to Jacqueline, overwhelming Jacqueline with his skill, bringing Jacqueline to orgasm—and all the while knowing his employer's daughter was not for a peasant boy from Sicily.

Now . . . now he had Jacqueline in his hands, and he was too turned on to do anything but plunge his tongue repeatedly into her mouth. He taught her nothing except how desperately he wanted her.

That seemed exactly what she wanted to know. She reveled in the lesson, her tongue meeting every thrust, her body writhing against his. When she stroked his thigh with her bare foot, he caught her knee and pulled it around him, and slipped into the cradle between her legs. He moved against her, matching the rhythm of his tongue with the rhythm of his body.

She rose to meet each thrust, rubbing herself against him, and when she did, she made a humming noise into his mouth. She was like a bee, flying to him for honey, darting in and out while he barely held on. The clothes between them made no difference; they might as well have been naked . . . and that thought brought his lust-induced frenzy to another level.

She pushed him away, and yanked at the yellow belt around her waist.

He helped her with the knot, opened the heavy white cloth—and looked.

Her skin was flushed and dewy from the workout. Her belly was flat and strong; her shoulders were muscled. Her exercise bra irritated the hell out of him; it mashed her boobs flat and completely concealed the erotic lines he had only imagined. He wanted to see her, know her, explore every inch of her. Sliding his hand under her back, he groped for the snaps. And groped. And groped.

She laughed abruptly and painfully. "There are no hooks. I pull it on over my head."

"Son of a bitch." He had never sworn so earnestly.

She laughed again, this time with real amusement.

Tugging her up to face him, he started to drag at her sleeves.

In one swift, efficient movement, she shoved him away, removed the top, and removed the bra.

She had the best, most glorious breasts he'd ever seen— because they were hers. He cupped one lightly in the palm of his hand, savoring the sweet weight, the silky skin, the pale pink nipple. He used his thumb to circle the areola.

She caught her breath and pressed her hand over his. Took his other hand and put it on her other breast.

He squeezed lightly, watching her face as she reveled in the sensation. She was so responsive, glowing with the joy of discovery, and he wanted her. Now.

He lifted her off the floor and onto the weight bench. Kneeling before her, he found her nipple with his mouth. He sucked, lightly at first, outlining the small, sweet circle with his tongue, then with more strength, letting her feel his raw desire.

She dug her fingers into his shoulders. She writhed in his arms, moaning. She was a flame that burned and enticed him.

He spread his fingers wide on her back, enjoying the flex of her spine as he kissed her other breast.

And then . . . she bit his ear.

The tiny pain tipped him over the edge into madness. He found himself on his feet, looking down at her upturned face. "You don't know what you're doing."

"No. But you said I was a good student." Her lashes lowered over gleaming amber eyes.

When had she changed from hesitant girl to alluring temptress?

"If you knew how much I've restrained myself, how much I've suffered over you, you wouldn't dare—"

Putting her hand on his thigh, she slid it around and up.

Her touch transformed him. He became a machine, smoothly catching her wrist, twisting her around and pushing her down to lie lengthwise, her spine resting on the bench. Hooking his fingers under her waistband, he pulled, taking the gi pants and the sports panties off in one effortless movement.

She tried to sit up, pull her legs together, regain her modesty even as he stole it away.

"No," he whispered, pushed her back and followed her down. He pressed his chest against hers, and the sensation of skin against skin was torture—and glory. She was naked, and he wanted to do her.

Yet if he took her, he'd be a cad and worse.

Yet he wanted to do her.

It was an argument he couldn't win.

So he kissed her. Kissed her hard and long, using his tongue as he wished to use his dick, with strength and speed and precision, seizing control with no intention of relinquishing it.

And she . . . she kissed him back.

It was like flinging rocket fuel on a forest fire. The resulting explosion broke his will.

Swiftly and with wicked intent, he kissed her neck, her breasts, her belly. He pulled her to the edge of the bench, put her legs on his shoulders, and kissed her pussy, tasting her and, when she came, drinking of her. Then as he rose above her, he shed his pants. "If you want me to stop, you have to tell me now." His voice sounded deeper, more demon than human, strained with the effort of making the offer.

Her chest heaved from the power of her fading orgasms. "After that . . . you think . . . you can run away?" Reaching up, she took his hips. She pulled him down to her.

"Finish it," she said.

Thank God.

He adjusted their bodies so that he sat on the bench with her legs on his thighs, so that she was stretched out before him like a feast, so that he held the globes of her bottom in his hands. Leaning over, he lifted her, tilted her hips and placed himself at the entrance to her body.

She was warm and wet, slick from his mouth and her climax.

She whimpered when he pressed inside the first inch.

"Okay?" He couldn't believe he even had the ability to form that single word.

"You're driving me crazy. Please." She sat up on her elbows and tried to work herself onto him.

As her pussy enveloped him centimeter by centimeter, lust burst like fireworks across his every nerve and synapse.

Closing his eyes, he concentrated on restraint. He was a fourth-degree black belt. He was an expert marksman. He had thrived on survival training. He was a man who understood discipline. Nothing and no one broke him.

Until she sat all the way up, pressed her chest to his, wrapped her arms around his shoulders, and whispered, "Please. I need you."

He lost his mind. He lost his control. He tried to lunge forward.

But he couldn't. Not entwined as they were.

Their eyes locked, challenging each other.

He rocked his hips.

She rocked hers.

He penetrated her body by fractions of inches, moving so gradually, his erection throbbed and grew, his balls tightened, and he ground his teeth in agony . . . and pleasure.

He had never imagined, never suffered such a luscious, tight, heated hell. She was virgin territory, and he couldn't bear it. . . . He could not stand another moment. . . .

In slow motion, he fell backward, bringing her up on top of him, breaching her swiftly, completely.

She threw back her head, panting with the shock of having him deep inside her. Her fingernails dug into his chest, and her feet hit the floor on either side of the bench.

"Move," he ordered. Because if she didn't, he would.

She did.

Her thighs flexed. Cautiously she lifted herself a few inches, then lowered herself onto him.

He arched his back as his whole body went into a spasm of ecstasy.

As if that motion was all she needed, she smiled with fierce, brutal joy, and started a rhythm that wiped every thought from his brain. As if she'd been born to drive him mad, she rose and fell, rose and fell, making each moment a dazzling glory.

He wanted to come.

He moved and groaned. He lived for the next rise and fall of her body over his.

He needed to come.

But her eyes were luminous with restless enthusiasm. She had never experienced the power and splendor of sex, she held mastery over him, and she ruthlessly used his body. She experimented, leaning backward and forward, flexing her muscles inside, trying every trick any woman from the dawn of time had ever imagined. He wondered—when he could think—what the hell she'd been reading, who the hell she'd been talking to, if she'd been watching some crazy sex therapist on Oprah. Then she'd lift her hands to lift her hair off her neck, her breasts would thrust forward, and he'd forget anything but this moment, this woman, this adventure.

Finally he couldn't take it anymore. Taking her hips, he forced her into a regular pace, moving her up and down so that he penetrated her slowly, completely, time after time. He made her feel each inch of his penis as it moved inside her . . . and passion caught her in its trap.

Her breath caught, and caught again. She placed her hands on his chest, looked into his eyes, and moved with ever-increasing violence and speed.

Frantic and desperate, they raced toward satisfaction. It was elusive, always out of reach, but they hurried, and it caught them from behind, surprising them, overwhelming them.

He came hard and fast, grinding her hips down on his hips, coming, filling her . . . making her his.

She struggled, whimpering in torment until he was done with his orgasm. Then he lifted her again, letting her work herself up and down his erection, rubbing herself against his pelvis until she cried out and convulsed, coming again and again in great waves of ecstasy.

They shuddered, as gradually the tempest retreated, until finally, it was over.

Except that it wasn't.

Because she was still his.

She would always be his. Every day of that week, Caleb branded her with his body, with his words, with his care, teaching her to laugh with him, love with him . . . depend on him.

And then . . . he had walked away.

Now he leaned over her as she slept. He brushed her hair off her face, and smiled at the boneless, child-like relaxation that possessed her.

He would always want her.

He thought no one knew of his obsession, but when he'd gone home to gather his clothes and collect something for Jacqueline to wear, his mother had listened to his voice, and something in his tone made her say, "Caleb, I hear what you do not wish to tell me. You love this girl. You have always loved her. And now you fear for her, too. Have a care, my son, for I know you. You are like me. You will love only once in your life, and if you lose her, your life will be desolation."

Caleb adjusted the white lace at Jacqueline's neckline.

To celebrate her happiness at her son's choice, Niccola D'Angelo had sent her wedding nightgown for Jacqueline to wear.

Chapter 18

———◆———

"**W**e've come to see Gary White."

The night nurse stared at Irving and at Martha, her mouth slightly open as she tried to decide what to do about two senior citizens visiting a man in a coma. "Visiting hours are over."

Irving and Martha exchanged relieved glances.

The nurse's words were a sign of normalcy for which they were sincerely grateful. Intruders hadn't forced themselves into the hospital, as Martha feared, and Gary was still alive.

"I know." Irving folded his hands before him and lowered his head, trying to look as old and feeble as possible. "But dear Martha's plane was late coming in to La-Guardia, and she's going back to Omaha first thing in the morning. If she can't see Gary now, she can't see him at all, and who knows if he'll be alive next time she's here."

Martha played along, covering her eyes with her hand and sniffling loudly.

"So, Martha, you're family?" the nurse asked.

Martha gave an indistinguishable murmur of agreement.

The night nurse looked them over again, then stammered, "I . . . well . . . I suppose it's all right. It's not as if you'll disturb him. You do realize he won't know whether you're here or not."

Martha looked up, her eyes remarkably dry. "So there's been no change in his condition?"

"No. He's unconscious, as he has been since he arrived here four years ago. Let me show you to his room." She stood and started down the corridor. Irving and Martha trailed her. "It's a shame, really. When he arrived, he was a man obviously in the prime of his life. I'll never forget how handsome he was, and strong-looking, as if he worked out every day. Now his muscles have wasted away; he's gaunt and . . . Forgive me, but if it's been a while since you've seen him, I thought you should be prepared." She opened the door of room 106 and walked in.

"Thank you." Martha followed her. She viewed the emaciated, twisted body beneath the sheets on the hospital bed, and tears rose in her dark brown eyes and trickled down her cheek.

Gary's face was still. His formerly black hair had thinned. An IV fed him liquids and nutrients, and his chest barely rose and fell under the meager force of his breath.

"This is a tragedy," she whispered.

But unlike Irving, Martha believed it.

Irving had always kept his opinion of Gary White to himself. Gary had come to the Chosen as a charismatic young man. He had been elected leader of his group right away and they'd willingly followed him into every danger every day. Even as he grew older, all the most challenging missions had been entrusted to him and his team. Until the day so many had died . . .

Except for Gary. Gary hadn't died. He'd been reduced to this helpless piece of human flesh.

Irving didn't know what happened that day. He only knew Gary had been the kind of guy who always got Irving's back up. He had been too brilliant, too compelling, too coordinated, too powerful. The men of the Chosen Ones had rallied behind his leadership. The young women of the Chosen visited his bed with consistent enthusiasm. Even more important, he'd charmed all the influential women over forty.

That was why Martha stood beside the head of the bed now, dabbing her eyes on a tissue.

Irving had been very much aware he might be jealous. But mostly, he thought his years as the director of the Gypsy Travel Agency had made him cynical.

Yet as he wearily sank into a chair, he knew he owed

Gary protection. Ugly opinions couldn't change the fact that Gary had been a Chosen hero.

Today, far too many of those heroes had died.

As he remembered them, conjured their faces from the vault of his mind, brought forth their vanished names, pain clawed its way up from his gut to his heart. With shaking hands, he loosened his tie and opened his starched collar.

He had given his life to the Gypsy Travel Agency and the Chosen Ones whom it supported, and now they were gone.

He'd seen the news reports, but even now, he couldn't comprehend the loss of so much talent, of so many gifts.

Dully, he watched the nurse change the IV bag. "Has anyone visited recently?" he asked.

"No. You're the first in months." Her voice was thick with reproach.

Torn between relief that the Others hadn't found Gary and killed him, and guilt that Gary had been so neglected, Irving said, "If you don't mind, Martha and I will sit here for a few minutes and talk to the boy. I imagine he misses hearing a friendly human voice."

"Whenever we come in, we talk to him." The nurse's judgmental tone upped Irving's guilt. "We play the television, too, in the hopes that will jog his brain to activity. We don't give up on our patients, sir, until the day they pass over."

"How much longer do you think he has?" Irving asked.

The nurse looked into Gary's face, and smoothed his hair back from his forehead. "Not long. I've seen it before. His spirit is fading. Unless something happens to bring him back to consciousness, he'll die. And perhaps . . . that would be best."

The Chosen Ones didn't have the resources to care for Gary White, and while Irving had not understood Gary at all, he knew one thing for sure—Gary would hate this helplessness.

Guilt swamped Irving, but . . . he couldn't help but agree. Gary would be better off dead.

Chapter 19

———◆———

Jacqueline woke and stretched, and smiled. She had slept marvelously well. Not once had Caleb strolled into her dreams to taunt her with pleasure unfinished and promises not kept, and that was just fine with—

Her eyes popped open.

She hadn't dreamed about him, because she'd been in bed with him.

And he was sitting in a chair, showered and dressed in a blue golf shirt and jeans, elbows resting on his knees, hands clasped, watching her sleep.

She sat up hard and fast. The covers were kicked back, this silly damned nightgown was hiked up around her thighs, and she'd probably been snoring, or drooling or, God help her, moaning his name. "What are you doing?"

"Thinking you're the most beautiful woman I've ever seen." He said it with a straight face.

So she had been drooling. "Luckily for you, you have great resistance."

"How do you figure?"

"Two years ago, you taught me to fight, you screwed me, and you left me without a backward glance." She finger combed her hair and discovered the left side was stuck sideways. She must have slept on one side for hours. "Two days ago, you found me in California, you screwed me, and yet managed to ignore my begging and pleading, and dragged me into the biggest, most horrific mess ever seen by the Chosen Ones."

"To be fair—"

"By all means"—she was proud of her tone, just sarcastic enough—"let's be fair."

"I am not a seer, therefore I had no premonition of yesterday's explosion. You weren't begging and pleading— you were throwing a tantrum. And I never screwed you, we made love." He was motionless, quiet, and logical.

She hated that. "Would begging and pleading have changed your mind?"

"No."

"Exactly. So a tantrum was more satisfying." She hated that he always seemed in control. Even when he made love to her, he was in control. Except for that one time. That first time. If they could somehow go back to that moment . . .

"Do you not have something smart-ass to say about the distinction between screwing and making love?"

"No." No, because she was still in bed and rumpled. And easy.

"Then I want to talk about what happened two years ago between us."

No way, mister. She rolled to the other side of the mattress and swung her feet off the bed. "You go ahead. I'll go into the bathroom and shut the door."

"Did you know after we'd been together that week, your mother had a vision about you and me?"

Jacqueline swung her feet back up and faced him. "When? *Then?*"

"She called me."

Jacqueline thought back on those perfect days of learning karate, making love, eating, sleeping, and knowing, for the first time in her life, that she belonged to someone. "She had a vision about us . . . together?" The mere thought was beyond embarrassing.

"Perhaps I should call it a hunch brought on by my continued absence at her side. At any rate, she called me."

"Did she?"

"She asked me what in the hell I was doing with her little girl."

"And you said?"

"I said very little. I listened, and I . . . agreed."

She didn't like this conversation. She didn't like

where it was leading, and really didn't like the fact that she so greedily wanted the information. "Agreed?"

"I agreed that you were twenty, a college girl."

She knew this was funny, in an awful way, but she couldn't smile. "I knew what went where."

"I seduced you."

She did laugh now, but bitterly and briefly. "That wasn't a seduction, my dear. That was a mutual and very satisfying release of pent-up lust. Besides, I don't know that your penitence is worth much. I was younger than you then. I'm younger than you now. Sometime between two years ago and two days ago, you decided I was old enough to screw."

"You are older than you were two years ago. I made love to you, and . . . in two years of ample opportunity, you had found nobody you loved. So you can love me instead."

Her palm itched to slap him, and she closed her hand into a fist to contain the urge. "Do you think it's that easy? I found no one, so I must take you? And why would I, when you left me on my mother's command?"

"I left you so you could go back to college."

"But I didn't." A cruel imp made her taunt him. "Do you know why I didn't?"

"Because I . . ." He stopped.

"Don't flatter yourself. It had nothing to do with you. When you walked out to return to your job as Zusane's primary bodyguard, I had nowhere else to go but back to college and that was where I was headed. It was Wyatt King who convinced me that running away was the best thing I could do with my life."

Caleb slowly straightened in his chair.

She was enjoying herself now. "Yeah. I'll bet that crushes your poor, meager little ego. It wasn't you who sent me flying across the country. It was a phone call from Wyatt King."

The color bleached out of Caleb's blue eyes until they resembled pure, hard diamonds. "What did he say to you?"

"He told me that his father's lawyer had gotten him off on all charges. He told me I'd better never come back to that school." Every word she spoke hurt her, like knives stabbed to her heart. "Because he made sure everyone knew I was a freak."

"I'll kill him." Caleb's lips barely moved.

"For what? Telling me the truth?" She spread her hands toward herself. "Look at me. Here I am, in a nightgown that's too small and forty years out of date, in a house with a bunch of other freaks, afraid to go out in case someone kills me."

He disregarded that, intent on pursuing one subject at a time. "You traveled the country. You supported yourself with all kinds of jobs. You took care of yourself. You should be confident."

"Oh, I am."

"I am proud of you."

"I'm glad of that."

"So why would you believe something a little piss-ant like Wyatt King told you two years ago?"

"Because knowing what I can do isn't the same as knowing I'm worth caring about. Wyatt thought I was a freak. Mother adopted me because she wanted a clone. You think I should take you because I haven't found anyone else." That maddened Jacqueline beyond any of the horrible, terrible facts of her life. "I don't really know what it is that makes me inherently unlovable, but I deal with it pretty well."

He would have spoken.

She didn't give him a chance. She didn't want to listen to him mouth platitudes about her desirability. Swinging her legs off the far side of the mattress again, she got up, and walked to the bathroom. "I don't need you to pretend a grand passion for me. We have great sex together. Whoo-hoo! But let's not get carried away."

The blue came back into his eyes, and they almost twinkled as he stood up.

She talked faster. "After all, you have a job to do. My mother told you to keep me safe." She clapped her hands together and made a shooing gesture. "So you better hit the streets and find out what you can about yesterday's explosion." Stepping into the bathroom, she shut the door. And locked it.

There was more than one way to have the last word.

Chapter 20

Tray in hand, Jacqueline stood outside Irving's bedroom and tried to figure out how to knock. Finally, she used her toes to thump on the wide wooden door.

At once, McKenna opened the door and looked her over from top to bottom, his gaze lingering disdainfully on her bare feet.

She smiled brightly. "I have Irving's lunch."

"Yes." McKenna stood unyielding, like a broad Celtic boulder.

"Let the child in!" Irving called.

With an infinitesimal bow, McKenna stepped away from the door.

She walked into Irving's bedroom—and stopped short. This cavernous room was more than a mere bedroom. It was a study, a library, a repository of relics. Jacqueline gaped as she looked at the bookshelves, crammed with leather-bound texts and parchment scrolls, with empty-eyed skulls and skilled glasswork and jewelry. African war masks hung on the walls between pieces of exquisitely rendered Italian Renaissance art. An illuminated world globe rested on a tall maple stand.

When she could catch her breath, she said, "This is spectacular. Where did you get all this stuff?"

"Here and there." Irving sat in a large easy chair set in the sunlight streaming through the window, his legs up on an ottoman and covered with a throw. "McKenna brought up my most treasured possessions from the library. Sadly, I spend more time here than I used to, and I like to be surrounded by my things." A long library table was beside him, stacked with books and artifacts. He shoved them aside, clearing a space. "This is pleasant of you to bring me my tray."

Pleasant? He'd specifically asked for her. But perhaps the old man had had a brain glitch. He seemed sharp enough, but he *was* ninety-three.

Or maybe he knew she'd once worked room service at a Marriot in Phoenix.

She put the tray down and uncovered the dishes, indicating each one as she named the contents. "An antipasto plate, field green salad with Italian dressing on the side, pasta primavera, garlic bread, and for dessert, tiramisu. Martha made it all."

Irving tossed the throw aside and turned toward his lunch. "Well, Martha is a very good cook."

McKenna *harrumph*ed in discontent.

"McKenna, you're a miracle worker, conjuring dinner for all of us last night out of thin air," Jacqueline said.

"Thank you, Miss Jacqueline." Amazing how McKenna managed to infuse those four words with such rejection.

"That will be all, McKenna." Irving flicked his fingers at McKenna. "Shut the door behind you."

Jacqueline watched McKenna bow again and march out, his spine as stiff and straight as an exclamation point. "He didn't like me bringing up your lunch."

"He's a fussbudget who thinks he is the only one who can care for me." Irving winked with good humor, picked up his fork and spoon, and dug into the pasta with the appetite of a young man.

"Easy for you to say. He won't punish you with undercooked chicken." She had enough people mad at her. Caleb. Her mother. The other six seerless Chosen. Adding McKenna was the icing on the cake.

"Did Caleb go off with our new Chosen?" Irving asked.

"He's got the men in tow, picking up toothbrushes, clothes, and other essentials. He figures with four guys, if they're attacked, they've got a fighting chance."

"*Will* they be attacked?"

"How would I know?" she asked in irritation. Books lay open on the table, and she pulled them toward her. They were old—medieval, perhaps—written in languages she didn't recognize, much less speak. One had an inkblot in the middle of the page, as if the monk had suddenly died in the middle of scribing a word. She looked beyond the books at the artifacts. They were an unsettling collection of history: a glass jar full of yellowed teeth, a Mesopotamian fertility goddess, a lava lamp.

Worst of all, Irving just happened to have a crystal ball, a beautifully rounded glass ball sitting on a primitive carved wood base.

Was it mere accident that it was out?

She doubted that.

"Sit down." He waved his silverware at the chair opposite.

She eased herself down, hoping he wasn't going to demand she produce a vision like some conjurer producing a coin out of thin air.

Instead he said, "Before all this started, I was going through my wine cellar and I found a few bottles that need to be investigated. I know you're the wine expert—I thought perhaps you could help me out."

Pleased, because she was off the hook, and because Irving was noted for his fine wines, Jacqueline said, "I'm not an oenophile, by any means, but I have tasted a few wines in my time."

"I'm holding the Sunset Vineyards cabernet sauvignon you sent me." He leaned forward. "That was very kind of you to remember me during such a difficult time in your life."

"I think I can safely say that that difficult time is only beginning," she said gloomily.

"Let's worry about that later." He brushed her concern aside. Leaning down beside his chair, he picked up a bottle, and placed it on the table. "This is an '06 Seghesio San Lorenzo zinfandel."

"I know Seghesio! An excellent winery." She inspected their pale cream-colored label with the distinctive swooping font. "They're known for their big zins."

"Here's my '97 Sanford pinot noir." He placed another bottle on the table.

"Before my time, but I've heard of it."

"And a 1989 Chateau de Beaucastel Hommage a Jacques Perrin." He produced the dusty bottle with a flourish.

She wrinkled her brow as she thought. "Isn't that the Chateauneuf-du-Pape red blend? The one with the ninety-eight rating?"

"Very good!" He approved her knowledge.

"But this is rare." She picked up the bottle, wiped it clean, and examined it. "And expensive. It sells for over two thousand dollars a bottle."

"I bought a case long before the price reached such an exorbitant level."

"Oh. Good." Somehow, she suspected his idea of exorbitant and hers differed wildly.

He placed a cork remover on the table by the lineup of bottles. "The thermostat on my cellar has been malfunctioning. I need to find out if my wines are still drinkable, or if I should throw a party and invite a lot of neophytes. Who better to assist me than you?"

Relieved to hear that was all he wanted, she laughed, stood, and started opening the bottles. "By all means, let me help you with this project."

"Glasses are over there." He waved his fork in the direction of the china cabinet.

She got a collection of fine crystal and filled each with a taster's sip. "We'll try the pinot first, then the Chateauneuf-du-Pape, then the zin."

Irving took the first glass she handed him and held it to the light. He swirled the wine to aerate it and put his nose to the glass.

Jacqueline watched him with affection. "I remember when you taught me how to taste wine."

"You had just graduated from high school and your mother scolded me for corrupting a minor."

"Tasting that Chardonnay was the wildest thing I did for graduation." She had always been the odd man out. "Everyone else in my class was running wild, going for a senior all-nighter on the beach, and Mother was personally making sure I remained sober and virginal."

"You can't blame her for wanting that."

"Of course I can," Jacqueline said lightly. Picking up her glass, she looked, swirled, and sniffed the wine. "This has a beautiful strawberry color. The nose is cherry, but more floral than fruit."

The two smiled at each other, clicked the glasses, and sipped together.

"Ahhh." Irving half closed his eyes in appreciation. "Burgundy-esque with cherry notes."

"And what a finish! If this is representative of your wines, I can't see that there's anything wrong with your storage."

"A little past its prime, though." He poured his glass full, held out the bottle for her.

She let him fill her glass. "It *is* a '97 pinot. It would have been at its peak two or three years ago."

He applied his fork to his salad. "Help yourself to the antipasto plate."

While she sampled the prosciutto, the cantaloupe, the black peppercorn cheese, the roasted vegetables, he polished off the pasta, the salad, and half the bread. Both agreed the pinot went down easily. The Chateauneuf-du-Pape was wonderful, but Jacqueline said it was too expensive, and they had a spirited discussion about value versus cost. The zinfandel . . .

She frowned. "The zinfandel smells a little smoky, and not in a good way."

He sniffed the wine. "I don't get that at all."

She lifted her nose out of her glass and sniffed the air. "It's in the room. It smells like something electrical shorting out. I hope there's no problem with your wiring." A fire was the last thing they needed.

"I can't smell smoke. And it's certainly not the wine." He tasted it. "This is excellent, deserving of all its praises."

Jacqueline sniffed again. Irving was right. The smoky scent had vanished.

Jacqueline took a cracker to clear her palate, tried the zin, and agreed with Irving's assessment. In her opinion, this was the best of the three. And by the time she had finished three glasses of wine, half of Irving's tiramisu and the ruby port he insisted she try, she was mellow enough to say, "Irving. There's nothing wrong with your wine or your wine storage. So why did you ask me up here?"

"I never can fool you, can I?" He leaned back in his chair, his eyes suddenly sharp.

With a shock, she realized the wine that had mellowed her had not affected him in the least.

He went right after his goal. "It's time to release your fears and become the seer you were meant to be."

She slapped her palm to the table. "I knew it! I knew we were having this pleasant little stroll down memory lane for a reason!"

"Do you get a shock when you hit your hand like that? Can you feel that tattoo speaking to you?"

He watched her, his dark eyes alive with a probing curiosity.

"No. I can't feel it speaking to me." Standing, she stalked over to the curio cabinet and stared blindly at the contents. Then she realized what she was looking at, and asked, "What are you doing with a collection of shrunken heads?"

"I was given them on my trip to New Guinea."

She looked around the bedroom again. He owned texts and treasures that belonged in museums—and why? "When I came in, I asked where you got all this stuff. You never answered me."

"Some are mine, collected while on my travels. Some my Chosen Ones brought me as souvenirs. Some I was lucky enough to borrow from the Gypsy Travel Agency and thus save from the blast."

"Because . . . ?" She trolled the shelves, finding more and more precious manuscripts, relics, and oddities.

"I've been doing research on speechless communication. It's a marvel that occurs so rarely among the gifted that some say it doesn't exist."

She stopped and stared at a display of uncut crystals. Gems? "Does this have to do with the lady whose nose had been split down the middle?"

"I don't know. Does it?"

She swung around in a fury. "That is really irritating. If I knew the answer, I wouldn't ask it."

"I don't have answers, either, and I need them." Irving was suddenly intense, the formidable leader who had guided the Gypsy Travel Agency through disaster to stability. "I need to know what happened yesterday, and how. Until this team chooses a leader, I can direct you, but I need a focus, and you are the only one who can provide it. Find the place where you should be and *see*."

"Sure. It's easy. *Go to the attic, Jacqueline. Don't worry about what's up there.*"

"The attic?" It was almost funny to see Irving go on alert, like an English pointer at a bird.

"When I was little, I was afraid of your attic. I thought there was something up there that would get me." He still had that wide-eyed, I'm-on-the-scent expression, and she sighed. "Really, Irving. It was a kid thing."

"All seers have a place where they can best call their visions in. Where they can control them. Where all is clear. Zusane needed to be near the earth. She told me when she had her first vision, she was locked in the cellar."

"Locked in the cellar? Who would have locked her in the cellar?" Jacqueline caught a whiff of smoke again. She looked around, but saw nothing. "Are your smoke alarms working?"

"McKenna replaced the batteries last month. Stop trying to change the subject." Irving pointed one finger at the ceiling. "Perhaps you need to be close to the sky. To go *up*. *Up* to my attic." Then in a totally prosaic tone of voice, he said, "If it doesn't work, what are you out?"

"Nothing. I guess." But that attic still creeped her out, and the smell of smoke was getting stronger. "Why don't you bug Tyler? He's a psychic, too."

"I intend to. But you . . . you are destined to be the greatest psychic we've ever had."

"What if I just want to be an oenophile?"

"You can be that, too. You can be whatever you want. Those roles are like clothes you don and discard. But a seer is who you are in your soul." Using both his large hands to pluck the crystal ball off its stand, he held it up for inspection. The globe glowed in the sunlight, colors moving, melding, sliding over its smooth surface and vanishing into thin air.

Jacqueline couldn't take her gaze off it.

"I am not one of the Chosen Ones. But my mother's great-great-grandmother was an African slave imported into the Bahamas to work the cane, and she knew her voodoo. My father's grandmother was Romany. She made her living with this"—Irving lifted the ball high—"traveling from town to town, enticing the women into her tent to tell their fortunes. The globe is nothing special, something she tossed into a trunk when she was traveling, and most of what she said was hokum, of course. But sometimes, I don't know why or how, she did see the future. Maybe she saw it in this globe. Maybe she simply had a gift. Take it. See what you can do with it. Consider it a present."

"With strings attached." Going to him, she knelt at his feet and looked up into his dark eyes. "Why should I do this thing?"

Taking her wrists, he stripped off her gloves. He placed the globe between her palms, and put his hands over hers. "Jacqueline, if you don't help us, we are destined to fall, and all the children like you, the children who are abandoned and without hope, will go straight to the devil. Please. We need you. Will you help us?" He looked so fragile, so ancient, so appealing. . . .

The old charlatan.

Then, from the depths of his soul, a painful cry of anguish. "Most of those people who died yesterday were young enough to be my children or my grandchildren or my great-grandchildren." He faltered. Tears welled in his eyes, and he fumbled for his handkerchief. "I should have died first. *I should have died first.*" Putting his hand to his face, he sobbed out loud.

It was a horrible, gut-wrenching sound, torn from a man deceptively strong, a man who never broke down, a man now tortured and in pain.

Jumping to her feet, Jacqueline placed the globe on its stand. Sitting on the arm of his chair, she put her arm around his shoulders, trying to impart comfort where none could be found. "I never realized that you thought that way," she whispered.

He blew his nose. He lifted his head. His eyes were bloodshot, tears still wet the creases in his cheeks, and he looked suddenly as old as his age. "You're young, but . . . can you understand? I have been preparing myself to pass into the next world, hoping that I've lived a good, productive life, that I did my best, that I was leaving a legacy. Instead, I've lost everything I've built for the last sixty years."

"The Gypsy Travel Agency."

"No. Not the institution. That never mattered. I built that so the people, the Chosen Ones, those talented, gifted few, could fulfill their destinies and do good. I took a personal interest in each one of them. I was so proud of them." He thumped his chest, his voice grew gruff, and again he fought for composure. "Now they're gone. Jesse and Monica and Olivia. Jack, Kevin and Natalie. Fred, Mildred, Erin, Carol, Owen. So many gone; their names are written on my heart. They were my children, and no father should ever have to see his children die."

Damn him. He meant it. She knew he did. He had always lived and breathed the Gypsy Travel Agency and its secret mission. He knew every employee, every travel guide, every one of the Chosen Ones. He sent e-mails for each birthday, he praised each achievement and he congratulated each one on each marriage and offspring. And now, with their deaths, the old man's hopes and dreams were shattered.

"All right." Jacqueline, heir to the same gift and sign as the world's first seer, picked up the crystal ball. "I'll do it." She walked to the door, opened it, hesitated, and turned back.

Irving watched her with such hope on his face and tears in his eyes.

She said, "But damned if I ever come up to share wine with you again, Irving Shea."

Chapter 21

———❦———

Crystal ball in hand, Jacqueline stepped into the attic. She'd played here when she was a kid. Large, bright, and empty, it hadn't changed.

The walls and floor were painted white. Dust motes floated along on the sun rays pouring through the big windows on the west side and covered everything in a fine layer. A door on the far wall led to another room like this one, and a storage closet filled the corner.

She'd run through this room, pulling a toy dog on a leash. She'd played with her dolls, and read her books.

Then one day, when she was eight, she'd stopped coming. She didn't remember why. She only remembered being afraid.

Now she wasn't afraid. She was a little tipsy. She was a lot disgruntled. The smell of smoke tainted the air, and that stupid crystal ball was not only heavy; it was so slick, she tucked it under one arm to keep from dropping it.

Wandering through the big room to the cupboard, she opened it. Old coats hung on hangers, and old drapes were folded on the shelves. She went to the door and tried the knob, and looked inside. The room beyond matched this one—the same windows, the same sunlight, the same cupboard—but the shadows seemed deeper. She couldn't see a source of the smoke, though, so she shut the door and meandered into a square of sunshine on the floor.

She held the crystal ball in the light and watched the colors, blue, gold, green, slide across the shiny surface.

Zusane effortlessly slipped in and out of her visions, but mostly Jacqueline felt silly trying. How did a person bring on a vision? Chant? Do yoga breathing? Perform a rain dance?

The wine had relaxed her. That would probably help. . . .

This wasn't going to work, and worse, the smell of smoke was getting stronger. She should go back downstairs and tell McKenna that they had a wiring problem or something up here. It could cause a real problem if a fire started, and they didn't need any more problems. The explosion was enough. . . .

Man, this was boring.

The smoke made Jacqueline's eyes feel funny, and she was briefly alarmed.

Then the colors disappeared from the surface of the crystal ball. Deep in its center, a flame glowed red, followed by a blast of yellow. The globe slid out of her hand. In slow motion, it twirled in the air and landed on the floor with such a heavy thud shards of wood blew into the air—and froze in motion.

The world became sepia-toned, and she realized . . .

This was it. A vision. Irving was right. She might not want to, but she had the ability. *This was a vision.*

Then someone screamed in her ear, high and panicked and pure terror. The shriek jerked Jacqueline back to the real world, but when she looked . . . she wasn't in the attic.

She stood in the aisle of an airplane, a private jet with a dozen luxurious seats set around tables and a flickering fifty-inch television dominating one wall. A young woman stood in front of it in a black silk YSL gown, arms at her side, fists clenched. She was the one screaming. And screaming. And screaming.

Jacqueline recognized this plane. She'd been on it before, with Caleb on the way from California to New York City.

Everything was different now. Thick, black smoke filled the cabin. The oxygen masks hung from the ceiling. An alarm shrieked in the cockpit. A dozen people shouted and stumbled from wall to wall while the plane pitched back and forth like a bronco ride in a cowboy bar.

The aircraft twisted, throwing Jacqueline off balance. She slammed against the table, scattering playing cards and breaking a bottle. For one second, the sharp licorice smell of ouzo washed the air clean.

Her hand hurt. She looked down. A shard of glass stuck out of her bare palm, cutting her tattoo in half. She pulled the glass out. It was sharp and wide and thick, and blood welled up, bright and crimson.

She'd been flung headfirst into a disaster.

But it was only a vision. Only a vision.

The electricity flickered and went off. It was dark outside. And Jacqueline saw sparks blowing off the left wing.

Low-level emergency lights flashed on in the cabin.

As if the smoke had found her again, it rose off the floor and like a boa constrictor coiled around her, blinding her, filling her lungs. She coughed, tried to get a breath, coughed again.

A vision. This was only a vision.

The jet pitched. She slammed into the far wall, banging her hip against one of the seats.

But this didn't *feel* like a vision. She *was* choking on the smoke. The blood *was* sticky in her hand. Her hip *was* bruised and throbbing. She wanted to close her eyes, plug her ears, get out of this vision, but she didn't dare. She was here. On this plane. And it was disaster.

Another alarm went off. Some guy in a uniform shouted, directing the passengers, handing out life jackets.

No, not life jackets. Parachutes.

My God. The steward—or was he the pilot?—was going to open the door. She wanted to look out the window, see if there were lights, if they were over land or headed into the sea.

Then across the cabin, something moved and caught her eye—a woman, speaking calmly to the man in the uniform. But . . . that dress, sparkling with gold sequins. That form, so opulent and curvy. That elegant coiffure of glorious blond hair, held up with a diamond clip . . .

"Mother!" Jacqueline screamed.

Zusane looked up.

Their eyes met.

And Zusane *saw* her.

Jacqueline was truly here.

The lurch and roll of the aircraft grew in intensity.

Zusane fought her way toward Jacqueline.

Jacqueline fought her way toward Zusane.

"I never saw this," Zusane shouted. "You shouldn't be here!"

"Mother, you have to take a parachute. You have to save yourself!"

"It's too late for that."

Jacqueline made a grab for her.

Zusane evaded her. "Don't touch me!"

Hurt, Jacqueline dropped her hands, and looked at them. The one still bled freely, blurring her tattoo.

Was Zusane worried about blood on her gown?

Or was she worried that Jacqueline had ruined her gift with the slice through her palm?

"Darling, don't be that way," Zusane said. "I don't know why or how, but you *should not* be here. Don't make it more real than it already is."

Jacqueline didn't understand what she meant. She didn't know what *any* of this meant.

The uniformed man got the door open. Cold blasted into the plane, clearing the air . . . except where Zusane stood. There the smoke coiled, dense, dark and oily. Zusane waved her hand. Her gesture seemed to call the smoke. It wrapped her, wrapped Jacqueline, tightening its coils.

Frightened, Jacqueline shouted, "What is it?"

Zusane looked over Jacqueline's shoulder, through the dense smoke. She saw something, something that made her eyes widen and her head jerk back as if she'd been slapped. Lifting her arms as if to ward off a blow, she clearly said, "Oh, Zusane. You fool."

Bewildered, Jacqueline turned and followed her mother's gaze.

A man stood there, bald, middle-aged, of slight build and dressed in a black, tailored suit. He looked like just another of her mother's wealthy boyfriends . . . until he looked straight at her.

A blue flame lit his eyes . . . from the inside.

In panic, Jacqueline gasped, choked on the smoke, and coughed, and coughed.

She knew who he was. She had always heard tales about him, always been warned about him . . . but no one ever really saw him. She had thought, hoped he was a myth.

Now she knew better.

One by one, the passengers donned their parachutes, rushed to the door, and leaped into space. The girl in the YSL gown jumped without fastening her parachute. It flew back into the cabin, and they heard her scream as she plummeted toward the ground.

Dear God, this was hell.

"Not yet." Although she hadn't spoken aloud, the man answered her.

"Mother, come on!" Clutching her aching chest, Jacqueline headed toward the uniformed steward.

Zusane followed close on her heels.

A freezing wind blasted through the opening.

The smoke hung close to them both.

Grabbing a parachute, Jacqueline shoved it at her mother. "Take it," she shouted. "Take it!"

"There's no point in jumping." Through the alarms, the shrieks, the blasting wind, Jacqueline clearly heard the man with the flaming eyes. His voice was quiet, calm, informational—and pervasive, invading every molecule of air, speaking in her head and in her ears.

"The ground's too close. The parachutes won't open. You're both going to die."

Fear gripped Jacqueline by the throat.

He was right. Of course he was right. He had engineered this whole scenario to destroy them both.

Her mother knew it, too. Knew it, and blamed herself. Yet she smiled. She was calm. "Darling Jacqueline," she said, "there's only one thing to do. Come on. Let's step close to the door."

As they did, the man in the uniform strapped on a parachute, and jumped. And screeched.

Only three people were left on the plane.

Zusane. Jacqueline. And the man with the flaming blue eyes.

With a panicked glance over her shoulder, Jacqueline saw him moving toward them. He walked with an ease that belied the rocking plane—because he was making it rock.

"Always remember, I love you." Zusane almost touched Jacqueline, almost cupped her cheek.

Jacqueline wanted to scream in fear. But the smoke still clung to her, filling her lungs, making her voice nothing but a scratch. "Mother! Hurry!"

"Yes." Zusane jerked the parachute out of Jacqueline's hand, throwing her off balance. Placing her hand flat on Jacqueline's chest, she shoved her backward out of the plane and into nothingness.

Chapter 22

———————◆◆◆———————

"Jacqueline." Caleb held her in his arms and spoke sternly. "Jacqueline, stop shrieking."

At the sound of his voice, Jacqueline froze. Her eyes were still closed tightly. Her fists were still clenched, her knees drawn up.

But the wind no longer blasted her face. A battered airplane no longer plummeted through the air beside her. The screams of the falling passengers no longer assaulted her ears. The lights on the ground no longer hurtled toward her.

The lights—close. Too close. They were all going to die.

The memory was so clear, she jumped and, in an agony of fear, opened her eyes wide.

Caleb's face was the first thing she saw, so close she could feel his breath, his worry.

Beyond that . . . she was in the attic. *In the attic.* Earlier this afternoon, she had stood in this same spot. Now the square of sun had moved on, and she shivered with cold and shock.

So the airplane, the crash, her mother . . . none of that was real.

But it was.

"Jacqueline," Caleb said. "Speak to me."

Lifting her hand, Jacqueline looked at the gash in her palm. The blood had obliterated the mark of her gift.

If the eye had been blinded, was she no longer a seer?

"The crystal ball broke one of the floorboards," he told her. "You cut your hand on the wood."

She looked where he pointed. The globe was burrowed into the floor, and shards of hardwood were scattered like . . . like a broken bottle. . . .

In her brain, she heard words chanting over and over. *If he looks into it, he will die. If he looks into it, he will die.*

She tried to speak.

She couldn't.

The smoke.

She put her hand to her throat.

"You've been screaming. And screaming." Caleb looked pale, strained. Angry.

"My head." Her voice. A hoarse whisper.

"You bumped it when you fell."

"I didn't fall. Mother pushed me."

The silence in the attic was deep and dark and concerned.

"What do you mean, she pushed you?" Caleb asked, his voice carefully neutral.

"She pushed me out of the plane. She pushed me out of the plane. *She pushed me out of the plane!* How much more clear do I have to make it?" Jacqueline was sitting up, her lungs ripping with strain as she yelled at Caleb—and she faced another nine pairs of horrified eyes.

Irving. And Martha, McKenna, Isabelle, Charisma, Tyler, Aaron, Samuel, and Aleksandr. They looked shell-shocked, embarrassed, curious, frightened. . . .

In a clear, calm voice, Isabelle asked, "What plane?"

"She was in his airplane. We were. The jet. Caleb, you remember, we used it to get from California to New York City. His . . . It was him. . . . He did it. . . ." Jacqueline started out loudly, insistently, wanting them to see, to believe. But her head hurt so badly. Inside her brain, voices babbled and screamed, memories flashed and flamed, and over and over, the oddest phrase repeated in her head.

If he looks into it, he will die. If he looks into it, he will die.

Wildly, she whipped her head around, wanting to cover the crystal ball, to make sure no one looked into it and died. But she couldn't hold herself up anymore, and collapsed.

Caleb caught her.

Her head throbbed and throbbed. Lifting her hand, she touched her aching forehead, and again she heard the words.

If he looks into it, he will die. If he looks into it, he will die.

Her hand felt funny, numb and burning at the same time. She looked at it, tried to move her fingers. Nothing worked right—had the nerves been severed? More blood oozed from the two-inch wound.

She tried to explain again. "Mother's boyfriend . . . his plane was in flames. Mother saw him. I saw him." The constriction in her chest got worse and worse. She could barely breathe. She coughed. She clawed at the neck of her T-shirt. Her lungs felt scraped and raw.

"All right." Caleb wrapped his arms around her. "We need to take you to the hospital."

"No!" Irving spread his arms and pushed the men back. "Let Isabelle help her."

Jacqueline stared, trying to understand what Irving could mean.

"How is she going to help her?" Caleb demanded. "Is she a doctor?"

Isabelle stood quietly. She wore a pair of jeans, scrounged from a secondhand shop, a large blue

T-shirt that looked sloppy on her slender form, and a pair of cheap flip-flops. Yet still, she looked every inch the lady, and not happy about being in the spotlight.

"She's a physical empath," Irving said. "That is her gift."

"What does that mean?" Tyler asked.

"She can absorb Jacqueline's pain and injuries. She can share them, and heal her." Irving turned to Isabelle. "If she will."

Samuel crossed his arms, the epitome of knowledge and skepticism.

Lifting her chin, Isabelle knelt beside Jacqueline. In that precise Boston accent, she said, "If you will let me, I can be of assistance to you."

Caleb held Jacqueline against his chest, his face still and cold. "I want to take her to the hospital."

"We *can't*." Irving sounded impatient and dictatorial. "She just had her first vision, and it was powerful enough to do *this* to her. We can't drive her to a hospital and try to explain how all this occurred, and take the chance she'll tell them her mother pushed her out of a plane. At the very least, they'll take her in for a psychiatric evaluation. Probably they'll decide you're abusing her and demand she press changes. She's a new seer. She can't control what's happening to her, and while she's there, she might have another vision. *And* we cannot have her visit a hospital without attracting the attention of the Others. I assure you, Caleb, there is no one they want to eliminate more than our psychic."

Isabelle paid no attention to Irving's rant, or to Caleb's resistance. Her focus was on Jacqueline. In her soft voice, she said, "I have to touch you. I won't hurt you. Can you trust me?"

Jacqueline stared into her eyes.

Isabelle was completely calm, and completely secure with her gift.

Jacqueline needed help; blood oozed from the cut on her hand, her brain hurt, and the tightness in her chest continued to grow, robbing her of oxygen. She hadn't died in her free fall from the plane, but she feared she would die here and now. She nodded, and whispered, "Please."

Caleb tensed.

Isabelle placed her fingers on Jacqueline's forehead right over her eyes, then on her chest over her heart.

The pain did not diminish. But Jacqueline's mind began to grasp the reality of this place and this time. Her heart rate slowed as the fight-or-flight instinct moderated. She was safe here. She was secure in Caleb's arms. And whatever had happened on the jet needed to be dealt with, but not yet. Not until she felt better—or at least as if she would live.

Isabelle pulled away now, and ran her palms over Jacqueline from head to toe . . . yet she never touched her. Her cupped hands hovered mere inches from

Jacqueline's skin, pausing here and there, assessing and deciding. When she was done, she came back to Jacqueline's face and said, "We'll start now." Sliding her hands around Jacqueline's head, she cupped it, and sighed and swayed as her fingers found the lump on Jacqueline's head . . . and as Jacqueline's headache eased, Isabelle's eyes filled with tears.

She drew her hands away and sat quietly, her face contorted as she fought her way through the pain.

Jacqueline realized that somehow, Isabelle shared her injury to heal it.

"I'm better," Jacqueline said—and coughed. And coughed.

Quickly, Isabelle passed her hands over Jacqueline's chest. For a long moment, the pain tightened its grip, and Jacqueline couldn't breathe.

Then in unison, they coughed, took a desperate breath, and went into a frenzy of coughing.

Jacqueline rolled into a tight ball of agony. That smoke . . . it shredded the tissues in her lungs. It clung in her airways with hooks and claws. Isabelle couldn't help her with this. This smoke . . . even together, they couldn't fight it.

Caleb gripped her shoulders.

Dimly she could hear him shouting at Irving. "Why did you send Jacqueline up here?"

"Because we need guidance or a prophecy or *something*," Irving shouted back.

A few feet away, Jacqueline saw Samuel crouched beside Isabelle as she spasmed and coughed.

They were going to die. They were going to die.

And just when it seemed they would . . . the coughing stopped.

The pain eased.

They could *breathe*.

Jacqueline collapsed in limp relief.

Isabelle rested on the floor beside her, holding her throat and wheezing.

They lay, exhausted, sweaty with exertion.

Jacqueline reached over and touched Isabelle's hand.

Isabelle turned her head to face her.

"Thank you," Jacqueline whispered.

"That smoke . . ." Isabelle began. Then, with a quick glance around at the watching eyes, she changed her mind and replied only, "You're welcome."

Caleb touched Jacqueline's cheek, looked into her eyes. "You're really better?"

Jacqueline nodded.

He looked up at Isabelle. "What about her hand?"

Samuel still knelt beside Isabelle, and he looked up sharply. "Give it a rest, asshole. She almost died helping your girlfriend."

Isabelle didn't stir, didn't glance, didn't acknowledge Samuel's defense in any way.

Scowling, he stood and strode out, leaving a small, strained silence behind.

Sitting up, Isabelle pushed the hair out of her face. Her voice was hoarse, but still cultured and cool as she said, "Believe it or not, Jacqueline's hand was the least of her problems."

Jacqueline sneaked a glance at her palm, brown with dried blood, wet with new blood. It was *not* the least of her worries. But how could she explain what that man with the flaming eyes had tried to do to her?

Carefully, she cupped her injured hand in the good one.

Pulling his handkerchief out of his pocket, Caleb wrapped it around her hand, masking the damage.

Martha stepped forward. "In my day, I've had plenty of experience stitching up wounds. Never lost a patient, never had one not heal clean."

"Let's get her to our bedroom, and you can take care of that." Caleb helped Jacqueline to her feet.

Aleksandr helped Isabelle.

"Wait." Irving stopped them with a raised, trembling hand. "First, I must know—Jacqueline, what was your vision?"

Jacqueline shook as she realized . . . she *had* seen it; she *had* been there. . . . In a slow, halting voice, she told Irving, told them all, about Zusane aboard the failing aircraft, how Zusane had seen her and been horrified, how Jacqueline had tried to save her and instead been pushed out of the plane by her mother's own hand.

She told them everything . . . except seeing the man with the flaming blue eyes.

Some caution, some lack of trust for these people she barely knew, held her back.

"So . . . your mother saved your life," Tyler said.

Jacqueline turned her head and looked at the quiet, handsome man.

"She *did*." Tyler sounded very certain of his facts. "If you'd gone down with the plane, or strapped on the parachute, you would have been tied to that place and time, and you wouldn't have escaped. When she pushed you out, she pushed you back here to the attic, where you were having your vision."

"How do you know that?" Charisma asked.

He shrugged. "I don't know *how*. I just do. I am a psychic, too, you know."

"Sure. My mother's great," Jacqueline said. "Pushing her daughter out of a plane should clinch that Mother of the Year award."

The awkward silence fell again, an almost familiar presence in the attic.

"Enough discussion. Jacqueline needs to go to bed," Caleb announced firmly, and led her toward the door.

Everyone followed, a solemn procession down the stairs and into her bedroom.

Irving indicated that Isabelle should take the chair.

Caleb helped Jacqueline onto the bed. "Okay?" he asked in a low voice.

"I'm fine. See what you can find out about Mother." Not because she was in any doubt, but because he had been Zusane's bodyguard for years. He'd once walked away from Jacqueline on Zusane's command; he was loyal to Zusane, and she could sense the unease behind his calm facade.

With a nod, he left.

Martha left, too, and returned with a medical bag. Unwrapping the cloth, she examined Jacqueline's hand, and even her voice sounded pinched and disapproving when she said, "If I might make a suggestion, Mr. Shea? In the future, when you send Miss Vargha off to access a vision, perhaps it would be wise for her to draw a circle on the floor around her. A circle drawn by one of the Chosen Ones promises at least a little protection, I believe."

Picking up the remote, Irving turned the television on and flipped through the news channels. He wasn't paying attention when he said, "Yes. Good idea. Make sure you do that, Jacqueline."

Martha sighed audibly.

McKenna left the room and returned with bottled water and a plate of nuts and cheeses. Opening a bottle, he handed it to Jacqueline. "Here, miss, you'll need this after your ordeal."

He didn't look or sound any different than he ever did, but Jacqueline was pleased. She'd helped Irving, and with that, she'd won her way back into McKenna's good graces. Thank heavens; she wouldn't have to worry about undercooked chicken now.

Aleksandr fell on the food as if he hadn't eaten for months. The others took the water with thanks.

Martha's bag proved surprisingly well-stocked. As she worked on Jacqueline's hand, she saw Jacqueline peering anxiously at her work, and said, "I can't do what Isabelle can do, but when the Gypsy Travel Agency recruited me, I was a nurse."

"I thought you were a—" Jacqueline stopped when Martha shot her a dark glance.

"A maid? A cook? A housekeeper? I've been all that, too." Her sutures were small and neat. "I've been everything they've ever asked me to be."

"For which we are thankful." Irving never took his gaze off the television.

Neither did Aleksandr or Aaron. The small room was crowded with everyone in the house—except Caleb and Samuel. They watched the TV or nibbled at the appetizers. No one seemed to want to leave. They wanted confirmation of Jacqueline's vision.

And when they got it—what would they do? Be awestruck? Thank her?

Treat her like a freak?

With a shock, she realized—no, they wouldn't. Because among the Chosen Ones, she was not a freak— she was gifted.

Leaning close to Martha, she whispered, "Can you sew my tattoo back together the way it was?"

Martha looked up into Jacqueline's face, and what she saw must have satisfied her, because for the first time in Jacqueline's memory, she smiled. Smiled and said, "I will do my best."

"That's all I ask." Leaning back, Jacqueline relaxed, at home for the first time in her life.

Chapter 23

Martha was packing her medical bag when Caleb returned. He looked stern, older, as he said, "I can't get Zusane on her cell, which doesn't surprise me, but I can't get any of my men, either, and that is unusual."

"Damn." Irving flipped off the television in disgust. "There's nothing here. Aleksandr!"

Aleksandr jumped and dropped a slice of cheese on the carpet. "What, sir?"

"You're good with the Internet."

"I am?" He scooped up the cheese and popped it in his mouth.

"You're a college student. Of course you are."

"If you're looking for porn," Aaron said out of the corner of his mouth.

Aleksandr's fist shot out and smacked Aaron's arm hard.

Tyler gave a crack of laughter, hastily muffled, then said, "I'm a fair hand at searching the Internet myself."

"Good. Come on, let's get on my computer and you can find me the news story about—" Irving stopped, and shot Jacqueline an anxious glance.

Jacqueline met his gaze. She wasn't going to get hysterical, if that was what he worried about. But the confirmation he sought was a certainty in her mind.

Her mother was dead, one more casualty in the battle between good and evil.

Jacqueline wanted to ask who was winning.

He must have read the truth in her face, for he looked suddenly old and weary. "Come on, gentlemen. Let's go and leave the ladies alone." Irving tucked his hand into McKenna's arm and used him as support as they walked from the room.

Aaron grabbed Aleksandr's collar and shoved him out the door. "Go on, kid. Show us what you can do with a Google search."

Tyler followed, a little apart, a tall, graceful Tolkien elf among brash, brawling humans.

With the five men gone, the bedroom felt roomier, but colder, too.

"You're going to be uncomfortable with this hand," Martha told Jacqueline, and handed her a small, plain bottle of pills. "Take two of these every four hours. I'll be back with something to eat." With an efficient nod, she bustled out the door.

Her exit left Isabelle and Charisma, Jacqueline and Caleb, and an unnatural hush in the room.

Caleb sat on the bed beside Jacqueline. He picked up her bandaged hand and looked at it. "Did she fix it?"

"She did her best." Jacqueline repeated Martha's assurance, taking comfort from the implied promise.

"Good." Caleb glanced up swiftly, capturing her gaze with his. "Why did you finally go up to the attic?"

"Irving thought I could access my visions there."

Caleb half stood, looking as if he wanted to kill someone.

Hastily, she added, "And he was so sad."

"He pulled on your heartstrings, huh?" Caleb couldn't have looked more cynical.

"Don't be like that, Caleb. I thought he was faking it, too, but he's really broken up. He lost his friends and his comrades. Think about it." She tugged at his hand. "This disaster has hurt him . . . so much."

"All right." Caleb put his hand on her head. Speaking to Charisma and Isabelle, he said, "You'll stay with her, keep her company, until we find out exactly what happened?"

"Of course, Mr. D'Angelo. We're glad to do that." Isabelle stood and spoke calmly, but he noted that she looked drawn and tired, and like Jacqueline, she cradled one hand in the other.

Had she somehow acquired a gash on her hand, too?

Charisma was less of a lady, and more of a bully. "You go check stuff out, Caleb. I'll keep an eye on them both."

On the first floor, Aaron observed as Irving wandered between the television room where the news stations blared and the study where Aleksandr and Tyler argued over which keywords to use in their search.

When he had made the circuit twice with increasing impatience, Aaron went to him and offered, "Let me help you, sir."

Irving looked at him sharply, glanced at the two guys, then took Aaron's proffered arm. "Thank you, my boy. It's been a long day for this old man." He walked with a fair imitation of feebleness down the corridor and into the TV room. Once there he straightened, seated himself at his writing desk, and muted the television. "Close the door behind you."

Aaron did as he was told.

"What's on your mind?" Irving asked.

"Depending on a seer, or rather a pair of seers, for our next move seems a precarious proposition. There are other ways, probably just as accurate, to tell what is forthcoming."

"Prophecies." Irving's lips curled in scorn.

The old man was really opinionated. And irritating.

"In my business, I've seen a lot of them carefully preserved and guarded in manuscripts and scrolls."

"And you've stolen them."

"And I've stolen them," Aaron agreed. He was, after all, the foremost retriever of stolen fine art—which was exactly how he'd gotten his ass in such big trouble.

"In my time, I've seen lots of them, too. Hundreds, maybe thousands, in the library at the Gypsy Travel Agency and here." Irving waved a hand at his well-stocked bookshelves. "I've met self-proclaimed prophets, and even read that charlatan Nostradamus in the original. Real or fake, well-tended or treated like trash, it doesn't matter. Trying to figure out which prophecy applies to this day is like finding a needle in a haystack."

"You need a librarian."

"Our librarian went up with the building."

"I am sorry about that, but it's not so difficult." Aaron's lips quirked. "There is a librarian, a Dr. Hall, an expert in ancient languages and prophecies, who works in the Arthur W. Nelson Fine Arts Library antiquities department here in New York City. . . ."

Chapter 24

"**J**acqueline, we'd better wash your face." Charisma sounded prosaic as she headed into the bathroom.

"Yes." Isabelle collapsed in the chair. "You're all bloody."

Instinctively, Jacqueline lifted her hand to the still-tender bump on the back of her head.

Isabelle shook her head. "You rubbed your hand on your face. You look like a wounded soldier."

Charisma appeared in the doorway holding a wet washcloth. "In a way, that's what she is."

Jacqueline got off the bed, leaned over the dresser, and looked in the mirror. She was pale, with brown stains marking her cheek and her forehead, and her eyes were shocked, like a deer who'd escaped a forest fire. "I look like I'm wearing war paint. Couldn't someone have told me?"

"We had other things on our minds." Charisma handed her the washcloth.

Jacqueline scrubbed at the brown stains, then paused and cocked her head. She could hear water dripping. Slowly. Steadily. Constantly. "Charisma, did you leave the water on in the bathroom?"

"I don't think so." Charisma checked and came back. "No, it's off."

"Okay." Jacqueline went back to work on her face and wished the constant dripping sound in her head would just stop.

Just . . . stop.

"It's just me, I guess," she said. "A hangover from getting hit on the head."

"You *hit* your *head*. When you fell. Remember?" Charisma peered at her in concern.

"You're right, I guess." In the mirror, Jacqueline could see the women exchanging glances.

The guys had brought back jeans and T-shirts for all the women, so they all dressed in approximately the same outfit. They should have looked like triplets, but they were each so very different.

"How are you feeling . . . otherwise?" Isabelle asked delicately.

"My head feels fuzzy, like I just recovered from a concussion, and my lungs feel . . . odd . . . as if I've shared them with someone." Jacqueline met Isabelle's gaze in the mirror. "Which I guess I did, and I thank her most gratefully. But considering what I went through, I feel good."

"I think she meant—how do you feel about your mother?" Charisma raised her eyebrows at Isabelle.

Isabelle nodded.

"You mean—how do I feel about a mother who pushed me out of an airplane without a parachute when I was trying to save her life?" Jacqueline found herself squeezing the washcloth as hard as she could.

Charisma plucked the washcloth away. "If Tyler is to be believed, she saved your life."

"Oh, what the hell does he know?" Jacqueline snapped.

Charisma and Isabelle both looked surprised, and then laughed.

"It's true. What does he know?" Isabelle asked.

Charisma filled up the sink in the bathroom and put the washcloth in to soak. "For that matter, what do any of us know? We're all just stumbling around, doing nothing when we should be . . ."

Jacqueline and Isabelle looked inquiringly at her.

"Be doing something that . . . that helps the fate of the world," Charisma finished dismally.

"I feel so helpless, but I don't know what to do. This morning, when I called, my mother wanted to know why I didn't come home," Isabelle said.

"What did you tell her?" Jacqueline sat cross-legged on the bed and patted the mattress. "Sit down here."

"Yeah. You don't look so good." Charisma had apparently assumed the role of the tactless one in their little group. She was good at it.

"I told Mother that I'd agreed to be part of this organization and I couldn't abandon you because times got rough." Isabelle got up and moved to the other place at the head of the bed, rearranged the pillows behind her, and reclined with her feet out and her ankles neatly crossed. "That's the only way to talk to my mother. If I'd told her I couldn't leave because I'd be hunted by the Others, she would have freaked. Telling her I have an obligation put it in terms she understands. *Noblesse oblige* and all that."

"She really thinks that way?" Charisma flopped down on the foot of the bed on her side and propped her head on her hand.

"Oh, yes." Isabelle didn't know it, but her voice held a sigh. "My mother's family landed on Plymouth Rock, and ever since then, the men have been leaders and the women have remained invisible and invincible."

"You're tugging on my lariat." Charisma stared in wide-eyed fascination. "That's archaic!"

"I know, but she means well, and she does get a lot done that way. She pulls strings and serves on committees and everyone in Boston does her bidding, or else."

"You do her bidding, too?" Jacqueline asked.

"Me more than anyone. She has never in thought,

word, or deed suggested that I owe her anything for adopting me, and that guarantees my constant devotion. And I know she hates my gift; it embarrasses her because it's not . . . normal, so I don't use it much." Isabelle smiled, a cool lift of the lips.

Charisma sat up. "But you should still get to do what you want! With your life, I mean."

"I moved from being president of my college sorority to president of her pet charity, I am engaged to a man she suggested, I will become one of Washington's top hostesses, and I did it all so when something came along that I really wanted to do, I could do so without guilt. That's why I'm here."

"You go, girl." Charisma gave her a thumbs-up.

"We'll see. The one other time I rebelled, it turned out badly. And it was not my mother's fault; it was . . ." Isabelle's composure cracked, and she cackled. "Heh, heh."

Charisma's eyes got wide. "Wow. I've never actually heard someone laugh like that."

A surprising color rose in Isabelle's pale cheeks. "Sorry. I'm sitting here talking about myself when Jacqueline has suffered shock and injury and possibly a painful loss."

By which Jacqueline understood Isabelle didn't intend to talk about her mother any longer. And Jacqueline didn't want to even think of her mother, but she couldn't seem to help it. Every time a silence fell, indignation seemed to burgeon out of her. "Zusane was always going off with her boyfriends and her husbands. I should have realized one of them would kill her sooner or later."

"It wasn't exactly his fault," Charisma pointed out.

Yes, it was. Yet Jacqueline still couldn't talk about the man with the blue flame in his eyes.

"Besides, I suppose he's as dead as she is." Charisma bit her lip at her inadvertent bluntness.

Isabelle made a warning sound.

Jacqueline didn't care how blunt they were. She was still mad. "She didn't have to go. Abandoning us like that in the subway right after she has a vision that the Gypsy Travel Agency is up in smoke and there's a good chance we're going to be toast. I mean, how careless and thoughtless can anybody be? You'd think she'd done it on purpose. . . ." She froze, as the thought worked its way into her brain.

"Well. If it makes you feel any better." Charisma slithered back onto the bed, flat on her back, and stared at the ceiling. "My mother's about as careless as anyone you've ever met. She married her one husband on a whim, then decided to adopt me on a whim, then sold their house on a whim while he was at work, and when he objected, she divorced him and took me on the road with her. I've lived all over the West Coast and Pacific Islands . . . Hawaii, Tahiti, Yap. . . ."

"Yap?" Isabelle asked.

"Trust me. It's a place. One year she got a wild hair and decided we were going to rough it in Alaska in the winter. We almost died before we were airlifted out."

"Okay. You win the my-mother's-crazier-than-your-mother contest." For now, Jacqueline pushed aside the thought that Zusane had deliberately joined her boyfriend for some reason. . . .

"I always win." For the first time since Jacqueline had met her, Charisma sounded weary. "The big problem came when I went through puberty and she realized I had a gift. Did you two ever see the musical *Gypsy*?"

"Oh, no." Jacqueline had seen the movie, she instantly understood, and her heart ached with sympathy.

Isabelle looked between the two of them. "I never saw it."

Charisma gestured widely at Jacqueline.

Jacqueline explained, "In the play, the mother has two daughters. When she realizes one of them has a *gift*—not like our gifts; this kid could sing and dance— the mother decides they're going to go into show business, and she pushes and prods and forces and manipulates them every miserable inch of the way."

"The ultimate stage mother," Isabelle said.

"That's my mama," Charisma agreed. "In the summer, we traveled to every farmers' market in the Pacific Northwest and California. We'd set up a stand and sell crystals that I had blessed. She called it *blessed*. I called it aligning the molecules. Once the customers found out they worked—"

"What do they do?" Isabelle asked.

"I can fix a crystal to ward off harm or illness, or improve your health or your mind."

"Wow." Jacqueline had never heard of such a talent.

Despite their makeup blackout, Charisma's black eyeliner was intact, so Jacqueline surmised it was tattooed on. Her lips were red, so they'd been done, too. The purple streaks in her black hair were as vibrant as ever, and a small climbing rose tattoo curled along her spine and out of her T-shirt to bloom behind her left ear.

Charisma was different from Jacqueline and Isabelle, and at the same time, when she talked about her mother, she was so very, very normal.

"As a matter of fact"—Charisma took off two of her bracelets—"I want you guys each to wear one of these until we get some idea what kind of trouble we're in. They're mine, so not fine-tuned to you, but they are really well-balanced."

"What about you?" Isabelle allowed Charisma to fasten one around her arm.

Charisma shook both her wrists, showing them another set of bracelets, and marks beneath them, too. "Since I didn't know what I was getting into, I brought extras."

"You're a good friend." Jacqueline examined the jewelry as Charisma wrapped it around her arm. The chain was silver; the charms were different-colored stones trapped in silver cages. This didn't look like a powerful charm, but Jacqueline wasn't about to be scornful. Not here. Not now. Not after her experiences today. "So your mother treated you like the road show?"

"More than that. She wanted to open a shop and have me be the main attraction. She wanted to dress me as a gypsy, which I am not, and pass me off as a psychic, which I am not, and make a fortune lying to desperate people and giving them false hope." For the first time, Jacqueline heard Charisma sound less like an enthusiastic girl and more like a woman whose hard-won maturity had cost her dearly. "So I left home and went to college. I didn't tell Mom where I was for two years."

"Did she leave you alone?" Isabelle asked.

"Yeah. Eventually. When I went to work in a lab testing soils. She thought that was . . . pedestrian."

"It sounds real," Jacqueline said.

Charisma's face lit up. "It's interesting. I love the earth sciences."

"I don't know anything about science." Isabelle stroked her throat. "But tell me if I'm wrong, Jacqueline—there was something not right about that smoke."

Jacqueline froze.

Slowly Charisma sat up.

"I'm not mad. I know you couldn't have warned me, but—was it enchanted?" Isabelle asked. "Because I thought I was going to die from having it in my lungs."

Jacqueline nodded stiffly, afraid to say too much. "It wasn't an accident that my mother's plane went down, and I think everything was done to make sure the crash was fatal to *her*."

"So this was murder, part of the plot by the Others to destroy us." Gravity sat oddly on Charisma's bright face.

"Especially to destroy Jacqueline. Irving said it. Killing our seer would do irreparable damage. That must be their main goal now." Isabelle touched her throat and chest. "Today, they came very close."

"It's so weird. All my life, I've been saying I don't want to be the seer." The pain reliever must be taking effect, because Jacqueline was babbling.

"I don't blame you. That was a pretty horrific vision you suffered," Charisma said.

"But now I'm afraid the mark of the eye has been severed"—Jacqueline stared at the white gauze bandage that wrapped her hand—"and that murdered my gift, and I *can't* be the seer. I feel . . . just . . . I feel at a loss. How dumb is that?"

"Maybe it's about having a choice," Isabelle suggested.

Jacqueline turned and faced the other two. "Or perhaps Irving is right—I can have different jobs, but a seer is who I *am*. I'm so scared that that's the truth, and if my psychic ability is gone, then . . . who am I?"

"That's deep," Charisma said in awe. "I can't help you with the answer, but that near-death experience really puts it all in perspective, doesn't it?"

"I guess it does. I'm sorry to dump on you two, but who else is going to understand?"

"You mean who's going to understand besides freaks like us?" Charisma slid into the middle of the mattress and opened her arms.

Jacqueline and Isabelle slid into her embrace, and the three of them hugged for one long, comforting moment.

A knock sounded at the door.

The three women jumped and looked in alarm. Then they laughed at themselves.

"Come in!" Jacqueline called.

Martha opened the door and walked in with a tray of finger sandwiches, with the crusts cut off and olives and pickles on the side. She looked at the three of them sitting together, and Jacqueline wasn't sure, but she thought she saw approval on her sour face.

"Girl food," Isabelle said with deep satisfaction.

"Yes!" Charisma pumped her fist.

"Thank you, Martha," the women chorused.

Martha put the tray on the dresser. Wrapping her

hands in her apron, she looked at Jacqueline, her eyes dark and still and calm.

Jacqueline had been waiting for this moment all evening. But even though she had seen the truth in her vision, even though she knew, she still wasn't ready. Getting to her feet, she concentrated on her breathing, trying to comprehend the finality of this moment. "Is there news?"

Isabelle placed a supportive hand on Jacqueline's arm.

Charisma leaned protectively close.

"Yes, miss. The news of a plane crash on the Turkish coast is starting to break." Each word from Martha struck like doom.

"Then I have to call the authorities," Jacqueline said in a voice that didn't seem quite her own.

"Do you wish to call from here? Or would you prefer the privacy of the library?"

Chapter 25

For the second time that day, Caleb went into the attic, but this time, he was walking up the stairs slowly.

The first time, he'd been sprinting, guided by Jacqueline's unearthly screams. He'd found her writhing on the floor, fighting something terrible, something that ripped at her flesh. A fall from an airplane, if she was to be believed.

Pausing, he called Zusane's cell phone again. And again he got her voice mail.

He put his hand to his forehead. That just figured. He left the woman alone for twenty-four hours, and she disappeared from this earth.

Forever?

If Jacqueline was to be believed, she had.

Disaster piled on top of disaster. The Chosen Ones

were inexperienced and bewildered. Caleb wasn't sure whom he could trust and whom he couldn't—right now, he wondered if Irving had sent Jacqueline up to the attic and into her vision in an attempt to kill her and Zusane at the same time. And he had a crime scene that had been contaminated by everybody. Because, despite the fact he worked for a seer, he wasn't convinced Jacqueline's injuries were the result of some mumbo-jumbo psychic experience.

Yeah, he was a suspicious son of a bitch.

Standing in the middle of the room, he donned his latex gloves and carefully looked around. The room was big, empty, with sunshine slanting in the windows in long, afternoon light. The dust on the floor had been undisturbed for months—until today. Now there were dozens of footprints, mostly leading from the door to the place in the middle of the floor where the crystal ball had fallen and shattered one of the floorboards, which was damned weird. One set of footprints led to the door at the far wall. A woman's footprints, leading to the door and back. So . . . Jacqueline's footprints.

He followed them to the door and opened it. The room beyond matched this one, except only one set of footprints walked through the dust—and they led toward the other door. Large footprints. A man's footprints. Caleb knelt beside one and examined it, leaning backward and forward, using light and shadow to get an idea of what kind of sole it had been.

No visible tread. So a loafer or some kind of business shoe.

He sat up straight. Helpful. With a lawyer, a faith healer, a sophisticated thief, a gentleman servant, and Irving in the house, he'd eliminated exactly one man—the student in his athletic shoes.

Following the footsteps to the far wall, he opened that door. The footsteps led up the stairs, and hey, maybe someone had raced upstairs from the kitchen when Jacqueline started screaming. And maybe someone had sneaked up here when she was having her vision and beat the crap out of her.

He looked in the closets and cupboards in both rooms. Nothing. So he returned to the crystal ball and the broken floor. He picked up each shard of wood, and discovered, to his dismay, none of them had blood on them.

So *had* Jacqueline cut her hand on the broken glass bottle on a jet somewhere over Europe?

Briefly, he closed his eyes and concentrated on the idea of Jacqueline falling into a vision and being swept away into a blazing plane. . . . Opening his eyes, he stared coldly across the empty room.

In all his years with Zusane, he'd never seen a vision touch her. As he understood it, they were like movies that played across Zusane's mind, carrying her away with the emotion of the events, but never physically affecting her. But she had said Jacqueline had the potential to be the greatest seer of all time. Did she realize that Jacqueline could be hurt by what she witnessed?

He knew Jacqueline better than anybody on earth. He'd viewed her struggles to avoid being what her mother was, what her mother wanted. He'd seen her soul torn asunder by what she desired to be and what she *was*. And he had wanted her to finally reconcile the separate parts of herself, to surrender to her fate—to grow up—because until she did, she would never be happy.

Had there been more to her resistance than he thought? Had she realized she could be injured? Had he urged her toward a goal that could kill her?

Was he really the smug bastard she accused him of being?

How could he be smug, when he couldn't even do his job well enough to discover if someone had come to Jacqueline while she was in a trance and hurt her?

Using only his fingertips, he picked up the crystal ball. It was heavy for its size—but not heavy enough to have shattered the floor as it had. It was slick and warm and beautiful, with colors that slid across the surface and drew his gaze deep into its center. And as if it had been waiting for his touch, an image darkened the surface—a handprint took form, smoky white, with long fingers and a broad palm. A man-hand.

Clad in a latex glove?

Perhaps.

And on the other side, a small, dark red blot—blood?—materialized and violently exploded, as if this ball had been used as the weapon to knock Jacqueline out of her vision. And kill her?

As he stared, the handprint and the blood spatter both disappeared.

That was all. The end of the show. The globe had shown him all it intended to show. The images shrank toward the middle and disappeared. The colors returned to play across the surface of the globe.

He was left with the conviction that he held the weapon that had given Jacqueline a blow to the head, and the knowledge that the perpetrator was a man.

Not McKenna; the stocky Celt's hands were broad, but stubby. Not Aleksandr, if the footprints were to be believed. Oh, and Aleksandr's burned and ruined hand made the crime impossible for him.

But every other man in the house was a suspect.

Sitting in that attic room, Caleb faced some hard truths. He had spent his adult life serving Zusane, and through her, the Gypsy Travel Agency. He believed in them, believed in their mission, and he, who had seen so much of the ugly underbelly of life, knew very well what could happen now that the fate of so much good work depended on seven gifted, inexperienced, and unallied Chosen. They desperately needed a seer.

But right now, he was of the opinion Irving and his Chosen, and the whole damned rest of the world, could depend on Tyler Settles. Because damned if Caleb was going to let Jacqueline risk her life for a shot at greatness.

Caleb walked back down to the bedroom he shared with Jacqueline, and stopped cold.

Isabelle and Charisma stood in the room, motionless and waiting.

At his appearance, Isabelle said, "She's in the library, on the phone with Turkish officials."

He turned and headed down the stairs. The door of the library was closed; he listened at the door, but heard nothing. He turned the knob and pushed into the room.

Jacqueline sat at the desk by the phone, hands in her lap, staring out the window into the garden surrounded by a stone fence. Her expression was pensive, thoughtful.

He knew without a doubt she'd been given the official word. "Jacqueline?"

She turned her head, a slow, graceful arc, and in a preternaturally calm voice, said, "I called. The plane went down—I get confused about the time difference, but I think it's tonight there now—and the wreckage is scattered along the coastline and in the water. They found Zusane's body washed up on the beach."

He went to Jacqueline and knelt before her, picked up her hands and chafed them.

"I'm so sorry." She passed her fingers through his short hair, and her beautiful eyes were wide and dry and terrible. "I know how close you were."

Standing, he picked her up and cradled her in his arms, then sat down in the chair and held her tightly.

She started trembling, but still she spoke in that abstract voice. "There was a survivor."

Startled, he said, "You're joking." But of course she wasn't. "Who?"

"The owner of the plane. Her new boyfriend. He walked away from the crash." Jacqueline wrapped her arm around his shoulders. "Did you know his name? Did you meet him?"

"No, to both questions. This romance came on fast, and she was unusually secretive. . . . Why?" He already knew he wasn't going to like the answer.

"His name is Osgood."

He was right. He didn't like it. "Son of a bitch."

"So you know who he is."

"He's famous in the underworld. Or infamous. Nobody knows what he looks like, but he owns half of New York City, and the rumors that swirl around about him are terrible. That he tortures and murders people who owe him money—or whoever he wishes; that he controls the politics all along the East Coast; that he smuggles in cigars, liquor, drugs, electronics; that everyone, even organized crime, pays him protection money." Caleb held Jacqueline tighter. "Did you see him on that plane?"

"Yes."

"Did he see you?"

"Yes." She curled up into the chair, scrunching herself as close to Caleb as she could get. "Caleb, I saw him, and he saw me. He spoke to me . . . in that voice. And I saw his eyes."

Caleb knew he didn't want to hear this. "What about his eyes?"

"Deep inside, they were lit by a blue flame. Caleb, Osgood is every evil thing you said, and more. Osgood went one step further. He invited the devil into his soul. Because of Osgood, the devil was on that plane—and the devil walked away from the crash."

Chapter 26

———⟨❈⟩———

Jacqueline woke to the sound of a knock on the bedroom door. Memories of the previous day rushed in; for a moment, she clung to Caleb, and he stroked her head. "Okay?" he whispered.

"Yes." Except that her mother was dead, and Jacqueline couldn't feel anything except anger. And she could hear something dripping, slowly, constantly, like a Chinese water torture. And she was scared. Scared as she had never been before.

But she knew Caleb was scared, too. Last night, when she'd told him about the devil, she'd seen it in his eyes. Somehow, knowing he believed her and understood the significance of the devil's hand in their affairs made her feel . . . braver. More capable.

Because no matter what he felt, he did what had to be done, and she would do the same.

She watched Caleb get out of bed, walk over to the door, and ask, "Who is it?"

"Tyler Settles."

The sound of Tyler's warm voice relaxed Jacqueline, and Caleb must have felt the same way, for he opened the door a crack. "Yes?"

"Just wanted you two to know we've decided to have our first official Chosen Ones meeting this morning at nine in the library."

"All right. We'll be there." Caleb shut the door and turned to look at Jacqueline. "You up for it?"

"Of course." She threw back the covers. "Should we tell Irving?"

"About Osgood?" Caleb watched her with warm appreciation, as if he liked her in that too short, too wide white nightgown and the jiggling charm bracelet Charisma had given her. "Why didn't you tell him in the first place?"

She shrugged her shoulders uncomfortably. "Because . . . because . . . this is an awful thing to say, but I don't know if I trust Irving."

"I don't know if I do, either."

Caleb's sentiment surprised her—and comforted her. "I hate feeling this way," she burst out, "but I don't know who to trust at all."

"Except me."

Startled, she looked at him. "Of course. I've always

trusted you." She shut the bathroom door on his half smile.

Because of Caleb, she had clean clothes to wear, which was more than the other women could say, and she was showered, dressed, and ready to go in fifteen minutes. It took Caleb five. Her leather gloves had made their way back to her via McKenna's obsessive management, so while Caleb was in the bathroom, she carefully pulled the right one over her bandage, then easily donned the left one. The gloves gave her a sense of security, a knowledge that her hands, her tattoo, and her injury were protected. Today, more than ever, it was a feeling she cherished.

She felt the same way about the bracelet Charisma had given her. She donned it not because she felt the stones would protect her, but because her friend had given it to her. Friendship provided a protection all its own.

Together, Caleb and Jacqueline walked down to the dining room. They picked up breakfast from the buffet and headed into the library.

"Ah, the two lovebirds." Irving didn't sound as if he approved.

Jacqueline didn't care that everyone thought they were a couple. She didn't care what Irving thought at all. Her suspicions of Irving had tainted everything she saw and touched and heard. It was a miserable way to live, but right now, she was stuck.

Maybe the meeting would help.

The Chosen Ones were dragging chairs into a circle in front of the window, and chatting desultorily about the weather, the comfort of their beds, how much weight they'd gained on the good cooking. Irving was already seated. Martha and McKenna bustled around, refilling coffee cups and offering tea and juice.

Only Caleb stood alone in one place in the middle of the room, observing . . . everything.

Jacqueline accepted a coffee cup, with thanks, and let Tyler place a chair for her.

He touched her shoulder. "How's the hand?"

She looked at the leather glove. "Good. A little tender." A lot tender, but she refused to take any more pain relievers. Today, she suspected, she would need her wits about her.

A small, round, antique mahogany table with ornate Chinese carvings on the face and legs had been positioned beside Irving. That damnable crystal ball had been placed in the middle on its carved wood base. As she seated herself, the globe inevitably drew her gaze, pulling her into the play of colors on its surface, and into the complex maze of visions it cradled deep within. The sound of dripping water grew louder in her head. . . .

Someone spoke right in her ear, startling her.

If he looks into it, he will die. If he looks into it, he will die.

She jumped. Looked around.

Next to her, McKenna was filling Charisma's coffee cup.

"What did you say?" Jacqueline asked.

McKenna glanced behind him, then back at her. "I didn't say anything, miss."

"Well . . . did you hear that?"

McKenna and Charisma looked at Jacqueline oddly, and McKenna said, "Hear what, miss?"

"Nothing." *Just some dripping water and a disembodied voice.* "I thought I heard . . . My ears are still ringing from the concussion, I guess." Searching the room, she found a silk throw tossed over the back of a chair. With elaborate casualness, she stood, walked over, picked it up and shook it out, then placed it over the crystal ball to hide it from sight.

Turning back to her chair, she discovered every eye was on her.

She smiled with carefree insouciance, and seated herself.

If she behaved with a little more circumspection, the men in the white coats would come to take her away.

"Could everyone be seated, please, so we can get started?" Tyler gestured in a circle.

There was the usual shuffling and coughing; then everyone looked at him expectantly.

"I called this meeting because I don't believe we're getting anything done sitting here waiting for doom to take us." Jacqueline didn't need a gift to know Tyler had assumed the leadership of the group.

Caleb interrupted. "Where is Samuel?"

She also didn't need a crystal ball to know Caleb had disputed Tyler's leadership.

Irving sighed deeply. "Yesterday, after Jacqueline's vision, he left the house."

"He hasn't returned?" Caleb asked.

"He hasn't returned," Irving confirmed.

For a moment, anguish touched Isabelle's face. Then her expression smoothed, and she was serene once more.

"Damn it. I'm going to search his room." Caleb lifted his eyebrows at Jacqueline.

She nodded. She would be fine here with the others.

Caleb slipped out.

Tyler waited until Caleb was gone, then rapped on the table with his knuckles to reestablish his authority.

Personally, Jacqueline didn't give him a lot of chance.

Tyler said, "With all due respect to Caleb, who is doing his best, and Irving, who is retired, it seems to me that hiding in this house is counterproductive. If the Others don't know we're alive, it would be best to get out there and do something to thwart their evil plans before they can be carried any further."

"Their evil plans?" Aaron raised his eyebrows. "Is that what we're calling them now?"

"With all due respect to you, Mr. Settles, you're a faith healer. What makes you the expert on our next move?" Irving had obviously been stung by the *retired* comment.

"I ran a huge corporation based on my talents, Mr. Shea, and no one questioned my guidance." Tyler was obviously stung in return.

"My family said to do exactly as Irving instructs, and in matters concerning the Chosen Ones, he's the expert." Aleksandr was young, but he spoke like a man, and one who knew his mind.

"But then, you're a *student*," Tyler said.

"*Exactly.* Which is why I listen to my *family*." Obviously, Aleksandr wasn't about to take trouble from anyone.

"What does Jacqueline think?" Charisma asked. "She's our seer. She's the one who's proved herself."

With that, everybody started talking at once. Arguing. Trying to make their views known.

Jacqueline looked wildly from one to another. "We've got to be calm. This is just the kind of chaos the Others want for us."

Nobody was listening.

Then she noticed Tyler. As if something drew him toward the crystal ball, he leaned toward it and with an elaborate flourish, drew the silk throw away.

The globe shone with the colors that slipped across its surface, and he stared into its depths. He stretched out his hands to cup the globe between his palms, and froze.

One by one, the Chosen Ones noticed and fell silent.

"A vision?" Charisma murmured to Jacqueline.

"I don't know," Jacqueline whispered back. "It doesn't look like one of my mother's, but—"

With an unearthly cry, Tyler snatched the crystal ball off its stand and held it before him. His arms shook as if it weighed him down. With a surge, he came to his feet, and said, "He's here." He whispered the words, but they rolled through the room like thunder. "He's here. He's in New York City. He's directing their operation himself. He knows our every move before we do it."

Jacqueline swallowed, her mouth suddenly dry.

"Who is here?" Irving asked his question calmly, as if he'd directed many a vision.

"He's middle-aged. Thin. Short. Unassuming. But he possesses a soul of pure evil, and when he looks at you . . ." Tyler suddenly turned his head, stared into Jacqueline's eyes, and his voice swelled with power. "You saw him. You saw him on the plane. He saw you, too. How could you not tell us about the man with the blue flame in his eyes?"

Right away, Irving knew whom he meant.

So did Charisma and Isabelle.

Aleksandr tugged at his crewneck T-shirt. Of course. With his background, he knew, too.

Aaron muttered, "Shit," so he'd been reading the Chosen Ones manual.

Everyone faced Jacqueline, accusation in their eyes.

But she didn't owe anyone an explanation. Certainly not a man in a trance. "Go on, Tyler," she instructed in a cool voice. "Tell us what else you see."

"I see an explosion." Tyler still held the globe at arm's length, and he swung around in a circle. "An explosion, greater than the last one! Wiping out all remnants of the Chosen Ones, leaving only a legend that will soon fade from memory. . . ."

In a forgotten corner of the room, Martha stood against the wall. Now she gave a sob, then pressed her fist to her mouth.

Compelled by the drama, Jacqueline sat forward in her chair. "Where is this explosion?"

He halted, swaying, staring into space. His beautiful voice grew thick and harsh. "Here. The explosion is here. Before it's too late, we've got to get out of Irving Shea's house."

He collapsed onto the antique flowered rug.

The globe slipped out of his grip, and everyone watched in fascination as it rolled toward Jacqueline, and came to rest at her feet.

Then the room burst out in a cacophony of voices.

One rose above the others. "Shut up!"

Chapter 27

J ust like that, the library was silent once more, and every eye turned to the door and Caleb.

"What in the hell is going on here?" He observed Tyler, struggling to sit up. Jacqueline, white-faced and frightened. Aaron, tight-lipped and furious. Charisma, holding her bracelets. Isabelle, thoughtfully watching her cohorts.

Tyler staggered to his feet and put his hands to his head. "What happened? What did I say?"

"He had a vision," Isabelle told Caleb. "He says the devil is in New York City."

"I don't think there was ever any doubt about that," Caleb responded.

As if he'd caught her by surprise with his humor, Isabelle smiled briefly. "True, but he's talking about the real devil, the one who possesses and corrupts men's souls."

Oh, Caleb knew. So did Jacqueline.

But how had Tyler figured it out? Had he overheard Jacqueline talking to Caleb?

No. Not unless Tyler had planted bugs in every room in this house, and he couldn't have smuggled in the electronics. Caleb considered Tyler with new eyes. Perhaps the guy actually had had a vision.

Isabelle continued. "He also said the devil was on the plane and Jacqueline saw him."

Jacqueline gave Caleb a short nod.

"I see," Caleb said.

"So it's true?" Tyler demanded. "The devil was on the plane that went down with Zusane?"

"Yes, it's true." Obviously, Jacqueline had been caught, and she didn't see the sense of lying now.

"Why didn't you tell us? This makes all the difference in the world!" Irving looked toward Aaron.

Something passed between them, some message Caleb didn't understand—and he didn't like not understanding.

"Yes, Jacqueline. Irving's right." Tyler sounded both persuasive and reproachful. "Knowing what we know now, that the devil himself is in charge, means the danger is greater and more immediate than we could imagine. It means we've got to approach our defense differently."

"The devil's not in charge," Charisma said patiently. "He's not allowed."

Tyler swung on her. "What?"

"The rules are older than even the existence of the Chosen Ones and the Others. Moreover, they're eternal. The devil isn't allowed to take a direct hand in the running of the world. He can offer rewards, as he did with the Wilders, allowing them to turn into predators to work his will. He can corrupt men, as he apparently did with this man Osgood, who walked away from the plane wreck—and now we know why. But he isn't allowed to come here and put a bomb in Irving's house and blow us all up. He's not allowed," she repeated. "He's not in charge."

Tyler flushed. "I think it's not as easy as you imagine."

"I think he's right," Aaron said. "According to *When the World Was Young: A History of the Chosen Ones*, the appearance of demon possession signals new and terrible trouble in the world."

"What's this about the devil blowing up this house?" Tyler asked.

With an authority Caleb admired, Isabelle took over, giving him and Tyler the details of Tyler's vision. She finished with, "The question I'm sure we are all thinking now is—is Tyler's prophecy correct, and if it is, when will it occur? Should we abandon this house today, or investigate further?"

"My visions are never wrong," Tyler said.

"That may be true, Tyler, but I've never met a seer

who had put a date on her—or his—predictions," Irving replied. "Perhaps we should ask Caleb if he found anything in Samuel's room."

"There's nothing there," Caleb reported. "Nothing to indicate he ever occupied it. He took his clothes, his toothbrush, everything."

Isabelle looked down at her hands.

Caleb hated to ask, but he had no choice. "Did he say anything to you, Isabelle?"

Isabelle raised her gaze to meet his. "I haven't seen him since we were in the attic."

"If he's the man who has somehow activated this bomb, he's cleared out for a reason," Tyler said.

"A persuasive argument, Mr. Settles, but I won't leave my home." Irving nodded at them all. "I do understand if you all wish to flee, but please, be careful out there. This has all the markings of a trap."

"Maybe Jacqueline could have another vision?" Aleksandr suggested. "I mean, we've got two seers; we might as well utilize them."

"No, I won't. . . ." Jacqueline shuddered; she cradled her injured hand in her arm, and a sheen of sweat covered her suddenly pale forehead. "That is, I can't call them up at will."

It didn't take clairvoyance to know she feared another vision. She feared being hurt again.

Irving didn't care. "But you did when you tried."

Damn the old man. Caleb liked him less and less, for

he was willing to sacrifice anything and anybody for his cause. "Let's let her heal from the first vision before we ask for another one," Caleb said.

"When you're thrown, it's always best to get back on the horse at once." Irving glanced at Caleb's stiff jaw, and added, "But of course, we're grateful to have had a vision from both our seers."

Aaron cleared his throat. "If you would allow me to speak about something of which I do have some knowledge?"

"Please, Mr. Eagle, we would appreciate any guidance," Isabelle said.

"I have no parents, of course, but I was raised in the midst of a small Indian tribe in Idaho. Our reservation was poor, the roughest, steepest, most unforgiving part of the Sawtooth Range, and whether we liked it or not, we had to work to survive. So in ways you can't imagine, we lived as American Indians have done for thousands of years. I bathed in an icy stream every morning of my life. I learned to track and hunt. I was taught to smell danger as it approached, and dodge before fighting." Aaron spoke without pride, as a man would give his credentials, yet in his voice Caleb now heard the cadence of an Indian's speech. "The stench of danger is strong in this city, and I would leave Irving's home if I smelled danger. But I don't. I respect Tyler's vision as I would my own, but my advice is to stay together, and stay put."

"Tyler, what will you do?" Caleb didn't blame the

guy if he wanted to take off. "It must be difficult to ignore your own vision."

"I don't remember the vision, and that makes it easier to ignore." Tyler yielded easily, and smiled with crooked charm. "I can't leave the Chosen Ones. I believe we're stronger together than apart. But I still don't understand why Jacqueline didn't tell us about the devil. Did I miss that part, too?"

Caleb could see they weren't going to let this one go. "She didn't want to alarm you."

At the same time, Jacqueline said, "Because I didn't see what my vision got us except early knowledge of something we were going to know anyway."

"But it was an important element," Irving said. "For you to discover that the devil himself has found a willing servant who does his bidding and whom he protects . . . That's exactly what we were trying to discover when we—" He stopped in midsentence.

"When you sent my mother to seduce him?" Jacqueline's voice, her demeanor, grew icy.

"Not seduce." Irving's protestations were feeble, and he knew it. "We never suggested your mother do anything she didn't want to do."

"But you knew perfectly well she was attracted to powerful men." Jacqueline came to her feet.

Caleb had seen Jacqueline in the throes of passion, of fear, of anguish. He had never seen her in such a rage, flushed and trembling.

She had a right to her anger.

"We simply sent her out to check out people, men, of whom we were suspicious," Irving said weakly.

"You hit the jackpot this time, Irving. My mother's dead, but hey, at least you know the devil's abroad in New York City." Jacqueline walked toward the door.

Caleb moved aside to let her pass.

"Come on, Caleb," she said, her voice rich with contempt. "The rest of the Chosen Ones can stay with Irving Shea if they want, but I'm out of here."

Chapter 28

Caleb walked behind Jacqueline. He was sympathetic, yes. He was in agreement with her rage, yes. But however disreputable it might be, his attention was mostly taken up with his appreciation of her magnificent figure as she stalked toward the front door.

The woman knew how to convey displeasure, and look good while she did it. She'd learned more from Zusane than she'd realized.

McKenna hustled ahead of Jacqueline. "Miss Vargha, Mr. Shea would never have asked Miss Zusane to do anything if he thought it was dangerous."

"Don't play me for a fool." Her contempt widened to include Irving's manservant. "Am I supposed to approve of him sending my mother into a relationship with the devil himself?"

"He didn't know for sure. . . ." McKenna seemed to realize that argument wouldn't fly.

"He *suspected*." She swung on him. "Supposedly he loved my mother. Supposedly he admired her. Yet he willingly sent her into hell?"

"He did love and admire her," McKenna said. "We all did."

She trembled with fury. "Yet you know and I know Irving would sacrifice anything—including a woman he loved—if he thought it would keep his precious Chosen intact and the mission going."

"Well. Yes." Jacqueline's wild burst of emotion had McKenna almost cringing with dismay.

"Right." She turned and headed for the door once more.

If only she realized how much her anger betrayed about her relationship with her mother . . . but Caleb wasn't dumb enough to try to tell her. She needed to figure it out for herself. But damn, he was getting tired of waiting.

McKenna wrung his hands. "But regardless, Miss Vargha, it doesn't make sense to go out onto the New York streets when danger stalks you."

"It's all right. I'll be with her." In fact, Caleb knew better than to try to stop her now. "Get me one of Irving's hats. We'll disguise her Hollywood style."

Before Jacqueline left Irving's mansion, her platinum-colored hair was hidden beneath a large fedora and her face was half covered with a huge pair of black sunglasses. They stepped out briskly, walking for two blocks toward the Met before catching a cab.

Once inside, she turned to him. "I was right about Irving. He is our traitor."

Caleb hated to be the voice of reason, but— "Not necessarily."

"What do you mean?" She was loud. Too loud.

He put his fingers over her mouth and glanced toward the Asian cabbie. Softly he said, "The driver has an execrable accent, but he could easily be one of the Others or one of their employees. You know that."

She nodded once, resentful because he was right and angry at herself for being so indiscreet.

In a voice pitched to reach only her ears, he said, "Irving has done despicable things for the Gypsy Travel Agency, yes, and considers them justified by the results. But that doesn't mean he blew the place up. If anything, knowing he approved of sending Zusane out to reconnoiter for them makes me more inclined to trust him."

"You're crazy," she muttered, and sat back against the seat, her arms folded over her chest. "What about my mother?"

"I served Zusane for many years. She was a woman of strong will and fire. She loved drama. She loved intrigue. They could have never forced her to seduce those men. So I think the truth is—she enjoyed her work as a spy." He waited, but he got no outburst from Jacqueline, which meant she grudgingly agreed. "At the chalk circle, after the explosion, she ordered me to stay with you. I was glad to do it. I thought perhaps it was her way of giving her permission for me to . . . love you."

Jacqueline's head swiveled toward him, and her eyes were wary.

He continued. "But now I wonder if she realized how dangerous a situation she faced. Perhaps she even foresaw her own death."

"And she wanted you out of it," Jacqueline said.

"Yes."

"She always loved you."

"Yes." They stopped in Times Square to let the mob of tourists pass. Caleb pulled cash out of his pocket and threw it toward the driver. "We're getting out here." Grabbing Jacqueline's arm, he pulled her through the door and into the crowd.

He hustled her along until they reached an upscale pet store. "In here," he said.

"Are we being followed?" she asked.

"It never hurts to try to lose them, whoever they are." He especially didn't want that woman who spoke in his head to find them again. His gut, and Irving's reaction, told him she was dangerous. "I need dog treats, and I want to say—" He planted himself in front of her, so close their toes touched, so close she had to look into his face and see the truth in his eyes. "I protected your mother because above all else, I owed her my loyalty, and for that, she loved me like a son." Taking her arms, he pulled her toward him and kissed her once, hard, on the lips. Then he set her back, settled Irving's hat on her head once more, and said, "Dog treats."

"Dog treats," Jacqueline repeated, and touched her fingers to her swollen lips. "No, thank you. I'm not hungry."

"I thought I'd take you to visit my mother." Her double take gave him a great deal of satisfaction. "It's best to bribe her dogs."

"Your mother?"

"You said you wanted to meet her."

"Yes. I . . . Yes, I would like that." Jacqueline looked down at her jeans and T-shirt. "I'm not exactly dressed for meeting anybody's mother. Not yours, anyway."

"Ma knows what happened to you. To us." He dug around in the bin with the teeth-cleansing chews and picked out two, then grabbed a couple of hard biscuits. He flung them all on the counter and stared down the bored and obviously listening sales clerk. "Remember, she sent you her nightgown."

"Oh. Yeah. Do you think she'll like me?"

He picked up her fingers and kissed them. "I know she will like you very much."

Chapter 29

———◆❖◆———

Somehow, Jacqueline did not find Caleb's opinion reassuring. This was his *mother* he was talking about. This was his *mother* he was taking her to visit.

Usually, when a guy took a girl to meet his mother, it meant he had serious intentions. What if Mrs. D'Angelo didn't like her? What if she didn't like tall women? What if Jacqueline said the wrong thing?

Oh, that was the most likely. What if she said the wrong thing? She almost always did. . . .

And in the pet shop, he'd kissed her in a way that, if she were a woman who thrived on self-confidence, she would think meant he *did* have serious intentions.

But she'd thought that once before, two years ago, and her mother had crooked her finger, and Caleb had left Jacqueline without a backward glance. So Jacqueline wasn't going to allow herself hope, only anxiety. Because she was going to meet his *mother*.

They took two cabs, a limo, and a circuitous route through Brooklyn to a middle-class neighborhood of restored brownstones.

"Stop here," Caleb instructed the driver.

They were at the end of an alley.

Jacqueline got out and looked around as Caleb paid the driver. Kids played on the sidewalk, trees lined the street, and she saw an APARTMENT FOR RENT sign in a window.

Caleb joined her, took her arm, and hustled her down the alley. "My mother's place is not as nice as Irving's, but it's home."

"It's better than Irving's. I can relax here. If I break something at Irving's, I know it's a priceless antique. If I break something here—"

"It's not." He took her past garbage cans and up the back steps to a wooden door with a lace-curtained window. He knocked, tried the knob, found it open, and sighed.

"Shouldn't it be locked? Isn't that dangerous?" Jacqueline followed him into the utility room. She pulled off Irving's fedora and her glasses and placed them on the washing machine.

"Yes, but my mother likes for her neighbors to be able to come in for coffee whenever they want." He shouted into the house, "Ma! It's me!"

A wild barking started in the depths of the house.

"She has Lizzie as a doorbell. The problem is, Lizzie isn't as young as she used to be, and she doesn't hear as well as she once did. I never used to be able to touch the door before she was jumping at me." He handed Jacqueline a treat and warned, "Brace yourself."

She heard the thundering of feet; then a large, ecstatic golden Lab and a small German shepherd with a big bark burst through the door.

"Lizzie, down! Ritter, sit!" Jacqueline recognized Caleb's command voice.

Too bad the dogs didn't. The German shepherd's attitude changed from aggression to a polite disdain. The Lab continued to prance for the pure pleasure of their company.

Jacqueline took one look at Caleb's disgusted expression and burst into laughter.

"Lizzie, down! Ritter, sit!" he said again, and this time they obeyed—until they'd received the treat he offered.

Then Ritter frolicked over to Jacqueline and smiled, positively smiled, until she gave him the treat she held. He crunched it without bothering to stop dancing.

Lizzie was more subdued, more cautious; she daintily removed the treat from Jacqueline's hand and walked with it to the kitchen. Ritter slapped Jacqueline with his tail until she scratched his back.

"Come in. Come in!" Caleb's mother had a lyrical

voice and a pronounced Italian accent, and when she appeared in the doorway, Jacqueline realized why the nightgown fit the way it did. Mrs. D'Angelo was probably fifty, short and plump, with snapping brown eyes and short, dark hair that curled around her smiling, dimpled face.

She was also quite blind.

Jacqueline muffled her gasp of surprise. All her life she remembered hearing Caleb talk about his mother, and never had he said anything about a handicap.

"Darling boy, what an unexpected treat. I didn't expect to see you today." Mrs. D'Angelo held out her arms toward Caleb.

He walked into her embrace, put his arms around her, and gave her a hug. "I brought you some company."

"Jacqueline? You brought me Jacqueline at last?" She bussed his cheek, pushed him away, and held out her arms again. "I am so glad to meet you, child!"

What could Jacqueline do? She walked to her, hugged her, and said, "Thank you for welcoming me, Mrs. D'Angelo. I've wanted to meet you for a long time."

"Yes, but we had to respect Zusane's wishes, didn't we? Caleb, why did she yield at last?" Mrs. D'Angelo cocked her head and waited for Caleb's reply.

"She didn't exactly yield, Mama. She was killed in a plane crash yesterday."

"Oh, no! The poor, dear lady." Mrs. D'Angelo's

arms convulsively tightened around Jacqueline. "My poor little girl."

Jacqueline became aware of an unexpected stinging in her eyes. Until this woman, this mother, held her and gave her sympathy, she hadn't really experienced the sorrow of losing Zusane. Now melancholy nudged at her, wanting attention, and she thrust it back.

Not here. Not in this cheerful place. Not in front of Caleb. Not in front of his mother.

"Come in. Sit down." Mrs. D'Angelo drew her into the sunny kitchen/dining area. Italian terra-cotta tile covered the floor, the cabinets were painted a pale yellow, and the stainless steel appliances shone. Two dog beds were on the floor under the window. A small, round, polished wood table sat in the window alcove overlooking the street, and Mrs. D'Angelo led Jacqueline there, pulled out a chair, and pushed her into it. "A cup of coffee. Sugar? Cream? Caleb, fix it for her. Can you stay for dinner?"

"No, Ma, we can't stay away that long." Caleb poured two cups of coffee from the under-counter Mr. Coffee, and refilled his mother's mug.

"Of course not. Silly me. You have much to do. The outpouring of mourning for the famous Zusane must be heartbreaking." Mrs. D'Angelo squeezed Jacqueline's shoulder.

"The news of Zusane's death must be all over the media," Jacqueline whispered. She hadn't thought about the publicity. Her chest felt tight; whether she wanted it or not, grief was building.

"Lunch, then. A frittata." Mrs. D'Angelo worked her way across the kitchen to her cabinets and with uncanny accuracy retrieved a cutting board and an eight-inch chef's knife.

"Please, Mrs. D'Angelo, don't go to any trouble," Jacqueline protested.

"It's no trouble to cook for friends." Mrs. D'Angelo gave the hovering Lizzie a pat and told her to go lie down on her bed.

Lizzie obeyed her immediately.

"Reports of the crash were on the early-morning news." Caleb placed the coffee in front of Jacqueline and sat down across from her at the small table, watching her as if he knew the train of her thoughts.

Ritter pushed his wet nose under her hand, and when she automatically began to pet him, he sighed with delight.

With his soft head under her hands, the heartache retreated a little.

"What are they saying? Not that Zusane was"—Jacqueline glanced at Mrs. D'Angelo and lowered her voice—"psychic."

"No reason to lower your voice," Mrs. D'Angelo said cheerfully. "I *know*."

"Ma is right—she does know," Caleb confirmed. "But no, there's not a whisper of that on the news. Instead they're doing retrospectives of Zusane's life, her marriages, her glamour. They're showing her with royalty, with men of power, with actors and politicians. They're talking about her sequins and her diamonds."

"She would love that." Jacqueline took a freer breath.

"Jacqueline, are you allergic to mushrooms?" Mrs. D'Angelo leaned into the refrigerator and gathered ingredients. "Or shellfish?"

"No, I'm not allergic to anything." Except maybe visions. Visions that ripped her flesh, clogged her lungs, and left the bitter residue of panic in her mouth. Jacqueline wet her lips. "Is there anything I can do to help you?"

"Thank you. You are a dear girl to offer. But I have my knives sharpened at Sears. They are very sharp." Mrs. D'Angelo smiled wickedly. "It's best to stay out of my way."

Caleb said, "The press mentioned that Zusane adopted a daughter, but that she and the daughter were estranged and no one knows where the girl is."

"Thank God." Jacqueline had never meant anything more.

"Your mother was such a good woman. It seems a shame that her greatest good works must remain hidden." Mrs. D'Angelo shredded Parmesan and deveined shrimp with speedy efficiency. "She saved our lives, you know."

"No. I didn't know." Jacqueline's gaze lingered on Mrs. D'Angelo as she chopped mushrooms, zucchini, and green onions. "What did she do?"

A little skepticism must have leaked into her voice, for Mrs. D'Angelo scowled and cracked the eggs into her bowl with unnecessary vigor. "Tell her, Caleb. She deserves to know."

Jacqueline thought he would refuse. He'd always refused to tell her anything but the most superficial details about his life.

Instead he settled back in his chair, watching Jacqueline steadily, weighing her reactions as he talked. "I grew up in a small town in Sicily, and the first time I saw Zusane, I sold her some shells from the beach. She was a lady, so beautiful, like an angel, and she talked to me and listened to me. I was eight, almost a man, and I was very flattered. I strutted home."

"You really did." Mrs. D'Angelo vigorously beat the eggs. "When I saw you, I knew something had happened to make you look like the cat that swallowed the canary."

So Mrs. D'Angelo had not always been blind.

"But charming though I was, Zusane had other reasons for paying attention to me. She had seen the aura of pain around me. She followed me home, and warned my mother that death and violence would visit that night, and we should escape while we could. My father and older brother laughed at her. My mother cried."

"Because I knew what trouble your brother had stirred up, and I was afraid." Mrs. D'Angelo slid the chopped ingredients into the eggs.

"The rivalries in Sicily never really die," Caleb told Jacqueline, "and my brother was a hothead who lived to fight. He fought the wrong kid, and won."

"He was the best fighter on the island. My oldest. So smart. So handsome. So foolish." Mrs. D'Angelo stopped cooking, suspended in memories.

"I didn't realize what was going on, but the other family was rich and influential, and they had bragged they would eliminate us." Caleb gave Jacqueline a half smile. "Needless to say, we were *not* rich and influential. So my father and brother refused to leave with Zusane, and refused to let me or my mother go."

"Why?" Jacqueline asked.

"Pride. Manly pride." If Mrs. D'Angelo hadn't been in her kitchen, she probably would have spit on the floor.

"Oh," Jacqueline said. "That."

"They wrapped me in a mattress and told me to go to sleep. I refused, of course"—Caleb grimaced—"and fell asleep waiting. I woke to the sound of gunfire."

Mrs. D'Angelo came to him as he sat at the table, and put her hand on his shoulder.

He covered it with his palm, warming it as if knowing she needed the contact.

Lizzie came to Mrs. D'Angelo's side, sat at her feet, leaned against her legs.

"I peeked out and saw my father and brother gunned down." Caleb's voice was steady, but beneath his even tone, Jacqueline heard an old anguish. "My mother picked up a knife and killed one of the attackers, and she was shot."

"My God!" Jacqueline's hand convulsed in Ritter's fur, and he whimpered and huddled closer.

"In the head." Mrs. D'Angelo lifted the hair on the side of her head and showed Jacqueline the terrible scar.

Jacqueline covered her lips in horror. "How did you live through *that*?"

Mrs. D'Angelo shrugged. "It wasn't my time. But I have not seen anything but darkness since."

Jacqueline looked back to Caleb, helpless in the face of such fatalism.

He nodded, accepting her compassion and appreciating it.

Mrs. D'Angelo continued. "That's why your mother didn't want you to visit me. She didn't want you exposed to the ugliness of life. She feared it, so much, and she hoped she could protect you for always."

"And of course, she couldn't protect you at all," Caleb said.

"She was your true mother, for she worried, but no mother can protect her child from every bump and bruise. It's not good to try, although when I attempted to tell her that, she would not listen." Mrs. D'Angelo *tsk*ed in sorrow.

"No. She never listened," Jacqueline said faintly.

Caleb watched Jacqueline and his mother, and continued his story in a monotone. "The thugs set the house afire. I came out of hiding and dragged Mama outside. They would have killed us then, but Zusane had arrived with all her bodyguards around her, and those *delinquenti* didn't have the guts to go up against armed men who knew how to defend themselves."

"She saved us, your mother, and three weeks later, when I woke in the hospital, the first thing Caleb told me was that he would be Zusane's bodyguard someday." Mrs. D'Angelo looked fierce. "To my eternal pride, he kept his promise."

"Zusane paid for Mama's medical treatment. She brought us to New York City. She eased our introduction to American life, paid for my education, and employed me." Caleb laughed as if amused at himself. "All she demanded in return was my total devotion."

"Which you gave freely." Jacqueline had seen it with her own eyes.

"Jacqueline, if you owed someone such a debt, would you not give her what she wished?" he asked.

She couldn't meet his eyes, and that sense of grief swelled once more. "I do owe her such a debt."

"You owe her what every child owes her parents—your life—and you are like every other child in the world—you are ungrateful." Jacqueline jumped when Mrs. D'Angelo lightly slapped the back of Caleb's head.

"Ma, I'm devoted to you, too," he protested.

"You don't do what I want." She returned to her cooking, slamming a black cast-iron skillet onto the stove. "All I ask is that you marry and give me grand-children to lighten the burden of my old age. And do you? No."

Jacqueline slouched down in her chair to avoid the fight. She found both dogs pressed close against her legs, trying to dodge trouble.

"I want you to marry Mr. Davies down the block to lighten the burden of your old age, and you won't listen to me, either," Caleb said.

"I don't have to listen to you." Mrs. D'Angelo sprayed her pan with olive oil and poured in the egg mixture. "I am your mother. You are nothing but my boy! Now set the table and pour the wine. The lunch will be ready in a few minutes."

Chapter 30

After lunch, Caleb finished loading the dishwasher and wiped his hands. "Ma, you've got a headache. You should rest."

Jacqueline looked between mother and son, startled at his insight.

"Since she was shot, she gets headaches," he explained to her, but he never took his gaze off his mother.

"It's a foolish weakness." Mrs. D'Angelo was seated at the table, her blank gaze on her hands in her lap. "I hate it. It makes me feel old."

"I think you should instead feel as if you survived a terrible crime and the payment is your blindness and a few inconvenient headaches," Jacqueline said gently. "Not so great a price to pay, considering, is it?"

"You are a very smart girl." Mrs. D'Angelo raised

her head and looked her way. "Of course, when you came to visit me with my son, I knew you were."

Caleb came to his mother's side and helped her to her feet. "Besides, if you rest, then I am free to make love to Jacqueline."

"Caleb!" Jacqueline had been worried she would say the wrong thing. Instead, Caleb had put his foot in it.

But obviously all the clichés she'd ever heard about Italian sons were true. He really could do no wrong, for Mrs. D'Angelo shook her finger at him—but she said indulgently, "You are incorrigible."

"Ma, I'm just trying to get going on those grandchildren you want."

Jacqueline choked.

Mrs. D'Angelo looked concerned. "Jacqueline, are you well?"

"Fine." Or she would be after she throttled him. "I'm fine."

Mrs. D'Angelo smiled as she left the room, her son on her arm, Lizzie and Ritter on her heels.

Jacqueline heard the murmur of their voices, the click of a door, and Caleb appeared in the kitchen again. Holding out his hand to her, he said, "Come and see my apartment."

So.

She rose slowly from her chair and walked toward him.

Did he mean it literally? That he was going to make love to her? He had told her he wouldn't until she asked him, and so far, he'd kept his promise. Did he mean to forget it today?

She took his hand.

Would she mind if he did?

"Children? We are going to create children?" She lifted her eyebrows.

"Possibly not now. There's too much danger for us both, and a child needs both parents." He led her into the entryway and up a narrow flight of stairs. "Don't you agree?"

She had to admire the way he manipulated the conversation. What was she supposed to say—no? Of course she thought a child needed both parents, and she knew that after his own personal tragedy, he thought so, too.

But as to whether the two of them should even be considering having kids together . . . They didn't even have an established relationship.

But they knew more about each other than most couples who had lived together for ten years, because they'd known each other for so long, and because they'd gone through so many tough times together.

They also had too many unresolved issues.

But danger pressed them all around, and their time together might be short.

Points and counterpoints tumbled in her head, and

a quick glance at him didn't help at all. He seemed to be sure of himself and in control. Regrettably, he always seemed that way.

He frustrated her with his elusiveness and yet, at the same time, he excited her merely by holding her hand, and when he opened the door at the top of the stairs and ushered her inside, her heart started a slow, steady thumping.

He had told his mother they would make love, and for all their differences, in that one matter, they were in total accord. Together, they went up in pure flame.

Jacqueline took a breath and asked, "Do you have the whole building?" Innocuous conversation seemed like a good idea.

"Yes. If it was up to Ma, she'd rent out an apartment, but I've got a thing about intruders not coming into the house—"

"I get that."

"Not to mention I can have the whole second floor as my place."

Jacqueline looked at him.

"I know. I know. I'm a grown man, and I'm living with my mother. But I'm always traveling with Zusane—or I was—so Ma is here to watch my stuff." He waved his arm around. "Four rooms: kitchen, living, bath, bedroom. It used to be a three-bedroom walk-up, but when I moved in I tore out walls to enlarge the spaces."

"Nice." The apartment *was* a lot more open than was usual in New York. Whoever had decorated his mother's floor had done the decorating here, too. The walls were pale yellow, and he had the same terra-cotta tile on the floor, with contemporary area rugs of black and gray carved wool.

He saw her glancing around, and said, "Go ahead. Check it out."

She was too mesmerized at being in his home to pretend anything but fascination, so she meandered from room to room. His home wasn't fussy, but then, she didn't expect it to be. He had tables in his living room with nothing on them except a well-read paperback and a lamp. He had a kitchen full of the best appliances, still in pristine condition. He had photos framed on his fireplace. A young man who looked like him—his brother. A wedding photo of his mother and his father. A photo of Zusane, standing in front of the federal courthouse, her arm around a teenage Caleb.

Jacqueline's breath caught as she looked at that photo. Zusane looked so proud of him, proud as she had never been of Jacqueline, and for a moment, a gray sadness swallowed Jacqueline's anticipation.

"Do you want something to drink?" he called from the kitchen. "Wine? Beer? Water?"

She fought back the sorrow. Later. She would deal with it later. She called, "I'd better stick with water. One glass of wine at lunch and I'm ready for a nap."

Then, to her chagrin, she blushed again. Apparently even mentioning sleep when he was around was too erotic for her libido.

She ducked into his bathroom and found it stark, without a single brush or shaver on the counter. Only a bottle of shampoo marred the pristine expanse of his shower.

The toilet seat was up.

"This is really a guy's lair." She walked into the bedroom to find him stretched out in the middle of the bed, his arms wrapped under his head, two bottles of water open beside him on the nightstand. She halted in surprise. "Wow."

"All the women say that when they see me." He followed her gaze, and sighed. "I suppose you're talking about the bed."

The tall four-poster was the antithesis of the rest of the apartment. It filled the room. It was gorgeous, elaborate, huge and . . . "Nice. Antique?" She traced the reeding in the footposts. An elaborately carved basket of fruit accented the tall, curvaceous mahogany headboard.

"I saw it in the window of a shop in Manhattan on West Twenty-fourth. It reminded me of my parents' bed in Sicily. So I bought it."

"You didn't think about it? You immediately bought it?"

"When I see what I want, I know it, and I don't

waste time acquiring it." He was looking at her—and she didn't think he was talking about the bed.

She wandered closer to the head of the bed.

He looked good. Long and lean, muscled and competent. A man she had known all her life. A man she could depend on.

A man who was dangerous to his enemies—and hers.

Her hand hovered over his chest. Should she give in to temptation and touch him? Should she kiss him, hold him, take him into her body . . . ?

He caught her wrist and opened her injured hand toward him. Her leather glove and the gauze bandage covered the slash on her palm, and he touched it lightly. "How does it feel?"

Caught off guard, she stammered, "G-good. Mostly good. Martha is very competent."

"Then why do you keep cradling it in your arm? What are you afraid of? What do you think happened when your tattoo was slashed?"

She stumbled into an explanation. "It's been a part of me, part of my whole self. The eye, and the expectation that I could, *would*, see the future. If that's gone . . ." And how did he know she was afraid of *this* when so many other terrifying issues loomed before them?

"My mother lost her sight at the apex of her life. It broke my heart, and at the same time, I was so grateful to have her alive. That's why when you didn't want to *see*"—Caleb gently stroked his hand across her gloved palm—"you made me insane. To refuse the gift of foresight seemed foolish and perhaps . . . a sin. Then yesterday you took the plunge into a vision, and you were hurt." Impulsively, he yanked her onto the bed and into his arms.

She caught her breath as he rolled her onto her back, trapped her between his arms, and looked into her eyes.

He spoke earnestly. "The mark on your palm doesn't matter. What it says doesn't matter. What Zusane wanted from you doesn't matter. What matters to me is that you do what you want." At her surprise, he smiled that half smile that enchanted her so much. "I will admit—I want you to want to do *it*, whatever *it* is, with me at your side."

Being here with Caleb, feeling his heat, smelling his scent, hearing those words from him, made her realize how long she had known him and how much he had meant to her.

"Will you live with me here?" he asked. "Will you make my mother happy and marry me?"

He had rescued Jacqueline, taught her to fight, taught her to love, taught her to hate. . . . Even when they were apart, he had been the center of her life. Now, two years later, they were together, in danger . . . and he was the only man she had ever wanted. "Yes."

"Yes?" He gave a bark of laughter. "Yes—what do you mean, yes?"

"Yes, I would like to live with you here. Yes, I would like to marry you." Jacqueline had never meant anything so much in her life.

He sagged with relief.

She added sternly, "Although not for your mother, but for us."

Resting his forehead against hers, he said, "No, you're right. Don't stay with me for my mother. Stay for us. Because I've loved you for so long, and now, at last, you'll be mine and I can be truly happy."

"So." Reaching up, she wrapped her arms around his shoulders. "Please."

His smile blossomed, became whole. "Please what?"

Oh, two could play that game. "Please undress me. Please let me undress you. Please kiss my lips, my breasts, my belly. Please let me turn you over and kiss your spine, your shoulders, your extremely fine butt. Please go down on me. Please let me go down on you."

He jerked as if he'd been hit with an electrical current, then froze, immobile in the struggle to remain in control.

"Please make love to me. Please do it now." She slid her hands up from his shoulders to the back of his neck, and slipped her fingers into his hair. "Caleb, please, do it without restraint."

His lips barely moved as he spoke. "You don't know what you're asking."

"Yes, I do. I want you as wild as you were the first

time we made love. I want you out of control and savage. I want you—"

He vaulted off the bed, and for a moment, she thought he was going to leave.

Instead he ripped off his clothes, donned a condom, and was back beside her in thirty seconds. Another thirty seconds, and her clothes had been tossed aside, and she was naked and captive in the arms of a man as savage as she had demanded. He pressed her back on the pillows. Holding her head in his hands, he kissed her, probing her mouth insistently, dragging the air from her lungs and replacing it with his own. He bit her earlobe, swirled his tongue around the whorls, and bit her earlobe again.

He had taken the electrical current and directed it at her, for each lap of his tongue, each nip of his teeth, shot a bolt of pure passion through her nerves to her brain, her nipples, her clit.

And all the while, he held her down with his naked body, pressing her into the bed, letting her feel his weight and the heat of his erection. He pressed his penis between her legs, sliding it up and down in the dampness between her nether lips, teasing her, dampening himself as her body responded. He dominated her, and everything about him made her realize that this loving would be like nothing they'd ever experienced.

He nuzzled her breasts, exploring them with his mouth, finding each nerve and heightening each sensation with a gentle suction that became an insistent suckling.

Sounds began to break from her, moans of delight and insidious fear. Insidious, because she wondered if she would survive this, or if she would break apart from the constant and ever-heightening pleasure. She twisted, pushed at him, trying to escape, and he responded by clasping her wrists and clamping her hands close to her sides.

And he kissed her breasts again. And her belly. And then, using his knees to keep her legs wide apart, he sank his tongue into her.

Too much. It was too much. She went mad from anticipation, with need.

He tasted her, over and over, keeping her on the edge of orgasm, but not allowing her more pleasure than he could take himself. It was torture of the cruelest kind, and all she could think was, *Higher. Please. A little higher. If you would touch me there, just once—*

But he didn't. Instead he rose above her so that only their groins touched and, still holding her hands, he pressed his erection into her . . . slowly. So freaking slowly.

If he would just do it.

But he didn't. He eased inside her, filled her, taking care not to press against her clit. Clearly, he knew what she wanted. Clearly, he intended to drive her mad before she got it.

She tried to get her feet under her, to lift herself onto him.

He controlled her with his hands and elbows, and all the while, he watched her with a heated gaze that taunted her for wanting what he now offered.

"Please," she whispered. "Please. Caleb, I need . . . please."

"What do you need?" He eased closer. "This?"

"More."

"Honey, how much more can you take?" He slid closer. "This?"

His organ pressed so deep inside, he touched her womb. It stretched her, made her gasp and clutch handfuls of the sheet. It made her crave . . . "More. Faster. Caleb, for the love of God . . ." She was close, so close. . . .

"Ah. You want this." He pulled out almost all the way. He braced himself, and she waited, trembling. Then, hard and fast and without pity, he thrust in.

She screamed as the long-awaited climax hit her in a wave, tumbling her over and over, taking her thoughts, her words, her mind.

She could hear him laughing as he thrust again, his mastery complete.

But his grip on her thighs slipped, and instinctively she wrapped her legs around his hips and met that thrust.

Suddenly, he wasn't laughing. He wasn't moving. His eyes closed and his face grew taut.

She called the shots now. She tightened her muscles, stroking him on the inside, making him feel her on his every inch. She lifted herself to him, grinding herself against his pelvis.

When he opened his eyes, the Caleb she knew was gone. In his place was the savage she'd demanded. He let her hands go and, lifting her buttocks in his palms, he propelled himself into her with a rhythm and a power she had only imagined.

She dragged him down to her, exulting in the flex of his muscles beneath her fingers.

He was unrelenting.

She was formidable.

Between them, they were invincible.

Her climax built, growing with each movement, each groan, with the pure knowledge that she had driven him as mad as he had driven her.

A flush suffused his forehead and lust toughened his face. Remorselessly, he began to come, thrusting harder, faster.

Her whole body clenched around him. In a frenzy of hunger, she clawed at him, wordlessly commanding he give her everything within him.

And he did, pressing his whole body against her, into her, making her know his possession.

They hung, suspended on a precipice of ecstasy.

Then gradually, the frenzy that had gripped them rolled on.

He collapsed onto her.

She tasted his shoulder and savored his salty skin. She smelled desire rolling off him, and knew he was hers.

Whatever worries she had had before they started, they were gone now. She was absolutely boneless with depleted passion.

Turning his head toward hers, he looked at her through narrowly slitted eyes. "Are you all right?"

"I'm magnificent."

"Yes. You are." Groaning, he eased himself away from her. He sat, his chest heaving with each breath, and scrutinized her as if he wanted to memorize each inch of skin. "Jacqueline."

"Yes." Would he want to do it again?

"I've got to go."

"What?" She clutched at his arm. Now? He wanted to leave? Was he crazy? "Go where?"

"Back to Irving's." He kissed her hand, put it on her stomach, and climbed off the bed.

"To hell with Irving!"

Caleb paid no attention. "I want you to stay here. Take a nap. Read a book. Check on my mother, if you feel the urge. I gave her her medication, and she'll sleep for several hours, but even if she feels rocky, she'll get up and try to make a pie or something to prove she can."

"I'll check on her. I don't mind. You know that." She sat up and pushed the hair off her forehead. "But why do you have to go back?" It had better be an incredibly good reason.

"Because someone tried to kill you, and I'm going to look into it."

Chapter 31

———◆———

I'm going to look into it. The phrase echoed in Jacqueline's mind. *I'm going to look into it.*

She'd heard that phrase somewhere before.

If he looks into it, he will die. If he looks into it, he will die.

The words gained meaning, gained strength, grew larger and louder, like a snowball rolling downhill.

If he looks into it, he will die. If he looks into it, he will die.

"You can't!" She scrambled into a sitting position, resting on her heels among the pillows. "If you look into it, you'll die."

He straightened, his clothes in his hands, and stared at her. "If I look into . . . What are you talking about?"

"Yesterday. After the vision. And today. At the meeting." Her hands shook as she recalled, "I heard a voice in my head repeating over and over, *If he looks into it, he will die. If he looks into it, he will die.* I thought . . . The crystal ball was there, and I thought it was a warning not to let anyone look into the globe. But that's not it. It's you. You're not supposed to look into this crime!"

"You heard a voice in your head?" He disappeared into the bathroom. She heard water running, and when he came back, his face had been washed, and his hair was damp and combed. "Why didn't you tell me?"

"We were busy. I was hurt. You were gone. There were a lot of things going on." She could see he wasn't buying it. He was still moving around the room, getting ready. "Because that's crazy. I have a vision and then I hear a voice in my head. That's not normal. Mother never heard voices."

"How would you know? You never talked to her about her visions." Maybe he didn't mean for her to hear it, but his voice held a hint of reproach.

And it hurt. "Then maybe I should ask you. Did Mother ever hear voices?"

"I don't think so." He rummaged in his closet, pulled out a pair of clean jeans and pulled them on, and donned a crisp, white dress shirt. "Whose voice did it sound like?"

"I don't know. It was just your standard disembodied voice." She was sarcastic.

He was serious. "Was it a woman's voice?"

"I don't . . . think so." She tried to put a gender on

it, and shook her head. "I don't know. It was simply this . . . voice of doom." Remembering his report to Irving about the woman who spoke to him from afar, she followed his reasoning. "You think this is someone talking in my brain."

"Yes. Making mischief, scaring you to death." Sitting in a chair, he pulled on ankle-high leather boots. "Who was close by when it happened?"

"Everyone. Pretty much . . . everyone." Remembering, she shook her head. "Well, no. Today, Samuel wasn't there. But we don't know whether proximity matters, do we? Whoever it is—if it is someone—might be able to project clear across the universe."

"That's true. And whether someone's speaking in your brain, or the words are a prediction of the future, doesn't matter, either." Caleb stood and adjusted his belt. "I've still got to go back to Irving's and figure out the identity of our bad seed before something awful happens."

"What could be worse than you losing your life?" she asked urgently.

"A lot of things. Whoever it is could scare the Chosen so much, everyone runs screaming into the streets for the Others to pick off at their leisure. Or he could blow up Irving's house. Or he could come for you again." He put a knee on the bed and adjusted the covers across her lap, touched her lips with his thumb, then used it to circle her nipple.

Putting her hand over his, she pressed it to her breast. She wasn't proud of the tactic, but she wasn't above using sex to keep him with her. "You can't. Don't you see? Maybe it is your woman with the scarred nose talking in my head, trying to make me crazy. But what if it's a hangover from my vision? What if I know what's going to happen to you because I'm a psychic? You've been bugging me all these years to become the seer I was born to be. Could you at least respect my gift as much as you respected my mother's?"

"I *do* respect your gift. How could I not?" He drew his hand away. Reluctantly, but he did. "I saw what you can do—and what the vision can do to you. What you have is more powerful than Zusane ever knew, and if you never use it again, it will be fine with me."

She looked at her bandaged hand, and muttered, "But I might have to."

"Exactly. You have a job to do. As I have a job to do."

He frustrated her so much, she wanted to scream. "You were always asking Zusane's advice, giving her lip service about her marvelous talent. If she told you to stay, you would have stayed!"

"I showed her respect, yes." His voice was level; his eyes grew cold. "And paid lip service. Because she *needed* it."

"And I don't?"

"No. You don't need false flattery. You're fine."

"My mother was fine, too."

"No. She wasn't. Zusane was broken."

"Broken? What do you mean, broken? She was glamorous. She was desired. She was completely, horribly sure of herself." Unlike Jacqueline, who spent her gawky adolescence being compared to Zusane, and not favorably.

"She was one of the Abandoned Ones." When Jacqueline would have pointed out the obvious, he held up one finger. "Not like you. Nobody rescued Zusane from the Dumpster. She had to rescue herself." He strapped a leather holster across his chest, then extracted a pistol from the drawer, loaded it, and slipped it into place. "She grew up in Eastern Europe, in Ruyshvania—"

"No, she didn't!"

"During the worst of the Communist years. People there were afraid—the old superstitions hold them tight—and the family, or the village, or whoever, tossed her as an infant in a ditch in the middle of winter. Maybe because they were starving and couldn't support another baby. Maybe because she was marked with an eye on the back of her shoulder. She grew up in an orphanage, and they abused her for the mark, and when the woman who ran the orphanage realized Zusane had visions, she sold her."

"Did she tell you all this?" Jacqueline swallowed to subdue her nausea. "Because it isn't what she told me.

She said she was the daughter of a dispossessed Hungarian noble."

"She never lived in Hungary." He pulled a series of knives from the center drawer of his dresser and lined them up on the flat surface.

What he said horrified her. What he was doing horrified her. "I don't believe you." The idea of Zusane, pampered and cherished by her Hungarian nursemaid, by her servants and her father, was too firmly implanted in Jacqueline's mind to be easily expelled.

"She lived in Ruyshvania," Caleb repeated. "The dictator Czajkowski bought her, and he possessed her in every way. He dressed her in beautiful clothes, he trained her in elegant manners and he kept her by his side—and when she didn't have visions on his command, he beat her until she lost the child she had conceived."

Jacqueline flinched at the ugly pictures in her mind.

"Why do you think she never had children of her own?"

Because she didn't want to ruin her figure. That was what Jacqueline had always thought.

"She almost died, and she never was able to conceive again."

Jacqueline didn't believe him. She couldn't believe him. "Hungary . . ."

"At the age of seventeen, she met one of Czajkowski's guests, a wealthy, powerful man. She put herself into his bed, she used her arts to convince him to take her to the US, and when he begged, she married him."

"For the money."

"Of course for the money." Caleb understood if she didn't. "She needed the money to create the persona of Zusane. Glamorous Zusane, elegant Zusane, wealthy Zusane. Never again—poor, abused Zusane."

No. *No.* "How do you know this?"

He placed a four-inch throwing knife into his boot. He slipped on a sports jacket, checked to make sure no bulge betrayed the pistol and holster. "I wanted to know the truth, so I followed the trail back to Ruyshvania."

Caleb painted a different Zusane in her mind. Self-indulgent, yes. Spoiled, yes. Shallow . . . yes, but because she couldn't bear to plumb the depths of her pain.

"You said she adopted you because she wanted a clone. In its way, it's true. She rescued you because she saw herself and she couldn't bear to know another child would suffer as she had suffered." Caleb was ruthless as he recited his facts. "She wasn't a good mother. Motherhood is suffering for your child, and she never wanted to suffer again. But she loved you."

"I know." Jacqueline did know. She had always known.

He should have stopped talking. But apparently, he'd been waiting to say this for a long, long time. "You were constantly angry because your mother didn't act like a mother; she acted like a diva. By making me your bodyguard, she acted in your best interests—because she was your mother."

He was stubborn. So stubborn. Despite Jacqueline's wishes, despite the danger, he was leaving her. Leaving her after he'd asked her to marry him, after she'd admitted she loved him. He didn't love her, or he wouldn't go. "Okay," she said. "But are you sure she didn't act in the best interests of the Gypsy Travel Agency? Because of the mark on my hand?"

He was dressed. He was ready to go. And he put his hands on his hips with an impatience so manifest, he made her pull the covers up to hide her body. "Are you ever going to grow up?"

He had showed her a view of herself she didn't like, and despite her pleas, he had prepared for a battle from which he might never return. In a rage of shame and fear, she lashed out. "Maybe you *are* too old for me."

"Maybe I am." He slipped a second throwing knife up his sleeve. "But I'm still going to find the son of a bitch who tried to kill you and take care of him."

In as nasty a tone as she could dredge up, she said, "Because my mother told you to."

Leaning over her, he pinched her chin. "Because your mother told me to."

She jerked her head away and watched him walk out of the room. She waited, wanting him to return so she could take it back, so she could explain she didn't mean it.

Then the outer door slammed behind him—and she was alone.

He was gone. To his death? She didn't need a vision, or words in her head, to understand the possible consequences of their acrimonious parting. She might never see him again.

He was gone . . . as her mother was gone.

The memory of yesterday's catastrophe rolled over her again. The smoke, the fear, the screams . . . her mother's calm face and her hand shoving Jacqueline out of the plane and into nothingness. The mere memory made Jacqueline's heart pound and her lungs hurt, and finally, the grief that had haunted her like a ghost within her consciousness slammed into her with the force of a hurricane.

Her keen of sorrow was deep, wrenching, painful. She crumpled onto the bed, pressed her face into the pillow to muffle her sounds of anguish. She cried for Caleb. She cried for her dreams that had so briefly gleamed like gold and now crumbled into dust.

But mostly she cried for her mother.

She cried because Zusane was gone, and Jacqueline would never again see her come in, dripping with diamonds, glittering with sequins, all beauty and glamour. She'd never hear that rich, accented voice nagging her about finishing school and accepting her destiny. She would never have the chance to tell her how much she loved her laughter, the way she always saw the humor in herself. She couldn't explain how much she admired Zusane's generosity, giving away money and jewels with abandon to anyone in need.

As wave after wave of misery swept over Jacqueline, she pulled her knees to her chest and curled into the fetal position. She rocked back and forth, seeking relief from the sobs that ripped at her throat, from the pain that tore at her heart, but nothing could help her now.

When she was a child, she had adored Zusane's glamour, missed her when she was gone, loved those special moments when Zusane told her about her visions and assured her that someday, she'd have visions, too.

Then she became a gawky adolescent, too tall and too blond, and Zusane became an embarrassment. Worse, in her secret heart of hearts, Jacqueline hated the comparisons between them. She had known she could never be as sensational, as enchanting, as exotic as Zusane.

Jacqueline had been jealous.

So she told Zusane she was a lousy mother. She told Zusane she disapproved of her husband-hunting and her mad partying. She told her she was superficial and silly.

As if any of that mattered, because Caleb was right. Mrs. D'Angelo was right. Zusane had saved Jacqueline, she had done her best to raise her, and all Jacqueline's resentment was just crap.

In the end, Jacqueline knew the truth—Zusane had pushed her out of that plane to save her life, to save her from the devil himself. And Jacqueline knew, for that act of maternal defense, the devil had made sure Zusane suffered horribly, and died alone.

Oh, God. The torment was more than she could bear, because there was nothing to be done. Zusane was *dead*. Jacqueline was out of chances to tell her the most important thing. She could never tell her how much she loved her. "But I did, Mama," she whispered into the pillow. "I did."

Her own insecurity had hurt Zusane and chased Caleb away.

So what could she do?

She wasn't dumb enough to follow Caleb. If the Others were out there, they would take her at once.

But she couldn't lie here crying while he walked into danger. She'd already failed at her relationship with her mother. She would not do the same with him.

Zusane would tell her to sit up and stop crying.

So she did. She scrubbed at her face with a handful of tissues. She got off the bed and stood there, naked, unsteady, still hiccuping from the tears.

She thought hard, and she knew what she had to do.

No matter what the cost, no matter how much she feared the pain, she had to invite a vision.

She had to find out who had betrayed the Gypsy Travel Agency.

Chapter 32

Never before had Caleb gone to Irving's house prepared for an ambush, but he did so now. Two days ago, the explosion had ripped the Gypsy Travel Agency from its foundations. Yesterday, Jacqueline had had a vision and been attacked. Today . . . he was going to find out what snake lurked behind a mask of friendship.

He was pretty sure he already knew who it was, and if he was right, before long, the nasty little traitor would return—and finish the job he'd started two days ago.

Caleb rang the doorbell, and when McKenna opened the door, he walked right in.

"Good to see you again, sir." McKenna tried to take his sport coat.

Caleb shook his head. "Anything happening?"

"It's been quiet since you left." McKenna peered out onto the street. "Miss Vargha is not with you?"

"No." That was all the information he would give about her. "Has Samuel Faa returned?"

"If you had come a minute earlier, you would have met him on the doorstep. He said he was going to his room and then—" McKenna found he was talking to Caleb's back, and gave a *humph* of disgust. "Young people. No manners."

Caleb ran lightly toward the stairs, caught a movement by the library, and changed courses.

And there he was, Samuel Faa, standing in the shadows, looking in the well-lit library as if he couldn't quite decide where to set his bomb. At the last minute, Samuel caught a glimpse of Caleb. But it was too late.

Grabbing his collar, Caleb slammed him against the wall. "You son of a bitch. I can't believe you had the guts to come back here. You tried to kill Jacqueline."

"What the hell are you talking about?" Samuel twisted, freed himself, and thumped Caleb against the opposite wall. "I never hurt your girlfriend."

Caleb jumped at him and grabbed again, and this time when Samuel feinted, Caleb grabbed his wrist, twisted his arm behind his back, and spoke in his ear. "You went up to the attic where she was having that vision and smashed her with the crystal ball."

Samuel stood very, very still, but his voice was dark and pissed off. "Why the hell would I bother to do that? I control minds. If I'd wanted to hurt her, I would have had her fling herself down the stairs."

"Likely story." Caleb was right about this.

Wasn't he?

"It's what I do," Samuel said. "It's my gift and I'm goddamned good with it. Ask Irving or Martha if you're in doubt. Hell, ask my clients. It's the reason I'm such a highly paid lawyer."

"Not ethical, but highly paid."

"I'm ethical when the occasion calls for it. When I know my client is innocent while their client is guilty as hell." Samuel muttered as if he wanted to keep it quiet. "I've got a thing about not letting murderers go free."

Was Samuel messing with Caleb's mind right now? Because Samuel had implanted doubt, enough doubt that Caleb loosened his grip.

"Mind control is the reason I got my ass convicted of improper practice." Bitterly, Samuel added, "That damned judge . . . I'd like to know how he knew."

Yet Caleb had been trained by the Gypsy Travel Agency to detect the presence of someone else poking around in his thoughts, and right now, he was pretty sure he was alone in his brain. "If the Gypsy Travel Agency wanted you, they probably helped him figure it out. They weren't immune to a few unethical practices themselves."

"I wondered. Those *bastards*."

All right. Samuel really wasn't bothering to mess with Caleb. He was too caught up in his own resentment. "Why did you leave the house yesterday?"

"Because I am fucking tired of sitting around doing nothing but being cautious and talking about what we should do. I went out there and *did* something."

"What?"

"Let go of my arm and I'll tell you."

"Why don't I tighten my grip and you'll sing every word?"

Samuel struggled and snarled like a tiger with his tail in a trap. "You really think you're in charge here, don't you?"

"No." Caleb ratcheted up Samuel's pain by a few degrees. "But I think I'm in charge of making sure Jacqueline is safe, and I hate knowing I've done a bad job."

Samuel gave up, stood very still, and recited the facts. "I made contact with one of my lawyer friends who's into investment properties in New York City. I told him I wanted to buy the site where the Gypsy Travel Agency had stood, and asked him who the heirs were."

Good idea. Astonished, Caleb let him go. "What was the answer?"

Samuel straightened his tie and turned to face him. "Right now they've got no bodies, because the bomb—which the bomb squad is saying must be a gas leak and the fire department is saying must be a new kind of explosive—vaporized everything inside and outside the building. But the list of beneficiaries goes on forever, and there are only two my buddy knows are alive. One is that guy in a coma, Gary White. The other . . . is Irving."

"Irving? Is the heir? I don't want to hear that."

"Look. I don't care about Irving one way or the other—I haven't known him long enough—but it doesn't make sense that he would do it. The first thing the lawyers have to do is provide death certificates for everyone who is in front of Irving on the beneficiary list, and unless the old man has discovered the Fountain of Youth—and with these people, I'm not saying that's impossible—he's going to be dead long before he comes into the inheritance." Samuel had obviously considered all the angles.

Coldly, Caleb turned over the possibility in his mind. "I've questioned Irving's morals"—today, in fact—"and I know sometimes guys have to have more, whether it makes sense or not."

"I'm a lawyer. No one knows that better than me. But Irving hasn't got any heirs, and he doesn't seem to be banging anyone, so who would it be for?"

"Who, indeed?" Irving stepped out of the shadows at the end of the corridor. "No, gentlemen, I'm not your man. But I'm willing to bet Samuel got the list of beneficiaries out of his friend."

"I did," Samuel admitted.

"I have a list, too, and it's supposed to be the most current." Irving looked both grim and angry. "Shall we compare the names?"

"God, yes," Samuel said with harsh delight. "That might throw some light on our perpetrator."

The two men started down the corridor.

Caleb didn't budge. "I don't give a damn about the list. I want to know who picked up the crystal ball and smashed Jacqueline's skull with it."

Irving and Samuel halted, swiveled.

"You know that for a fact?" Samuel asked.

"Yes." Caleb had no intention of explaining the crystal ball had been the tattletale.

"Someone in this house?" Irving clarified.

Caleb met his eyes. "You set the enchantment, Irving. I'd say by your swift appearance you know who's coming and going, and when. So has a stranger sneaked in?"

"No," Irving said.

"Then yes, someone in this house." Caleb met his eyes. "If it wasn't Samuel, then who?"

"We could ask our second psychic if he knows," Irving said.

"Our second psychic?" Samuel stepped back. "I wasn't gone that long. Who the hell are you talking about?"

An ugly suspicion stirred in Caleb's gut.

"Tyler Settles. Didn't you know?" Irving stared hard at Samuel. "That's his gift."

"No, it's not." Samuel couldn't have sounded more scornful. "He controls minds, like me. I saw him manipulate Zusane."

A quick glance at Irving proved his chin had sagged and his eyes were round.

Okay. This was a surprise to him, too. Caleb didn't feel quite so stupid. "When you saw him do it, why didn't you say something?"

"Because I didn't want to be in that silly chalk circle. I didn't want to be part of the Gypsy Travel Agency. I didn't want anything to do with the whole stupid setup, and I figured the less I got involved, the better off I was." Samuel was frank to a fault.

"And now?" Irving asked.

"Now I'm stuck." A hot flush settled on Samuel's cheekbones. "For more reasons than one."

"Yeah. Women." Caleb could relate.

"Settles can mind-speak, too," Samuel said. "When he was testing me out to see which of us was stronger, he tried to make me think his thoughts were mine. I let him know that didn't work on me, and he backed off."

"Guys, have you got a minute?" Charisma stood in the door of the library. She'd obviously been listening for a while. "I've got something you'll be interested to see."

Caleb shifted impatiently.

She looked right at him. "Really. You need to know this."

He followed the other two men into the library.

She shut the door behind them. "Over there on the computer. When Tyler was having his vision, I kept thinking I'd seen something similar before. So I searched YouTube and guess what I found." She clicked the mouse and started the video in motion. "Check out the character actor on this episode of *Grey's Anatomy*."

"It's Tyler." As if his knees could no longer hold him, Irving sank into the desk chair.

"The dialogue's completely different, and he's holding a gun, but . . . Man, that's exactly the same routine," Samuel said.

"Is it." Caleb wasn't asking a question. He was making a threat he intended to keep.

"He's supposedly an epileptic patient who suffers from delusions." Charisma's gaze never left the screen. "In this version, in the end, instead of getting up off the floor on his own steam, he chokes to death on his own tongue."

"We should be so lucky," Irving said.

"I found a video of his faith healing show. He does the same routine there." Leaning forward, she clicked her mouse, brought up another video, and started it playing.

Caleb turned on Irving. "I'm confused. How could you not know what his gift was? I thought the top dudes always knew."

"They did. They do. I did know." Irving blinked as he concentrated. "I remember thinking he was a mind manipulator, but after the explosion, I was in such an uproar, and when he said he was a psychic, I realized I had been wrong."

"He never said that when I was around." Samuel planted his feet. "Or at least not loudly enough that I could hear him."

"Because you were the stronger manipulator and you would have called him on it." Caleb hated knowing he had been criminally unperceptive. "And he waited to have a vision until you were out of the house."

"How could I have been so gullible? I've been trained to recognize fakers." Irving could not have been more chagrined.

"You said it. You were in an uproar of grief and fury." Caleb balanced on the balls of his feet, ready to take action. "Where is he now?"

Irving squarely met his gaze. "He told me he was going out."

"You let him?" Caleb hadn't thought the state of affairs could get any worse. What a bitch to find out he was wrong.

"He had an important mission, so I encouraged him." Irving spoke slowly, his eyes unfocused.

"What important mission?" Charisma asked.

It took a minute for Irving to snap to the realization he'd been manipulated again. "I don't remember."

"When did he leave?"

"He walked out of the meeting right after you did."

"I'll just bet he did. Search his room. See what you can find. A computer, a GPS, a cell phone. Something he can communicate with. Something that lets them know where we are. I'm going to see if I can locate *him*." Caleb turned to the door.

"It's a big city," Samuel warned.

"I think I know where he is," Caleb said. "And I'm going to make him sorry he ever tried to hurt me and mine."

Chapter 33

Head down, Jacqueline walked with jerky determination up the stairs to Mrs. D'Angelo's attic,
and all the while fear buzzed like a thousand bees in
her head.

She shouldn't be here.

She was trespassing.

Mrs. D'Angelo wouldn't like it.

Caleb would be furious.

She could have a vision and be hurt.

She wiped a sheen of sweat from her forehead, and
with a trembling hand opened the door to the attic. She
stepped inside and tried to focus on something besides
her fear.

Mrs. D'Angelo's attic was the polar opposite of
Irving's—small, cramped, with tiny windows and a

low ceiling, stuffed with trunks and hung with old clothes and more of the inevitable lace curtains.

Jacqueline liked it. It felt cozy. Lived in. And without the spooky undertones of Irving's stark space. If only she didn't have to have a vision up here.

But second thoughts were useless. She would do what she had to do. She *would*. For Caleb.

The thought of him steadied her. Caleb wouldn't be having second thoughts. Caleb wouldn't be afraid. He always did what had to be done. The memory of his bravery pushed her forward. Shutting the door behind her, she looked around, and realized—she was too new in the vision business to know how to make it work. What if she needed the crystal ball to induce a vision? What if she had to be in Irving's attic?

Panic choked her . . . and a shameful relief.

Coward. She was such a *coward*.

Then she stiffened her spine. If pain and death were the price she had to pay to invite a vision, she would pay. She *owed* Caleb all the help she could give him. If anything happened to him—no. She wouldn't let it.

Spying an artist's easel and a collection of drawings on the wall, she hurried over to see a lineup of crayon works with Caleb's name scrawled in the corner of each one. Some of the pictures made her feel his passions—the young boy Caleb drew fire engines, firemen, big buildings, taxis, all the things he saw in his new world. Some made her feel his sorrow: He drew pictures of his father and mother, of his brother and himself, of a cottage overlooking the sea, and finally, of fire and his mother's blind brown eyes.

Jacqueline stared at that one, stared hard, imprinting it on her brain. Mrs. D'Angelo had defended her husband and her son, and paid a horrific price in pain and blood and darkness.

Jacqueline touched the place on her forehead and remembered the pain of her concussion. She took a free, clear breath and wanted never again to breathe smoke-filled air. She looked at her bandage-wrapped hand.

It was shaking so hard the stones of Charisma's charms clinked against the silver bracelet.

She tried to close her fingers into a fighting fist.

It hurt. It ached. The stitches pulled.

She felt sick.

She recognized a pencil sketch of Zusane, clad in one of her sequined gowns and sporting a fur around her neck. Picking it up, she whispered, "Were you ever hurt by a vision?"

No. Caleb had told her the truth. Zusane had been hurt by *life*.

Beneath the sketch of Zusane, Jacqueline caught sight of a drawing of herself on the baseball diamond, all gawky legs and stick-straight figure, dressed in a softball uniform and winding up to pitch. He'd perfectly captured that sulky adolescent cast of her mouth and the uncertainty in her eyes. She found one from her graduation, and another of her in a karate gi, scowling with her fists clenched. She located a series of photographs, each with a drawing attached. It took her a minute to realize the pictures had been taken in the last two years, as she traveled across the country trying to escape her fate. Caleb had reproduced them here in the attic at his easel, then hidden them out of sight.

So. It was the truth—he loved her. He had loved her for years.

She had to get this vision started. And there was no use lying to herself. She *did* know how to bring about her vision—she simply had to give herself, wholeheartedly, to the role of seer.

She peeled off her leather gloves, and placed them on the shelf. Finding the edge of the tape, she ripped it and the gauze away. She dropped the handful onto the floor, opened her palm . . . and couldn't bring herself to look.

What if . . . what if she couldn't help Caleb find the traitor? What if the devil had succeeded, and in cutting open her eye, he had destroyed her gift?

Oh, God. She was so afraid.

For so many reasons, she was afraid. Afraid of being cut again, afraid of choking on killing smoke—more than anything, afraid of seeing those glowing blue eyes coming to get her . . . and take her to hell.

Glancing around, she found a round powder compact with a broken hinge. She opened it; it had a mirror. Perfect.

In a corner on a shelf, she found a cheap plastic snow globe. Inside was New York City: the Empire State Building, Times Square, Central Park. Also perfect.

Rummaging around in Caleb's art supplies, she found a stub of green chalk. The chalk circle Martha had made was red and blue, but Martha had suggested a circle; she hadn't specified what kind.

Taking her findings, Jacqueline went to the middle of the attic, bent and used her outstretched arm like a compass to draw a circle around herself. She seated herself in the exact middle. Sitting guaranteed that if something hit her during her vision—like the wing of a plane—she wouldn't fall down, too. She checked the clasp on Charisma's protection bracelet, and took a long breath of preparation.

Man, she hoped all this helped.

She placed the snow globe and the mirror on the floor. Neither was particularly like a crystal ball, but they gave her something on which to concentrate. Unfortunately, sitting here, she felt nothing like a vision approaching. No sepia tint, no sense of skewed time.

Picking up the mirror, she looked at herself.

Caleb's drawings had done a good job of catching the nuances of her features, although she was grateful he couldn't see her now. She touched the still-tear-swollen and blotchy skin around her eyes and nose. She didn't want to explain her tears to him, not because he wouldn't understand, but because another crying bout hovered close to the surface, and she didn't have time to weep again.

Putting down the mirror, she picked up the snow globe. It was a silly thing, a child's souvenir. When she shook it, the snow cascaded over the plastic buildings and the plastic roads, filling them with winter. Whoever had designed the globe hadn't cared a bit about the arrangement of the streets or the placement of New York's landmarks. They had slapped the Statue of Liberty in the East River, Rockefeller Center on Broadway, the Metropolitan Museum of Art in SoHo, and beside that, they'd placed a church, a hospital, and a cemetery. . . .

That dripping sound grew louder and more insistent.

A church? A hospital? A cemetery? Funny things to put in a kids' snow globe. Funny to see that sepia tone creep over the cheap souvenir in her hand . . .

When she looked around, she stood on the quiet, snowy street.

Where had the summer gone? Where had the attic gone?

How had she fallen into the snow globe?

A vision. She was living in her vision.

The experience was fragile. If she struggled, if she panicked, she could break free, and she knew, she *knew*, she would never have to worry about another vision. She would be, at long last, as normal as she had always longed to be.

This was temptation, offered not by the devil, but by her own desires.

She looked up into the dim, gray sky. The snow fell, cold on her face. In the distance, she could hear the honking of cabs and, far away, see the flash of New York billboards. The landmarks matched the ones in the snow globe: a church, a hospital, and a cemetery.

Here the drip . . . drip . . . drip of water was constant and distracting. It was coming from somewhere close, and some instinct told her that if she wanted to *know*, she would have to *look*.

But she didn't want to look at the church. The masonry building was old, crumbling, surrounded by a fence with a sign that said CONDEMNED. The cemetery was attached to it, and its gravestones were uncared for, chipped and covered with moss. Some of the names had worn off, and they surrounded elderly trees that sagged under the burden of the heavy snowfall. A shadow dwelled in that church, a darkness that made her want to run away.

She was afraid. She could break free. She could quit.

With a shudder, she turned to the hospital. The building was small, no more than three stories. The walls were private, pale, and when she looked in the windows, she saw nurses and doctors moving silently through their rounds. She wondered if one of them would have put the stitches in her palm with more skill than Martha, or whether what had been done by the swift slice of a broken bottle could ever be undone.

Opening her hand, she at last forced herself to look.

The glass had slashed the outer line of the eye as well as the pupil and the iris, but Martha had carefully matched them up. The black stitches were small and neat, pulling the skin together. It wasn't Martha's fault that the cut was red. She had disinfected it. She had done everything right, yet when Jacqueline touched the cut lightly with her finger, she felt the heat of an infection.

Her mark would never look the same, but more important—if the devil had truly bent his malice toward her, might she not have lost her hand and her life to this injury?

A tear dripped off her cheek and onto her palm. It splashed, startling her from her terror. She blotted at her nose with the back of her hand, and looked up.

Yes, she was a coward.

So what? She could be afraid, and do this. Fear would not rule her now. For Caleb, for the Chosen, for her mother, she *would* do this.

The weight of years and years of fear and rebellion dropped away, and she walked along the street, armed by fear, yes, but also by determination.

Dear God. If only that dripping would stop. The more she heard it ... the longer it went on ... the scarier it got. It didn't sound like rain, or snow melting off the roof, or even a leaky faucet. The sound was too steady for that; it had a sense of eternity about it. The dripping sounded like ... like water in a cave, the movement of one molecule at a time, forming a drop on the tip of a stalactite, hanging there for an interminable second, then falling to the floor. And then starting again.

Maybe there was a cave under the church. Or one of the old graves had collapsed. Or ... she felt the cool touch of the floor against her back as she slowly lowered herself into a supine position. Or ... maybe she was dead.

Her hands are at her sides; she can't lift them. Her head isn't turned, but straight, the way they placed it. No matter how hard she tries, she cannot speak. She cannot scream. Her eyes are closed. Forever closed. Her friends are gone, abandoning her, uncaring of her loneliness. No one remembers her greatness. She has no air. She has no light.

She is dead.

A voice whispers in her mind. It goes on and on, sympathizing about her absent friends, offering life. . . . All she has to do is betray the ones who have betrayed her.

With a shock, she recognizes the voice; it is the devil.

She's afraid. So afraid. But she can't jump. She can't run.

She is held in place, forever in the dark, listening to the drip . . . drip . . . drip. . . .

Cursing those who had forgotten her.

Listening to the devil's promises.

Promises that sounded less and less like temptation and more and more like justice, and the only way to escape back . . . into life.

Chapter 34

"**D**arling, I know this is an important vision, and I am so proud that you overcame your fear, but I need you to wake up." The voice was familiar. So was the cool touch of a hand on her forehead.

Jacqueline opened her eyes to the cramped, warm, sunny attic. "Mother?"

Zusane knelt beside her. She wore a gold sequined gown, huge yellow diamond earrings, and an anxious expression that made Jacqueline sit up straight.

"Mother, I'm really busy here." The images of the snowy New York street still hovered close. "I'm going to find out who betrayed the Chosen Ones."

"I know you are, but if you stay in Mrs. D'Angelo's attic, you're going to get hurt." Zusane sounded calm, but she looked as she did when she was on the verge of an Eastern European tantrum. "I won't let them do that again."

Because last time Jacqueline had been hurt, Zusane had been . . . she'd been killed. The thought made Jacqueline's heart leap, and shocked her back to the present. "I thought you were dead."

"I am, dear. But I do get a few bennies for sacrificing myself so many times for the good of the Chosen Ones!"

"Of course you do," Jacqueline said automatically, then wondered what kind of bennies a dead person was entitled to.

"Although," Zusane mused, "I didn't mean to make the ultimate sacrifice of my life. If I had realized who Osgood harbored in his soul and that he could bring you on board before I got on that plane, I wouldn't have done it."

"I'm glad to hear you have at least that much sense."

"What do you mean? I have lots of sense."

"I mean, you loved the adventure so much you ignored the danger. How many times did you think you could gamble with your life and win?"

"You are the most annoying child."

"Because I'm logical?"

"Because . . . oh, for heaven's sake! We don't have time for this bickering. You can't laze around here all day. You need to get going, or you won't be able to bear the consequences." Zusane stood up.

She was fading. Leaving. An hour ago Jacqueline had wept for her and dreamed of one more chance, and now all she could manage was light chitchat. "Wait. Mother. Listen! I can't bear the consequences now. Mother, I'm doing what you wanted—I'm looking into the future."

"I know. Now, if you'll just finish college so you can get a day job—"

If Jacqueline had had any doubts that this was truly Zusane, they were vanquished now. Exasperated, she plowed ahead. "Listen to me, Mother. I never told you—"

"That you loved me?" Zusane smiled, and that smile was the same as always, filled with the truth of her vivacious personality. "One thing I've learned here on the other side—love is a very real emotion. I feel your love, as soft as a puppy's fur. I see your love, bright as a diamond's sparkle. The scent of your love is my favorite perfume. And I hear you cry when you miss me. Don't cry, Jacqueline. Don't miss me. I'm not far away."

Tear sprang to Jacqueline's eyes. "Oh, Mama . . ."

"Still . . . occasionally in life, I would have liked to have heard you tell me you loved me. It would have made me very happy."

Jacqueline gave a crack of laughter. "Guilt. The gift that keeps on giving."

"Always the joke." Zusane cocked her head as if

she heard something, and her voice sharpened with urgency. "On your feet, now. Get out of this vision. Trouble is coming, and you have to be ready to meet it."

"But I still don't know who the traitor is!"

Zusane stopped. She turned back and smiled. "You know one of them. Think!"

Jacqueline sank inside herself, looking for the clue, the thread. . . . *If he looks into it, he will die.*

"That voice. It's Tyler Settles." The fog that covered her memory cleared. It was Tyler who had come to Jacqueline while she was in a vision, picked up the crystal ball, and smashed her skull. He had been lifting it again, prepared to kill her, when he heard the pounding of feet on the stairs. He had dropped the globe and run for the other exit, and barely made it before Caleb came running in. . . .

"See? You know him, and you remember everything. Now go. Remember, I love you, and be careful!" Zusane disappeared with an incongruous little pop.

Jacqueline found herself standing in the middle of the green chalk circle, her eyes wide, listening to the sounds in the brownstone.

Nothing about the noises signaled a problem, but the atmosphere within the house curled and writhed like a gray sea fog.

The danger of which her mother had spoken was here.

Picking up the snow globe, Jacqueline walked to the stairs. Lightly, taking care to make no noise, she ran down into Caleb's apartment.

The door was locked. Mrs. D'Angelo was downstairs. . . .

With Tyler?

Moving with stealth and speed, Jacqueline opened the door to the stairway and started down.

Maybe Mrs. D'Angelo was still napping. But if that was the case, where were the dogs? Why wasn't Lizzie barking? Even if Jacqueline was wrong, even if Tyler wasn't here, Lizzie should be barking. But the place was as silent as a . . . as a tomb.

As Jacqueline descended the stairs, her heart started a slow, terrified thumping. She looked down at the snow globe in her hand. What a *stupid* weapon to pick up. But she'd grabbed it without thought, and now she had to trust her intuition.

As she set foot in the entryway, a voice spoke in her head. *You're going to die, and she's going to die with you.*

Tyler's voice. He *was* here—and he knew she was, too.

How could she have not recognized that dramatic flourish as his?

He'd killed a hundred people at the Gypsy Travel Agency, and destroyed countless priceless books and relics.

He'd hurt her. He'd tried to kill her.

And now he was trying again, and he intended to destroy Mrs. D'Angelo, too.

Jacqueline was going to make him pay.

She strode through the living room. It was empty. Then she looked into the kitchen—and stopped short.

A smear of blood wet the tile floor.

She ran the last few steps toward the door.

Mrs. D'Angelo sat at the table, staring blindly ahead, her hand on Ritter's head.

Tyler, handsome, blond, conceited Tyler, stood behind her, a pistol to her throat. With all the considerable charm at his disposal, he smiled at Jacqueline. "Mrs. D'Angelo is such a hospitable woman. When I got here, her back door was locked. I thought I would have to break it in, but her doggie barked at me. She hushed it and opened the door and invited me in. How hospitable she is! And with her personal history, how foolish!"

Jacqueline glanced between him and Mrs. D'Angelo.

Mrs. D'Angelo had no expression on her face. She was as remote and cold as an iceberg. Yet her fingers clenched in the loose skin at Ritter's throat, and the gentle Lab pushed closer to her side.

"So I shot her dog, the one that barks, and unless Mrs. D'Angelo cooperates, I'll shoot this one, too." The eye of the pistol swerved to indicate Ritter. "And unless you cooperate, I'll shoot Mrs. D'Angelo in the brain. I promise that this time, she won't recover. This time, she'll be brain-dead until she's really dead."

"Hasn't she had enough hurt in her life?" Jacqueline cried.

"What do you care? You're like me. You don't have a *mother*. People like us—we don't concern ourselves with *families*." His lip curled in contempt. "Only the weak yearn for something they can never have."

"Only the weak envy families so much they long to hurt them."

"I'm not weak, and I don't long to hurt this . . . *mother*." He dug his fingers into Mrs. D'Angelo's hair. "But since the chance has presented itself, I might as well enjoy it. So come in, Jacqueline Vargha, and let's talk about our plan for the Chosen Ones."

Jacqueline didn't want to talk about his plan for the Chosen Ones, because his only plan for the Chosen Ones was death.

And the Chosen Ones were Jacqueline's friends. They were her people.

She walked toward him, calm and quiet, trying to put him at ease. "Don't hurt Mrs. D'Angelo, Tyler. We can work this out."

His gaze shifted over her, appreciatively taking in her jeans, her rumpled shirt, her bare feet. "Do you know what he promised me if I ended the Chosen Ones?"

"I can't imagine."

"All the women I want. All the power I want. All the glory I want." He gloated. "My own television show.

I'll be bigger than Robertson. Hell, I'll be bigger than Oprah!"

"Wow."

He was so involved in his magnificent vision of the future, he didn't hear the sarcasm.

She balanced on the balls of her feet, ready to attack. "I don't know about the power and the glory, but I'm not available. I'm sort of busy with Caleb."

"Honey, he's not here, and he's not coming home." Tyler sounded way too certain.

Jacqueline wavered, eased back to stand solidly on the floor. "Why not?"

"He checked in with his mama before he left—such a good boy—and told her he was going back to Irving's." Tyler smiled.

He was so good-looking, so strikingly gorgeous, yet in that instant, Jacqueline saw the corruption that ate away at him, turning his mind into a cancerous mass, his flesh into a wasting disease.

"What did you do?" she whispered.

"What I'm good at."

"I don't think I really know what that is, but I'm pretty sure it's not being a psychic." She took a breath. "You're a mind speaker."

"Very good." The words were approving. His tone was not. He didn't like being caught at his games. "I'm a mind controller, too, and it turns out that Irving is an easy target."

If that was true, it was very bad news. "I would have never suspected that."

"In my business—"

"A faith healer, right?"

"That's right. In my business, you learn that the time to take control of a mind is when that person is distraught by a tragedy, or in anguish or in pain. The person has no guards then. They're not paying attention, their shields are down, and I can move right in."

"Yes. I can see how that would work." She thought it through, and said, "I imagine you convinced a lot of people to give you access to their bank accounts."

"You are such a smart girl."

"Yes. I am. But you didn't take control of my mind." She knew that because once she had the information she wanted, she still intended to beat the hell out of him.

"No." He turned sullen. "Some of the Chosen Ones have a protection I hadn't encountered before. You especially. You've got a Teflon mind. I couldn't get anywhere with you. At least, not until after that vision of yours. Then you were hurt and confused, and you sure heard me when I talked!" Now he smirked in a way that made her want to slap him.

But she kept her voice cool and distant. "I did. You told me, *If he looks into it, he will die.*"

"See? It was nice of me to warn you. It's too bad you didn't pass it on."

"I did pass it on. Caleb didn't care." The memory of that moment, when she and Caleb ripped each other to shreds with their words, made her want to give in to easy tears. But she couldn't; that *would* give Tyler a hold on her mind. "He wanted to find the man who tried to kill me."

"If he had realized I was coming here, he could have saved himself cab fare." Tyler laughed, long and low. "Not to mention a messy, inescapable death."

That laughter, that unmistakable air of triumph, chilled her to the bone. "Tyler, what have you done?" she asked.

"The same thing I did at the Gypsy Travel Agency. I rigged my room and my things."

"Rigged. Like with a bomb?"

"A *bomb*." He was scornful. "A *bomb* isn't necessary when the Others are willing to show me tricks with the supernatural. Your boyfriend has got such a dislike for cell phones, and I kept my spare, so that's what I used as a fuse."

"So it is a bomb."

"It's not!" he said sharply. "Nothing as crude as that. It's an enchantment. Sooner or later, your boyfriend or one of your friends will search my room. He'll turn on my cell phone to see who I've called and who's called me, and"—Tyler flipped his fingers—"Irving's home and everyone within the range of his containment spell will vaporize . . . including your boyfriend."

In a whirlwind of fury that startled Jacqueline and took Tyler by surprise, diminutive Mrs. D'Angelo came up out of her chair and rammed her head toward his chest.

Perhaps if she had hit him squarely in the breast-bone, she would have done some damage. Instead she thumped his left ribs, and she didn't have strength behind her.

Grabbing her arm, he tossed her aside, knocking her head into the cabinets.

She crumpled to the floor, unconscious.

"You . . . *mother!*" He made it sound like the worst insult he knew. He lifted his gun. He aimed at Mrs. D'Angelo.

Jacqueline cried out, "No!" and started toward him.

Ritter, gentle Ritter, sank his teeth into Tyler's thigh.

"God damn it!" With his other leg, Tyler kicked the dog in the ribs.

Ritter yelped and let go. On his belly, he crawled toward Mrs. D'Angelo.

Tyler pointed the cold, black eye of the pistol at the dog. Then at Jacqueline. Then at the dog again.

Lifting the snow globe over her head, Jacqueline threw it with all the considerable power of her well-toned arm. The cheap souvenir ripped through the air.

The bracelet Charisma had given her flew off.

Tyler flung up his hand to fend off the snow globe.

He deflected it, but not enough. With the weight of the water behind it, the snow globe smashed into the side of his face. The plastic shattered. The globe exploded in a splash of water and a slash of blood.

He yelled in pain and rage.

Jacqueline ran toward him.

Recovering, he steadied his gun on her.

She skidded to a halt.

He lifted his hand to his face. The Statue of Liberty, the Empire State Building, *something* had ripped into his cheek, leaving a jagged cut that extended from under his eye to the edge of his mouth. "You marked me!" Incredulous, he stared at the blood on his fingers.

That was as good an opportunity as she could expect. Jacqueline leaped toward him, her hips swiveling as she swung her foot around and up toward his groin.

He leaped up and back.

The kick landed squarely on his thigh, making him grunt with pain. He responded with a punch toward her throat.

She spun away, but now she knew—he had a long reach, he was trained, and he was good. Very good.

As he punched again, she kicked and caught his forearm hard. Followed up with a solid hit to the face that made blood spurt from his lip.

He roared with rage, and came at Jacqueline with a

lightning-fast barrage of blows that had her retreating across the kitchen.

Somewhere, Lizzie barked sharply and in agony.

As if that was just the sound he needed to hear, he stopped and laughed.

An opening.

She aimed a punch at his throat.

He caught her fist in his hand, swung her and flung her toward the door. "I'm going to kill you. Slowly. The way I did that dog-bitch, and the way I'm going to kill that mother-bitch."

Caleb had taught Jacqueline to save her breath, and she did now, fighting hard, making him shut up and back away.

He was panting, bleeding, hurt.

She watched for an opening. It came when he swung wide.

She kicked again, aiming for his soft belly.

With lightning-fast reflexes, he caught her ankle and flipped her around.

He wasn't as hurt as she'd thought.

She'd been suckered.

She hit the floor hard, on her chest. The impact knocked the air from her lungs.

He landed on her with all his weight.

Her ribs cracked; she gasped in agony, saw red stars explode behind her eyes, lost consciousness for a vital minute.

She came to on her back.

His pistol was gone. He sat on her chest, his blue eyes mad with fury. His hands pressed against her throat, cutting off her breath. "The devil picked this way for you to die. So die. Die."

She struggled desperately, clawing at his wrists.

His fingers tightened, crushing her windpipe. "You were almost finished yesterday because you couldn't breathe, but Isabelle had to show off. She had to save you. Let's kill you today."

Blood dribbled from his face onto hers. She had no air, and loudly, inside her head, she could hear the sound of dripping. If she didn't do something, the noise would never stop. She'd be trapped forever in that cemetery, alone, friendless. . . .

Instinctively, she brought her injured palm around and pressed it against his forehead.

A shock ran down her arm, through her hand, and burst like fireworks against his forehead.

He staggered back, holding his eyes and shrieking in pain.

Hand outstretched, she sucked in a long breath and went at him again.

Leaning down like a bull prepared to charge, he brought his shoulder forward. He fixed his crazed eyes on hers.

Still gasping, she tried to scramble backward. She

couldn't recover this time. When he hit her, she would never get up again.

He started toward her with the speed of a linebacker—and from the corner of her eye, she saw movement.

Caleb. It was Caleb. He was here. He was alive.

She crumpled to the floor, gasping for breath.

Chapter 35

Caleb slammed into Tyler from the side and smacked him sideways across the kitchen.

Holding her throat, Jacqueline dragged in one breath after another. The coolness of the tile seeped into her heated skin and slowly brought her back to consciousness, and relief, and gratitude.

Caleb was here. Oh, God, her lover was alive.

He was alive, Tyler's plan had failed, and Caleb had arrived in time to save Jacqueline and his mother.

Tyler hit the stainless steel refrigerator hard enough to put a dent in the door and make the metal ring. He fumbled in his jacket, rolled around, and faced them, pistol in his hand and aimed at Caleb's chest.

In a motion so swift Jacqueline almost couldn't see it, Caleb pulled a knife from his sleeve and, with deadly accuracy, threw it into Tyler's shoulder.

Tyler screamed and dropped the pistol.

Caleb rushed him, smashing his body against the refrigerator again.

Grabbing him with one hand at his throat, another on his forehead, he slammed Tyler's skull into the metal once, twice.

Jacqueline didn't care. Tyler had killed Lizzie. Hurt, maybe killed, Mrs. D'Angelo. Hurt Ritter. Hurt her.

She hoped Caleb killed him.

Crawling to Mrs. D'Angelo's side, she checked her pulse. Caleb's mother was unconscious, bleeding from a cut on her forehead—but alive. Ritter lay close against her, and he licked Jacqueline's hand as she dragged the phone off the counter and called nine-one-one. "Home intruder," she croaked, and folded a kitchen towel to press onto Mrs. D'Angelo's wound. "Need an ambulance."

"Address?" the emergency operator inquired.

"Don't know." The battering at the refrigerator went on.

"Please stay on the line," the operator said.

"Can't." Jacqueline hung up the phone, realized she didn't know Irving's number, and tried to shout at Caleb. It was justice of a kind that her voice was gone and she couldn't stop Caleb from beating Tyler. But she had to; this was more important than Tyler's punishment. She tried to stand and went down on one knee. Tried again and lurched to a chair. Grabbed the back and shoved it across the tile floor toward Caleb. It hit him in the backs of the legs.

His hands still wrapped around the whimpering Tyler, he looked at her, murder in his eyes. "My mother?" he asked.

"She's alive," Jacqueline rasped. "I've called nine-one-one, asked for medical assistance, but I didn't know the address."

"They'll trace the call."

Tyler clawed at Caleb's face.

Caleb slapped him in openhanded contempt.

"Caleb!" She was louder this time. "Irving's phone number. We've got to warn them. . . ."

Caleb saw her desperation, and discarded Tyler like a piece of trash. "Warn them about what?"

Tyler tumbled to the floor.

"He set a trap." She gestured at the moaning mind speaker.

"What trap?" Caleb grabbed the phone and dialed.

"Cell phone set to blow up the house."

Jacqueline had never heard Caleb swear in Italian, but he did it now. He was pale as he spoke urgently into the receiver. "Come on. Come on!" His gaze flicked over Jacqueline as he listened to the ringing. It lingered on the bruises on her neck, then snapped back to Tyler. "I *am* going to kill him."

"Okay." She sagged into a kitchen chair. "But first, *they've* got to answer the phone."

He punched a button, and suddenly, she could hear the ringing.

"Speakerphone," he said.

Someone picked up. "Hello." It was McKenna, and he sounded annoyed.

Caleb straightened. "McKenna. Listen to me. Don't go in Tyler's room. Don't touch anything. Especially don't touch the cell phone."

"But sir, Mr. Shea, Mr. Eagle, Mr. Faa, and Miss Fangorn have all gone up there and are searching the chamber."

Caleb snarled, "Well, stop them!"

"They're doing this on your orders, sir." McKenna sounded reproachful.

Jacqueline came to her feet. "Stop them. Stop them!" she croaked.

"If you don't stop them," Caleb said, "the whole place is going to go sky-high. McKenna, listen to me!"

The receiver on the other end clicked down.

Caleb and Jacqueline looked at each other.

"Do you think he'll do it?" Jacqueline asked.

"He'll do it. Do I think he'll compromise his dignity by running or shouting? That's a whole different question." His gaze shifted to Tyler, lying by the refrigerator.

Tyler's eyes were swelling shut.

"He won't be going anywhere soon," Jacqueline said.

"Not if he knows what's good for him." Caleb walked toward her, arms outstretched, face taut with relief.

On the floor, Mrs. D'Angelo groaned.

Turning back, he dropped to his knees beside her. "Ma. Can you hear me?"

"Yes." She put her hand to her forehead. "I can hear you. Stop shouting."

In relief, he leaned against the cabinets. "Can you move?"

"Do I have to?" she asked.

"Just a little. To prove to me you can." He watched her wiggle her arms and legs, lift her head and put it back on the floor. Looking up at Jacqueline, he smiled with joy and relief.

Then Mrs. D'Angelo stirred more violently. "Lizzie?" she asked.

Jacqueline looked around, followed the smear of blood on the floor toward the utility porch. "In there," she said.

Caleb stood and hurried to the door.

Three pain-racked woofs sounded.

He disappeared inside. Jacqueline heard cabinets open, heard a few gasping snarls; then Caleb came out and washed the blood off his hands. "She's not good, Ma. She's going to lose her leg." He gave Tyler a glance that promised retribution. "I wrapped her in some towels to keep her warm until we can get her to the vet. But if she can bark at me, she's going to live."

"Thank God," Mrs. D'Angelo murmured, and petted Ritter's insistent nose.

Caleb walked toward Jacqueline, holding out his hand.

Moving slowly, carefully, Jacqueline joined him.

Putting his arm around her, he pulled her into his embrace.

She gasped. "Be careful! Ribs!"

Caleb loosened his grip. "What did he do to your ribs?"

"Jumped on me."

Caleb glared at Tyler; then he turned her face to his. "I can see what he did to your throat." With light fingers, he traced the bruises there. "And your face." He traced a lump on her forehead, one she hadn't been aware of. He burst out, "How could I have left you alone? Why didn't I listen to your warning?"

"Because you're obstinate and think you always know best?" she suggested, then buried her face in his shoulder to hide her grin.

"I'm an ass."

"Yes." She lifted her head, and in a voice filled with her own worry, she said, "You can't be everywhere. Even now, you're almost twitching with the need to go back to Irving's and save them."

"I told them to go to Tyler's room and look for a cell phone. If the house goes up—"

"It's not your fault. You were the only one who suspected a traitor and went looking for him. Without you, we'd all be victims of a blast at Irving's and . . . oh, Caleb." She threw her arms around his neck, ignored the pain the sudden movement caused, and said, "God help me, but as we wait to hear, I am so glad you're here and alive."

"God help us both, then." He kissed her, a gentle touch of the lips that told her how much he had worried.

The phone rang shrilly, breaking them apart. They both jumped for it, and Caleb punched the button for the speakerphone.

McKenna's voice said, "Sir, I stopped Miss Fangorn from opening Mr. Settles's phone. Is there anything else you would like me to do?"

"Thank you, McKenna." Relief knocked the starch out of Jacqueline's knees, and she slithered down onto the floor and leaned against the cabinets.

Caleb instructed, "Get them out of the house until Irving, or someone, can take that enchantment off that phone."

"I've got the cell phone here, sir. What would you like me to do with it?"

Jacqueline sat up straight.

Caleb put his hand on his head. "You shouldn't have touched it."

They heard a woman's voice in the background; then Charisma came on the phone. "Last night, I was reading one of Irving's textbooks on magic, and I think

I know what this is. It's an enchantment meant to vaporize things like garbage or potato peels. You put a containment spell around a trash can—like the spell around the Gypsy Travel Agency or Irving's house—hit the trigger, and everything inside the can vanishes."

"What does *that* have to do with *this*?" Caleb asked.

"Don't you see?" Charisma said. "The explosion fills whatever space that contains it and does its job. This was a very clever usage of a very old technology, magically speaking."

"I think she's right." Irving's voice joined the conversation. "There's always a lag on the timer so a lid can be put on the can. The problem is, once a device like this is inside a containment, it can't be taken out without setting it off. In this case, if it left my house, it would blast the whole world. So I'm sending everyone out of the house, and I'll put it in the trash and see if I can contain the explosion."

McKenna's voice spoke coldly, formally, clearly as offended by Irving's intended sacrifice as it was possible for him to be. "I just escorted Miss Fangorn out the door. Now, sir, if you would leave—"

"I have no intention of leaving," Irving said, "nor will I let you sacrifice yourself in such a manner—"

"I am your butler, sir, and these duties are my responsibility—"

"I'm very old, and you're still a young man, and I will not permit—"

"I'm forty-nine, not young at all, and I've lived a full, rich life of service to—"

Jacqueline heard a muffled explosion in the background.

Irving and McKenna abruptly stopped talking.

Martha's voice spoke into the phone. "It's all right, Mr. D'Angelo. I took care of the matter. And the garbage is most definitely gone." Her heels clicked on the floor as she walked away.

A long silence followed.

Jacqueline grinned at Caleb.

In an unbiased tone, Caleb said, "I guess that resolves the problem, does it not, gentlemen?"

McKenna cleared his throat. "Indeed."

"That it does." Irving's voice changed. "And you? You caught Settles before he could do any damage?"

Caleb looked around the kitchen, at the blood, at his mother and her dog, at Jacqueline, at Tyler, and his face kindled. He was still starkly angry, yet anxious about her and his mother.

"No harm done," Jacqueline rasped. "We'll see you soon."

Caleb cut the connection.

Jacqueline looked down at the palm of her hand. The blast of magic that had knocked Tyler aside had healed her wound. The stitches had been burned away. The slash was nothing more than a thin white scar.

Yet her other palm tingled and throbbed.

She looked—and saw another eye, a mirror image to the first, etched into the palm of her hand.

She gasped.

Caleb leaped to her side. "What's wrong?"

She showed him her hands.

He took them in his, and stared in wonderment. "Have there been prophecies about this?"

"I don't know."

"What does it mean?"

"That I *do* know. I'm ready for the battle ahead, for I am going to be the best seer the Chosen Ones have ever had."

He smiled—not one of his patented restrained half smiles, but a joyous smile that transformed his face.

Keenly aware of how lucky she was to get a second chance, and how few second chances came along, she said, "I'm sorry I said those things to you. You were right about everything. Almost everything."

"No." He put his finger over her lips. "I'm the one who was wrong. No child receives a gift like yours unless she is discarded in the cruelest way, deprived of the love every child is owed. You . . . you've had Zusane as a mother, and God rest her soul, I saw how difficult she could be. I lost my father and brother, but I was always secure in my family's love, and I had no right to tell you about Zusane's past. She would have hated that, and she would have hated more that I compared your ordeal to hers. Because she wasn't always unselfish, but she understood how very much you have accomplished in your life."

"Yes, but she would have liked to be told more often that I loved her." And Jacqueline laughed.

He cocked his head curiously.

Soon she would tell him about her meeting with Zusane, but not now. Now she could hear sirens coming, and she knew she had only a few minutes alone with Caleb. "Caleb, you helped me so much. You protected me as you did Zusane. I know with you around, I can go into a vision and be safe. I know that with the Gypsy Travel Agency gone, we're going to be desperate for your kind of fighting experience. Somehow, your love makes my gift stronger and more magical." Again, she showed him her hand.

"It's not my love that makes you strong. It's that special soul that shines out of you like a beacon."

"I love you. I want you to marry me. You asked last time. This time it's my turn. Marry me and fight by my side."

He hugged her again, then quickly loosened his grip. "I have never wanted anything else." Her big, muscular, bodyguard-man's eyes filled with tears. "Jacqueline, I love you."

She was home at last, in his arms.

Chapter 36

On the other side of the kitchen, Tyler gasped so loudly, he sounded like he was dying.

Caleb's jaw clenched. "The big faker."

The sirens were coming closer, turning the corner onto Mrs. D'Angelo's street.

Tyler gasped again, and this time the sound rattled in his throat.

Jacqueline flinched. "That doesn't sound like faking to me."

"I didn't hit him hard enough to kill him. I wanted to, but—" At another one of those awful rattling noises, Caleb jumped to his feet. "Stay there," he told Jacqueline.

She paid no heed, but eased herself up onto her feet and followed.

Tyler's skin had a gray tinge, his fingers were swollen, and he rolled on the floor, holding his belly in apparent agony.

"He swallowed something, a drug of some kind. It's the only explanation for this." Caleb grabbed his shoulders and shook him to get his attention. "What did you take? Tell me! What did you take?"

Tyler shook his head. "It doesn't matter. There's nothing you can do about it." His voice was broken, his words slurred.

"He took poison? Like a cyanide capsule or something?" Jacqueline knelt beside them. "Who does he think he is? A spy for the . . ." As the truth hit her, she met Caleb's gaze.

"A spy for the enemy, one who won't allow himself to be taken and questioned," Caleb finished.

The sirens stopped outside.

"You Chosen . . . haven't got . . . a chance. Inexperienced. Irving . . . that old duffer . . . to lead you." Tyler gasped over and over. "I've been . . . talking to the dead man . . . and he . . . will . . . triumph."

Jacqueline stiffened.

"What's wrong?" Caleb asked. "Jacqueline?"

She shook her head, concentrating on Tyler.

Still compelled by that frantic need for attention, Tyler spoke through blue lips. "I'll . . . go . . . to the master. I'll be . . . at his side."

"The master?" Jacqueline drew away, appalled and disgusted. "You mean . . . the *devil*?"

"He . . . will . . . honor me." Blood oozed from the slash on Tyler's face, but it had turned a ghastly shade of brown.

New York's finest hammered at the front door and burst through the back.

"In here!" Caleb called.

EMTs, firemen, and policemen swarmed the house.

Caleb helped Jacqueline to her feet. "You fool," he said to Tyler. "Your master doesn't tolerate failure."

Tyler looked at him in astonishment. "Not . . . true!"

"You will burn in hell forever," Caleb said.

"No!" Yet Tyler recognized the truth, and as the idea took hold in his brain, he sat up and desperately clawed his way toward them.

Chilled, Jacqueline backed away.

Tyler stared at some vision beyond them. His blue eyes grew wider and wider. As Jacqueline and Caleb watched, blood vessels burst, obliterating the whites. He fell back.

He was dead before he hit the floor.

Caleb helped Jacqueline up the steps to Irving's front door and rang the doorbell. "We'll get you in bed and give you some pain medication, and you can sleep for the rest of the day."

"I think I must be surging with endorphins, because I don't feel too bad." Jacqueline belied her protest by leaning against him.

"The bruises will make themselves known tomorrow." He cursed himself again for leaving her alone to face Tyler.

But Jacqueline knew what he was thinking, and kissed his cheek. "The hospital is keeping your mother overnight for observation, but she's so annoyed you know she's going to be fine. And they were so unimpressed with my injuries, they couldn't wait to toss me out. So stop blaming yourself. Everything came out fine. Better than fine."

McKenna opened the door. "Ah. Good evening, Mr. D'Angelo, Miss Vargha. Come in. Will you be staying long this time?"

"I sense sarcasm, McKenna." Jacqueline peered around the dark, empty entryway. "Where is everybody?"

For one second, Caleb tensed. He had that creepy-crawly feeling of being watched.

Then—"*Surprise!*" The Chosen Ones filled the entry. They came from the library, the study, down the stairs, yelling, waving their hands, grinning.

Caleb relaxed. This was a friendly assault.

Jacqueline flung herself at her friends. "You *guys!*"

Charisma and Isabelle reached her first with their arms outstretched.

"Careful!" Caleb fended them off.

"Caleb, it's only a couple of broken ribs." Jacqueline scolded him and embraced the women at the same time.

Charisma took Jacqueline's arms and looked at her wrists. "Where's the protection bracelet I gave you?"

Jacqueline fished it out of her pocket and showed her. "The clasp broke."

"I'll fix it for you." Charisma put it in her own pocket, but a frown tugged at her forehead. Obviously, she didn't like that development.

"So you only have a couple of broken ribs," Aaron mocked, and hugged Jacqueline gently.

"I've had broken ribs; they're a bitch." Samuel gave her a token embrace.

"You've got to stop running into stuff with your face." Isabelle rubbed the bump on Jacqueline's forehead.

The redness and swelling receded.

"Thank you." But when Isabelle would have continued, Jacqueline stopped her. "The ribs aren't too bad, really." She moved her shoulders as if testing the waters. "I think I might have somehow developed some superhero healing power."

"Or it's a hangover from Isabelle's healing," Charisma suggested.

"Her work as one of the Chosen Ones has benefits, and a quicker healing is one of them." The crowd parted to allow Irving through. He put his wrinkled, bent hands around Jacqueline's face and looked into her eyes. "God bless you, Jacqueline Vargha. You saved us all." He looked up and caught Caleb's gaze. "And you, Caleb D'Angelo. Without you, we would be both dead and foolish."

"Yeah." Samuel offered his hand. "Thank you for alerting us in time. Charisma had just located the cell phone when McKenna came running in."

Caleb shook his hand, and Aaron's, and Irving's, then offered his to McKenna. "Thank *you* for running."

"It was more of a fast walk," McKenna said, his dignity untouched.

Charisma hugged Caleb. "I never wanted to be at the center of an annihilation."

Isabelle put out her hand. Caleb appreciated that she wasn't as warm and fuzzy as Charisma, but he pulled her into his embrace, anyway. She had healed Jacqueline and right now, she was his favorite Chosen.

Aleksandr scooted his way through the crowd to Jacqueline. With a grin, he presented her with a leopard-print gift bag. "We got together and decided to get you a present."

When she would have ripped into it, Caleb placed his hand over the package. "Wait. We can't stand here all day. Jacqueline has barely left the hospital. She needs to sit down."

"Shall I prepare the library for a meeting, sir?" McKenna asked.

"Meetings are such a drag in the library," Charisma said. With a start, she realized she had been tactless, and corrected herself. "I mean, it's a gorgeous room, but it's too big and there are all those antiques and I'm always afraid I'm going to break one. . . ."

In his coldest voice, McKenna suggested, "The study, then? The billiards room? The dining room, perhaps?"

"She's right. This is a gorgeous mansion, but it's like living in a museum. I'm always tiptoeing around." Obviously, Aleksandr didn't give a damn about tact.

McKenna was so annoyed, he snapped, "Then where would you suggest you go to allow the rest of you to speak to each other easily?"

Caleb knew where he'd rather be. "Let's go to the kitchen."

"Good idea!" Aaron clapped him on the shoulder.

"Yes, I'm always comfortable in a kitchen." Samuel glanced sarcastically at Isabelle. "It's my servant mentality."

"Really?" Isabelle proved she did sarcastic as well as he did. "I thought it was because you like to watch a woman prepare food for you."

Jacqueline stepped between them. "Great. Then it's settled. We'll hold our meetings in the kitchen."

"But . . . I . . . My home . . ." Irving waved his arms around the impressive foyer.

Charisma tucked her hand in his arm and started toward the stairs that led down to the kitchen. "It's not that we don't like your house, Irving. It's that we respect it too much."

Aaron smothered a grin and gave Caleb a thumbs-up.

"That's true." Caleb wrapped his arm around Jacqueline and followed them. "You have to remember that at heart I'm an Italian peasant."

McKenna skittered after the group, his round face pulled long in disapproval.

As they entered the kitchen, Martha was rattling the pans, preparing dinner. She straightened and stared. "What is it now? You've decided to raid the refrigerator?"

Caleb knew then neither Martha nor McKenna approved of the eccentric group of Chosen.

Too bad. They were stuck with one another.

The kitchen was a relic of a bygone age when the New York aristocracy catered parties for all of society, when three dozen servants worked for a week to prepare and decorate enough food to feed two hundred hungry mouths, when no one had ever heard the term "efficiency" in regard to the labor of cooking. The room itself was as big as a lobby, with open pantry shelves, cupboards that reached to the twelve-foot-tall ceiling, a gas stovetop with six burners and a grill, three ovens, a huge refrigerator, and a freezer built to hold an entire steer. The long granite tabletop was so heavy, it required a jack to lift it, and only a massive oak frame could support its weight. The floor was below ground level, the ceiling above. The windows were set high on the walls and looked out on the sidewalk, and as the Chosen Ones grabbed chairs and benches and settled themselves around the table, they saw the legs of pedestrians as they walked by.

Irving settled at the head of the table. Of course.

Aleksandr yelped and advised everyone not to knock their knee into the table leg, because it hurt like a son of a bitch.

Isabelle decided the table was too cold and asked for a tablecloth, and when McKenna and Martha glared, she searched in the pantry until McKenna gave up in disgust and found one for her.

The kitchen was warm, it smelled good, and everyone felt at home.

"This is exactly as it should be." Charisma nodded as she poured coffee for Jacqueline, Irving, and herself. "Friendly. Being sunk in the earth like it is, it has good vibes."

"Jacqueline, check out your present." Aleksandr set his Coke on the table, flipped his chair backward to the table, and straddled it.

Jacqueline opened the gift bag, tossed out the leopard-print tissue paper—obviously the wrapping was the work of the women—and discovered a box. She opened it to find a shiny red cell phone crusted with large rhinestones.

On the bench beside her, Caleb blinked. "That's bright enough."

Jacqueline pulled it out. "Wow. This is really . . . something." Obviously, she didn't know what.

"It was Aleksandr's idea." Irving looked befuddled by his Chosen, but proud, too. "I'm glad I suggested him."

The boy preened. "I may not have a woo-woo gift like the rest of you, but I can help in this way."

"We've all got one." Aaron showed Caleb his phone. It was black. "They've got a linking GPS. Unless you've got one of these phones, you can't access the location."

"Aleksandr did the programming for that, too." Samuel handed Caleb a package. In an undertone, he said, "It's yours, and it's black."

"Thank you." Caleb used the same quiet voice. He did not want rhinestones. More loudly, and to Aleksandr, he said, "Thank you. You solved one of the problems that has haunted me—how to keep track of and communicate with the Chosen Ones. Especially Jacqueline."

Jacqueline waited until the laughter had died, then in all sincerity said, "You guys are the best!"

"I picked out the phone, and set and aligned the stones to protect you from harm." Charisma smiled with satisfaction.

"You can align man-made stones?" Jacqueline asked.

"They're not man-made. Irving provided them."

Charisma leaned across and touched one reverently. "They're diamonds."

Horrified, Jacqueline tossed the phone in the air.

Caleb caught it.

"I can't have diamonds. I *lose* cell phones!" she said.

"You won't lose this one." Aaron looked grimly vengeful. "See that big diamond? The one surrounded by the little yellow diamonds? That's the button you push to call if you're in trouble. So if you lose the phone or, God forbid, someone steals it, and that guy presses that button, we'll all arrive at his side—"

"And he'll be sorry he was ever born," Aleksandr finished.

"Besides, no one's going to steal a cell phone that looks like that," Samuel said.

"I think it's pretty!" Charisma said.

Caleb wasn't sure, but she might have had her feelings hurt.

Apparently he was right, because Isabelle put her arm around Charisma, cast a dark look at Samuel, and said, "You're right. It *is* pretty."

Caleb had to give Samuel credit. He moved to correct his mistake at once. "I meant no *guy* would steal it. It's too froufrou."

"Thank you all." Jacqueline gingerly accepted it again. "No one's going to take it from me, and I will make sure I never, ever lose something as precious as the gift my friends have given me."

"You mean your fellow freaks." Aaron bumped her lightly with his shoulder.

"That, too. But first . . ." She held the phone in both hands and looked down at it, then up at them. Her face was serious. Her fingers trembled. "Caleb and I have to tell you what we've learned."

Chapter 37

"Tyler was our traitor. We all know that." Jacqueline slid her hand over the cell phone, over the expanse of glittering diamonds. "But while he was dying, he said something. . . ."

"About a dead man," Caleb prompted. "He said he'd been talking to a dead man."

"Yeah, right," Samuel said.

Jacqueline scooted closer to Caleb on the bench. "No, it's true."

The silence that fell in the kitchen was profound. The Chosen Ones glanced at one another.

Then Isabelle asked, "How do you know?"

Jacqueline slipped the phone into the pocket of her jeans. "I had a vision in Mrs. D'Angelo's attic."

Caleb whipped around to face her. "You didn't tell me that."

"When would I have told you?" She made a face.

"All right." He acknowledged that truth. "But why did you go up to the attic?"

"Because Mother was dead and you were in danger, and I had to do *something*." Remembering the tears and the crisis that had led to her decision put a husky edge to her voice. "I wanted to see if I could direct a vision, to help myself discover who had sold us out. And I did . . . sort of."

"Tyler sold us out," Aaron said.

Irving shook his head. "No. Or rather, he's not the only one. Without the codes, there is no way Tyler smuggled an explosive device into both the Gypsy Travel Agency and my own home. Not even all of the directors knew those codes. So who gave them to him?"

"A dead man?" McKenna sounded incredulous.

When everyone turned to face him, his Celtic face flushed a ruddy red. "I'm sorry, sirs, madams. I spoke out of turn."

"But you're right," Jacqueline said. "It was a dead man. I heard him. He's angry and he's hostile. He hates everyone, especially the people who were once his friends, and he feels betrayed."

"But how could a dead man communicate with Tyler Settles?"

"Tyler Settles was a mind controller and a mind speaker," Samuel said slowly. "He rummaged around in my head, trying to exert an influence, and I think he could do that with other people. I'm merely surmising, now, but if he could get into the wrong mind, that mind could communicate with him. Perhaps that mind could even take him over."

That made sense to Jacqueline. "I don't think Tyler Settles needed much of a push to become evil. From what he was saying, he had quite a lucrative business going, swindling sick people out of their bank accounts."

"How did he get picked to become one of the Chosen Ones?" Aaron asked.

"If he was already in communication with this dead man, he may have been able to use the dead man's knowledge of the Chosen Ones and his own skill in controlling minds to inveigle his way into the organization," Samuel suggested.

Aaron sat back and looked Samuel over. "The way you think is a little scary, too."

Samuel had never looked so wicked. "I *am* a lawyer."

Martha freshened Jacqueline's coffee, and as she poured, she asked, "But what about this dead man? He has to have been associated with the Gypsy Travel Agency to be able to give up the code. How are we going to find him?"

"Where is he buried?" Aleksandr asked.

"I saw a street in New York. There's a hospital, an abandoned church, and a graveyard. The only clue I have is that he can hear water dripping . . . a constant, eternal torment." Jacqueline listened in her head, and sighed. "I can hear that water dripping right now."

"So all we have to do is figure out who knew or *knows* the protective codes for both the Gypsy Travel Agency and this house and go looking for him in a cemetery." Aaron obviously didn't completely believe Jacqueline's vision.

Jacqueline didn't mind. She thought it was stupid herself. If only she hadn't heard it and seen it. "There was a voice speaking in his mind, offering him a new chance at life." She wrapped her hands around the warm cup. "All he had to do was betray the ones who had betrayed him. I recognized the voice."

"The devil's voice," Irving said.

Samuel shook his head and smiled.

Irving drew himself up with all his elderly dignity. "I assure you, Mr. Faa, I am not an enfeebled old man. I recognize the devil's modus operandi. Offering temptation is a tradition with him."

"Yes, it was the devil." Jacqueline was really chilled now.

Caleb took off his jacket and wrapped it around her, engulfing her in his heat and scent, reminding her how much she had gained when she fell in love with him.

Gratefully, she took his hand.

"What is the dead man? A vampire?" Aleksandr's voice rose incredulously. "Because my grandfather says there's no such thing, and in this case, I'd like to believe he's right."

"No. It's nothing like that." That hadn't even occurred to Jacqueline. "He's not hungry for blood. He's all human. But he's in the dark in a tomb where nothing ever changes."

"So in your vision, you were in the dead man's head." Charisma wet her lips. "I've been reading as much as I can of Irving's library, trying to see if I could help you, and your visions—they're dangerous. Only the first seer could transport herself to another setting and really be there, and only three other seers could be one with another person, and none of them could do both."

"Dangerous." Caleb repeated the word that had snagged his attention. "How?"

Trust him to go right to the heart of the matter.

"The other seers were all members of . . . the Others," Charisma told them.

Caleb gave a bark of laughter. "Then that is further proof that the world is changing, because Jacqueline could never turn to evil."

His certainty warmed Jacqueline's heart.

"What if she gets caught in a vision?" Charisma asked. "It's happened. People go mad."

"Charisma, don't worry so much." Jacqueline leaned forward and spoke earnestly. "When I had my first vision, I was in real danger of being killed. I think

Tyler was right. I think I could have been killed, and Zusane saved my life by pushing me out of the plane. But when I had that vision, I was alone and afraid. Today, when I went into the vision, I knew no matter what, Caleb loved me, and that love grounded me in the real world."

"Awesome." Charisma's bracelets rattled as she applauded Jacqueline and Caleb. "So his love strengthened your gift."

"Exactly." Jacqueline smiled as joy burst in her. "That's it exactly!"

Everyone in the kitchen joined in Charisma's applause.

Caleb lifted Jacqueline's hand in his. "I'd like you all to be the first to know—Jacqueline and I will be married as soon as the state of New York will allow."

Now everyone came to their feet to hug and kiss. Martha and McKenna gave up their displeasure with the invaders in their kitchen, and bustled around dusting champagne flutes, popping corks, and laying out another round of exquisite hors d'oeuvres.

Jacqueline hugged Caleb, wondering how she could have been fool enough to run from him when everything she wanted . . . was here.

In her lovely soothing voice, Isabelle said, "Jacqueline and Caleb have won us our first victory. We're starting to become a cohesive group, and I am so glad. But we have to decide what our next move will be. We have decisions to make and there will be times when we must make them."

Caleb pulled Jacqueline onto the bench. "Isabelle is right."

Everyone shuffled into their seats.

McKenna and Martha set the hors d'oeuvres on the table.

Isabelle remained standing. "I think it would be best if we first voted on a president, and then used Robert's Rules of Order to direct the meetings."

"She's right. We need a leader," Aaron said.

"It should be Isabelle." Samuel projected an authority as weighty as any judge's.

Everyone looked between him and Isabelle.

"Isabelle," he repeated. "She has been trained to run her sorority, to raise funds for charities, and to organize elaborate parties in honor of politicians and bankers. She never raises her voice, she never breaks a sweat, and she never fails. Is there anyone here who would resent taking orders from Isabelle?"

Aaron scratched his chin and declared, "I'm good with it."

"Me, too," Aleksandr said.

"That is too cool!" Charisma leaped to her feet and threw her arms around Isabelle.

Jacqueline beamed at Samuel. If he kept this up, she might come to like him. "See? I knew we could do this."

"You're warm and dry and fed, surrounded by safety

and by each other, and your first adventure came out well." Irving poured the first flutes of champagne and passed them down the table. "Are you prepared for the adversity that follows? The Others are better manned, more learned, and so far, they have defeated us in almost every way. I promise, until we find the prophecy that will give us direction, matters will only get worse— and even then, there's no guarantee of improvement."

"Irving's right. To merely survive will take all our skills and dedication." Aaron had never appeared more serious, more intense.

Jacqueline had to speak. "It's going to take something more important. I met you all only a few days ago. I didn't know you. I didn't want to know you. I didn't want to be part of this mission. But as I stood outside the chalk circle, I felt something . . . a blast of heat, and the cool wind of change, and I knew I couldn't be a coward. I had to step inside. With you. In the days since, I've gotten to know you all." She looked at Isabelle and Charisma. "I like some of you." She looked at Samuel. "Not all of you."

"Thanks." Samuel leaned back, unfazed.

She looked at Caleb. "And I love you."

Caleb kissed her once, hard.

She continued. "But now I know one thing. When we stand alone, we are all targets for our enemies. But if we stand together, we can defeat them."

As she spoke, she stripped off her gloves. "We are

only six—some call that the devil's number—and until the seventh makes an appearance, I swear on my soul I will watch your back. I want to know that you will watch mine." She put out her right hand, tattoo clear and bright and healed. Then she offered her left hand, with its newly etched mark of power.

A collective gasp went around the table.

"Yes. This is proof. Things can happen for the better." She placed her right hand on the table, palm up. "So will you swear on your soul and everything you hold holy to be true to us, to the Chosen Ones?"

Six hands came out and the palms slapped, one by one, on top of hers.

She looked toward Caleb. "You, too. And you, Irving. And Martha. And McKenna."

The two servants stiffened and looked around, uncertain of their place in this new order.

"It's really not proper," McKenna said.

"I have no gift," Martha agreed.

"And we are not seven, as we should be, but only six," Samuel said.

With the vigor that accompanied her every word, Charisma said, "Yet we can't sit idly by while we wait for the seventh to show her—or his—face. We have to forge ahead in a new direction."

"We have never needed our allies as much as we do now, and you all know more than we do. We depend on you to tell us the traditions of the Chosen Ones, and to be tolerant when we are forced to make new ones. Please do come." Isabelle was soft-spoken, yet her authority could not be denied.

Martha placed her soft, wrinkled hand on the pile; then McKenna placed his atop hers. Irving's long, dark fingers were next, then Caleb with his hand palm down, and Jacqueline's left hand atop them all.

It was as if she closed an electrical circuit. Something warm, bright, and hot flashed from the mark on Jacqueline's hand up through everyone's palms and back through her.

They all jumped.

They laughed, and slowly, one by one, they pulled their hands back.

"It's a sign." Irving raised his champagne flute in a salute. "We are doing something right."

Everyone raised their glasses.

"Because of you, Jacqueline." Caleb caught her bare hand and kissed her palm. "Because of you."

Not far away, in a private New York hospital, a nurse's aide bent over the comatose form of Gary White. She bent his legs, back and forth, trying to slow the atrophy that ate at his muscles. She rolled him from his side to his back, trying to ease the bedsores that had formed under his hips and spine. She switched the empty IV bag for a full one, checked to make sure the drip was the same steady drip as it had been for the last four years, delivering fluids and nutrients to a hopeless patient.

As she prepared to leave, to finish her rounds, something caught her attention. A movement from the bed.

She turned toward the patient, sure she was mistaken.

But for the first time in four years, his eyes were open. He was staring at her, and she froze, mesmerized by his gaze.

Slowly, using muscles that were thin and wasted, he worked himself into a sitting position. Balefully, he glared at the dripping IV bottle. Viciously, he ripped the tubes from his arm. "Get me my clothes. I'm getting out of here."

She backed away, groped for the door, and ran shouting down the corridor. "Doctor. Doctor! Come at once. Come and see. A miracle has happened!"

Read on for a sneak peek
of book two in
Christina Dodd's
The Chosen Ones series

STORM OF SHADOWS

Available from Signet in September 2009

"I'm looking for the antiquities librarian. I have an appointment. I'm Aaron Eagle."

"Yes, Mr. Eagle, I've got you on the schedule." The library's administrative assistant was gorgeous, lush, and fully recognized his eligibility. She smiled into his eyes as she pushed the book toward him. "If you would sign in here." She pointed, handed him a pen, and managed to brush his fingers with hers. "And here." She pointed again. "Then if you don't mind, we'd like your fingerprint. Just your left thumb."

"I'm always amazed at the security required to visit antiquities." Aaron smiled at her as he pressed his thumb onto the glass set into the desk. A light from beneath scanned his thumb.

"The Arthur W. Nelson Fine Arts Library antiquities department contains some of the rarest manuscripts and scrolls in the world, and we take security very seriously because of it."

"So if I made my living stealing antiquities, you'd know."

"Exactly."

"If I'd been caught."

"Thieves always eventually get caught." She had him stand on the line and took his photograph.

"I would certainly hope so." He stepped onto a grate that shook him hard, then through an explosives screener that puffed air around him.

She riffled through the piles of paper on her desk, compared them to the information on her computer screen, and smiled with satisfaction. "But you seem to be exactly who you say you are."

"I do seem to be, don't I?" He leaned back over the grate. "Perhaps we could discuss your job tonight over drinks?"

"I'd like that."

"I'll get your number on the way out, and we can arrange a time and place."

She nodded and smiled.

He smiled back, headed down the corridor, and as he walked, he peeled off his thumbprint and slipped the micromillimeter-thin plastic into his pocket.

"Just take the elevator down to the bottom floor," she called after him.

"Thank you, I will. I've been here before."

"That's right. You have." Her voice faded.

The corridor was plain, painted industrial gray, and the elevator was stainless steel on the outside and pure mid-twentieth-century technology on the inside. The wood paneling was obviously plastic, the button covers were cracked and the numbers worn, and the mechanism creaked as it descended at a stately rate.

But this was the Arthur W. Nelson Fine Arts Library, and their funding didn't include upkeep on nonessentials like a new elevator for the seldom-used antiquities department. They were lucky to have updated security in the last ten years, and that occurred only when it was discovered one of the librarians had been systematically removing pages from the medieval manuscripts and selling them for a fortune to collectors. If he hadn't decided to get greedy and remove a Persian scroll, he might still be in business, but Dr. Hall had been the antiquities librarian for about a hundred and fifty years and he caught on to that right away.

It was Dr. Hall that Aaron was on his way to see now. When it came to ancient languages, the old guy was a genius, and his specialty was prophecies, religious and otherwise. Which was exactly what Aaron needed right now.

The elevator door opened, and he strode along another short, industrial gray corridor that led to a metal door at the end. He rang the doorbell at the side. The lock clicked, he turned the handle, and he walked in.

Nobody was there. Whoever had let him in had done so remotely.

The place smelled like a library: dust, old paper, cracking glue, broken linoleum, and more dust. Rows and rows of gray metal shelving extended from one end of the basement to the other, clustered in rows, lined with books.

No one was in sight.

"Hello?" he called. "Dr. Hall? It's Aaron Eagle."

"Back here!" A voice floated over and through the shelves. A woman's voice.

They must have finally dug up the funding to get Dr. Hall another assistant. Good thing. The old guy could croak down here and no one would notice for days.

Aaron headed back between a shelf marked *Medieval Studies* and one marked *Babylonian Gods*. He broke out from among the shelves into the work area where wide library tables were covered with manuscripts, scrolls, and a stone tablet.

A girl leaned over the stone tablets, mink brush in hand, studying them. "Put it on the table over there." She waved the brush vaguely toward the corner.

Aaron glanced over at the table piled with Styrofoam containers and fast-food bags wadded up into little balls. He looked back at the girl.

Her skin was creamy, fine-grained and perfect, and that was a good thing, since she did not wear a single drop of makeup. No foundation, no blush, no powder, no lipstick. She was of medium height, perhaps a little skinny, but with what she was wearing, who could tell? Her blue dress drooped where it should fit and hung unevenly at the hem. He supposed she wore it for comfort. He didn't know any other reason any woman would be caught dead in it. The neckline hung off one shoulder; the bra strap on her shoulder was dingy, the elastic stretched and frayed. She had thin latex gloves stretched over her hands—nothing killed a man's amorous intentions like latex gloves—and she wore brown leather clogs. Birkenstocks. Antiques. As the crowning touch, she wore plastic-rimmed tortoiseshell glasses that looked like an extension of the frizzy carrot red hair trapped at the back of her neck by a scrunchie that had seen better days . . . about five years ago.

Yet for all that she was not in any way attractive, she paid him no heed, and he wasn't used to that treatment from a woman. "Who do you think I am?"

"Lunch. Or"—her glasses had slid down her nose— "did I miss lunch? Is it time for dinner already? What time is it?"

"It's three."

"Rats. I did miss lunch." Lifting her head, she looked at him.

He did a double take violent enough to give him whiplash.

Beneath the glasses, dense, dark lashes surrounded

the biggest, most emphatically violet eyes he'd ever seen.

Like a newly wakened owl, she blinked at him. "Who are you?"

"I'm. Aaron. Eagle." He emphasized each word, giving time between for the village idiot to absorb the name. "Who are *you*?"

"I'm Dr. Hall."

Aaron was immediately pissed. "I've met Dr. Hall. You are most definitely not Dr. Hall."

"Oh." A silly smile curved her pale pink lips. "You knew Daddy."

"Daddy?"

"Dr. Earl Hall. He retired two years ago." Her smile died. "He, um, died last year."

"Dr. Earl Hall was your father?" Aaron didn't believe that for a minute. Her "mentor" maybe, but Dr. Hall was way too old to have a daughter this girl's age.

Aaron frowned. Of course, Dr. Hall was way too old to be a "mentor," too.

Meanwhile, the girl babbled on. "I know what you're thinking. Nepotism. It's true. It's also true no one is as qualified for the job as I am. Daddy saw to that. He tried to teach me everything he knew, but really, with a brain like his, how is that even possible? What cinched it for the library, of course, is that I'm cheap."

"Yes. I see that." He also saw she wasn't as unattractive as he'd first thought. Hidden under that dress, she had boobs—B-, maybe C-cups—some kind of waist, and curvy hips. She had good bones, like a racehorse, and of course those amazing eyes. But her lips were good, too, lush and sensual, the kind a man would like to have wrapped around his— "So let me get this straight. You are Dr. Earl Hall's granddaughter?"

"No. I'm. His. Daughter." Now she spoke like *he* was the village idiot. "He married late in life."

"To somebody much younger."

"Not *much* younger. Ten years isn't much younger, would you say? Mama was forty-two when she had me."

"And you're twenty now?"

"I'm twenty-seven. I've got a BS in archeology from Oxford and a graduate degree in linguistics from Stanford, not to mention some more stuff like a stint teaching vanished languages at MIT." She waved at a desk overflowing with papers, artifacts, and atop it all, a new Apple laptop. Her voice got louder and more aggravated as she spoke. "I've got all the papers in there if you need to see them. I've had to keep track of all that stuff because everyone thinks I'm twenty!"

"Obviously, we're all dolts."

"Yes."

He could tell it never occurred to her to deny it, or flatter him in any way. The girl was clueless about the most basic social niceties, and worse, she didn't seem to notice he was a man.

Why did he care?

"When I was five, my mother died in a cenote in Central America retrieving this stone tablet." The girl waved her hand at the table.

He glanced at the tablets, then did his second double take of the day. He leaned over it, studied it with intense interest. "Central American. Logosyllabic. Epi-Olmec script. Perhaps a Rosetta stone for the transition between the Olmec and Mayan languages . . ."

"Very good." For the first time, she looked at him, noticed him, and viewed him with respect. Not interest, but respect.

"I had no idea these existed." His fingers itched to touch them, and he carefully tucked his hands into his pockets.

"No one did. After Mommy died, Daddy brought them here and shut them in the vault. He blamed himself, you see, for sending her down there." The girl was blinking at Aaron again.

He couldn't keep calling her "the girl," not even in his mind. "What's your name?"

"Dr. Hall . . . Oh, you mean my first name." She smiled at him, those amazing eyes lavishing him with happiness. "I'm Rosamund."

Didn't that just figure?

"My parents named me after Rosamund Clifford—"

"The Fair Rosamund, King Henry the Second's mistress, reputedly the most beautiful woman in the world." Could this Rosamund be any more unlike her? "Henry built Rosamund a bower and surrounded it by a maze to protect and keep her, yet somehow the wildly jealous Eleanor of Aquitaine poisoned her and she died for love."

"Most of that is romantic fantasy, of course, but you do know your history. And your linguistics." This Rosamund, plain, unkempt, and appallingly dressed, viewed him with approval.

"History. Yes. That's actually why I'm here." He might as well give her a shot at his question. "I wanted to talk to Dr. Hall about a prophecy—"

"My goodness." Rosamund blinked at him again. "You're the second one today to ask about a prophecy."

Penguin Group (USA) Inc.
is proud to present

GREAT READS—GUARANTEED

We are so confident you will love
this book that we are offering a
100% money-back guarantee!

If you are not 100% satisfied with
this publication, Penguin Group (USA) Inc.
will refund your money!
Simply return the book before
October 4, 2009 for a full refund.